ESCAPING HOME

A TIME TRAVEL HISTORICAL ADVENTURE

CHRISTY
COOPER-BURNETT

Black Rose Writing | Texas

First printing

ISBN: 978-1-68433-810-8
PUBLISHED BY BLACK ROSE WRITING
www.blackrosewriting.com

Printed in the United States of America
Suggested Retail Price (SRP) $18.95

Escaping Home is printed in Calluna

*As a planet-friendly publisher, Black Rose Writing does its best to eliminate unnecessary waste to reduce paper usage and energy costs, while never compromising the reading experience. As a result, the final word count vs. page count may not meet common expectations.

For my son Mychael. My inspiration for everything.

OTHER TITLES BY
CHRISTY COOPER-BURNETT

NO WAY HOME

A Time Travel Novel of Adventure and Survival

FINDING HOME

A Time Travel Romance Adventure

ESCAPING
HOME

ONE

Los Angeles, California 2072

The newscaster's voice trembled, her eyes widening as she read from the teleprompter.

"Water supplies in twenty-two states are tainted and now non-potable. Experts warn the public not to consume any water from these areas. Filtering and boiling do not make it any safer. They also advise against showering or washing with it until the contaminate is tested. They recommend people in the affected regions to drink bottled water only and to wash using prepackaged sanitary wipes."

"Up next, Jill Meriweather with the weather."

I waved my hand over the hologram control, turning the news off. I could not stomach any more of it today. The meteorologist's name never failed to make me cringe. Despite her name and apparent education, she could never get the weather report right. For all our technological advances, it remained unpredictable. I wondered what Jill would talk about when the weather no longer mattered.

I leaned back against the couch. The television shone like an enormous piece of polished obsidian embedded in the wall. A huge, gleaming, black monster. The bearer of bad news.

A major world war was brewing, and everyone knew it. The conflict was inevitable. I *felt* it. It was in the air and reflected on the faces of strangers everywhere I went. There were thirteen countries involved in the war, all of them blaming the others for attacks on their homelands. Never had the United States been so blatantly targeted. Our water supply was being poisoned now. What was next, biological warfare? Someone spreading smallpox or another obscure disease we have no immunity to any longer? It wouldn't surprise me, and I expected it to happen any day.

My name is Christine Stewart, and for the past twelve years I worked for the Cyber Criminal Enforcement Agency, the CCEA. I was a time-traveler, escorting prisoners back in time. I began my career there right after the government unveiled the exile program. In 2060 I found myself divorced with a young son and working as the manager of a mortgage company. Financially, the CCEA job wasn't an opportunity I could afford to pass up. My family thought I was crazy for applying, and to tell you the truth, I second-guessed that decision more than once myself. Being flung into history twice a week did not come without certain risks. Cowards and alarmists would not make it past the first month, but I considered myself neither.

So I made my living extraditing nonviolent cyber criminals hundreds of years into the past as a sentence for their crimes. We abandoned them in a time when technology was nonexistent, where society washed their hands of them.

Now the CCEA had suspended all inmate transports until things cooled off. Which meant at our normal pace, prisoners would overrun the system within four weeks. The government designed the facilities to rotate inmates out regularly, not keep them harbored for months at a time. They normally processed detainees through the program inside thirty days, maximum.

Once that happened, it would go from bad to worse quickly. People were already hoarding and installing steel shutters over doors and windows. They were trying to protect themselves from each other, but what they didn't understand was, we weren't the enemy. If another country attacked us with air or ground troops, our houses wouldn't offer protection. There would be nowhere free from danger if the entire world went to war.

Ethan, my fiancé, was a CCEA agent too, and we talked about this at length. We concluded the only logical, safe solution was to exile to the past. I knew it would be difficult. We had both been to many places and timelines; we knew exactly how unforgiving history could be. It was a tremendous gamble, but we believed the only way to survive our future was to exile to another timeline. Maybe permanently.

If we stayed here, the war would certainly affect us. Nuclear weapons had advanced to the point it could all be over in a matter of seconds. As the tensions mounted between the feuding countries, the risk of a few continents being annihilated was higher than ever. I, for one, did not want to stick around for that.

So Ethan and I did the only practical thing we knew to do. We invited the people we loved over for dinner to spring our brilliant plan on them. I only hoped they saw the logic in our strategy, but I expected them to meet our idea with some resistance. I mean, who wanted to live hundreds of years in the past, with no running water, modern bathrooms, medicine, or cars? Someone who recognized the danger in staying, that's who.

Besides, we would bring things with us. Items to help us survive and even thrive with some luck. But space limited what we took. We could each carry a large rucksack and a backpack. That was it. Our packs had to hold everything we wanted to transport with us in our jump pod. And we couldn't take anything that might disrupt history, such as weapons. That was just too risky. If a modern-day weapon fell into the wrong hands, well, who knows what could happen. And we'd have our share of secrets to hide and problems to overcome without an added burden. But honestly, survival was foremost on my mind at that point. I attempted to make a conscious effort to follow the rules, but when it came right down to it, our continuity was number one on my list.

I ordered dinner on my ChefAid, so I didn't have to cook for my guests. The ChefAid was like having a personal chef without the human interaction. I loved mine precisely for that reason, especially tonight. I wanted to concentrate on my speech, not cooking, which I didn't do well anyway. I was most concerned about convincing my son Michael and his fiancée Maddie to come with us. I could never go if they stayed. There was no way I was leaving them alone in such a mess. They both worked for the CCEA, Michael in population control and Maddie in IT. The idea of transporting would not be as alarming to them as it would be to someone who didn't work in the environment, so I felt confident this would make sense to them.

I opened a couple of bottles of wine and put some music on to help myself stay calm. The closer it got to six o'clock, the more anxious I became. This would be no easy topic to broach, and subtlety had never been my strong point. I was counting on Ethan to soften the edges of my spiel for me.

I paced and finally poured myself some wine to relax. That helped a little, and by the time Ethan entered the kitchen, I was pouring my second glass.

"Liquid courage?" he asked as he leaned in for a kiss.

"Something like that, yes. Don't judge me. I'm nervous about telling them."

"No judgements here. This is the only thing that makes sense. The whole bloody world has gone mad, Christine."

His British accent still took me by surprise now and then. He hadn't picked up any American slang since relocating here either. Which was fine with me. I thought it was sexy.

"Well, fingers crossed, they don't think I've lost my mind."

Before he could answer, a knock at the door drew our attention. I inhaled deeply, pasted a smile on my face, and reached for the handle.

"Showtime," I whispered to myself.

I opened the door to my best friend and fellow CCEA agent, Annabelle Harris, and her family.

"Hey, girlfriend. Sorry to arrive with a screaming kid, but Joe forgot Willow's favorite doll," she said, shooting her husband a glare.

"I told you, I figured you had it. Is there beer?" he asked, bouncing the crying toddler on his knee.

"Joe, you follow Ethan for beer. Annabelle, you come with me for wine. Heather, sweetie, do you want to take your sister and go see Max in the backyard? I'll bet he would love a game of fetch with both of you. He told me just this morning how much he misses you."

The youngster stopped sobbing and studied me with puffy eyes. "He did?" she asked.

"Yep, he sure did."

"Come on, Willow, let's go play with Max!" said Heather, grabbing her sister's hand as her dad put her down. He mouthed a silent *thank you* to me as he followed Ethan out of the entry.

"You okay?" I asked Annabelle.

"Yeah," she sighed. "With everything going on, I'm stressed out, and a hysterical toddler on the plane for an hour did nothing to improve that. Joe and I are sniping at each other because we're anxious. I'm just burned out."

Annabelle works for the Chicago division of the CCEA. We both fly between Los Angeles and Chicago often to see each other.

"Well, come on, let's grab some alcohol and sit on the deck to watch the girls wear themselves out for bedtime," I said, grabbing her arm and leading her to the kitchen.

Before I could get her out of the entry, the doorbell rang. "Go ahead, wine is breathing on the counter in the kitchen. I'll meet you out there in a minute."

I opened the door to Frank and Linda Rhoades. Frank was my supervisor at the CCEA. He was also a good friend.

Michael and Maddie arrived while I was still in the doorway.

"Hey, Mom," Michael said, stepping through to hug me.

"Hi, everyone, come on in. Annabelle and Joe just got here."

I hugged Maddie, and they took off in the backyard's direction, where I heard the girls giggling and Ethan and Joe laughing.

"I hope you have beer, Stewart. And something good for dinner. I'm starving," Frank said as he squeezed my shoulder and headed for the kitchen.

"Ignore him, Christine. I fed him a couple of hours ago," Linda said, leaning in for a hug.

"He's always hungry, I know. He tells me you starve him at home, which of course I do not believe."

"Ha! I force him to eat healthy and this betrayal is the thanks I get. He's not a young man anymore, a fact he seems to forget."

I felt a stab of guilt at her words. Maybe it wasn't fair to ask Frank to help me with this. But we could not transport to the past without his cooperation. I wasn't exactly sure of his age; he would never tell me. But I knew he was over fifty, closer to his late fifties. Which wasn't really old, especially by today's standards. Modern medicine had eradicated most communicable diseases like the common cold and the flu. We wiped out many of the hereditary afflictions that used to plague the population, so people expected to live much longer these days.

Unless war threatened to expunge humanity.

I shook off the thought and led Linda into the kitchen.

"What can I get you?"

"Some of that wine would be lovely," she said, pointing to a bottle on the island.

"You got it."

I poured myself another glass and followed her out to the deck to join the others.

Here goes nothing, I thought.

Everyone had found seats on the deck and the conversation flowed. I took my place next to Ethan and reached for his hand. I breathed a deep breath after he squeezed it firmly.

"So, I asked you all to dinner tonight because I want to talk to you about something."

"Is it wedding time?" Maddie asked excitedly.

I glanced at Ethan, who grinned at me. "Well, of course we'd like to do that as soon as possible, but with the state of the world at the moment, we aren't certain this is the right time," he said.

"Then what's up, Mom?"

I cleared my throat and inhaled another deep breath. "So, Ethan and I are really worried about the future. It's pretty clear war is imminent, and I'm not sure how the country is going to make it through that. We haven't had fighting on US soil since the attack on Pearl Harbor. And before that it was the Civil War."

"Look, what we're trying to say is that we don't believe we are safe here, no one will be," Ethan added.

"So what are you saying, we head for the hills?" Joe asked. "Because that's what we're planning. You know we've shopped mountain cabins. We are ready to make an offer on one. We want to get the girls out of Chicago."

"We realize large cities will be the most affected, so when it gets really terrible, we'll come here to the new place," Annabelle said.

Frank's eyes darted between us. "I think they're trying to say it's already got bad," he said.

Michael reached over to grab Maddie's hand. "So, what are you suggesting exactly, Mom?"

I studied each one of them for a second before I spoke again. "I'm saying we need to leave, before we no longer can."

"I think we can all agree on that, Christine," Frank said, taking a long pull from his beer bottle.

"Well, you may think I'm crazy for what I'm about to say, but just hear me out." I hesitated for a moment, then blurted it out. "We're convinced the only solution is to transport to the past and live there. It will be the only safe place in the entire world—another timeline."

My words hung in the air between us as everyone except Ethan stared at me like I'd lost my mind.

TWO

Los Angeles, California 2072

No one spoke right away as drinks paused midair. Frank was the first to break the silence when he laughed.

"Oh, come on, Christine. I'm a fairly go-with-the-flow kinda guy, but even I have my limits. That's an insane idea, especially from you two," he waved the neck of his beer bottle between me and Ethan.

"Why is it crazy, Frank? We both know if biological warfare breaks out here, there is nowhere safe. No mountain cabin will be far enough away. And there are so many countries feuding, where would we go to be out of danger? Don't tell me you haven't thought about that. The US has a long list of enemies right now, and if one of them spreads a disease or introduces a poisonous chemical into the air, it's over for everyone."

"It's actually not that crazy of an idea," Annabelle said.

"What? You cannot be serious, Annabelle!" Joe said. "You want to take our kids and live in the past somewhere with no modern conveniences? Have you lost your mind, babe?"

"I want to protect our girls, Joe. I survived the past once before. I can do it again if it means keeping them out of harm's way."

Joe scoffed and drained his beer.

"All we're asking is that you hear us out. No one is going to force anyone to do something they don't want to do," I said, glancing around the group. "Michael, I want you and Maddie to come. I won't go without you, but I feel strongly this plan is our only chance of survival."

Michael exhaled loudly and reclined all the way back in his chair, while Maddie resembled a deer in the headlights.

"This is really coming out of left field, Mom. I mean, seriously, I didn't see this coming. Let me just wrap my head around what you're saying for a minute."

My brow furrowed as I studied him. I would have more opportunities to talk to him later, but as I sat there, I couldn't help but regret not having this conversation with him in private before now.

"Look, last time Christine, Ethan, and I were living in the past it was completely unplanned. We had nothing. No supplies whatsoever. We had to struggle to survive. If we plan this right, we can prepare," Annabelle said.

"Exactly!" I said, casting her a thankful look. "I've done a lot of research, and if we are smart, we can do this. I think we should go to Alexandria, Virginia, in 1790. I was there last year, as you all know. It's a large, established port city. We can buy land and build. I walked the city. There is potential there."

I learned all about the risks of the job when on routine transport to 1867, Oklahoma two years ago. The CCEA stranded transporters all over the world, trapped with nothing but the clothes on our backs and malfunctioning devices. That's when I met Annabelle. After six months there, our instruments showed signs of working again, and we tried to get home. But instead, I transported to medieval England, and Indians captured Annabelle in Oklahoma.

Annabelle escaped, and Frank led the CCEA retrieval team, who rescued her right before they found me in England, where I survived with Ethan, his prisoner Malcolm, and three other transporters. I helped Ethan retrieve—okay steal—an astronomer's research after we uncovered a plot that involved two of the other transporters in our camp. The creator of the exile software, Jonathan Hoyt, discovered a devastating pandemic predicted for 2072, based on the astronomer's writings, and he needed a missing part of the treatise.

Frank coughed and snapped me out of the memory and back to the present when he choked, nearly spitting out his swallow of beer. Linda patted his back and twisted to stare directly at me.

"What do you mean, Christine? How could we possibly prepare for a move such as this?"

Frank's head jerked toward her. "Linda, no. You don't know what it's like in the past."

"I can always count on you to point out the obvious, Frank. I'm asking questions, not signing a contract. Calm down and drink your beer," she said, patting his hand.

"We all take a large pack. As long as we can hold it and it fits in the jump pod, it will transport. We can bring seeds and fertilizer, money, knives, medicine, all the vital things we'll need. I know this is extreme, but it's how we stay alive. This is how Annabelle and Joe give their girls a chance. This is how Michael and Maddie live to start their own family and keep them safe. Our way of life is circling the drain, and pretty soon there might be nothing left."

"Where would we live?" Maddie asked.

"Well, we obviously don't have the skill set to construct our own houses. We bring money to buy lumber and such, and we hire someone there. We build four cabins, nothing fancy. We will have to hunt for food and grow our own, but that's not impossible. I survived for seven months in the Cotswolds with zilch. I can bloody well do it in Colonial America with supplies," Ethan said.

"We can do this. Buy the right clothes, research the timeline, get vaccines, and then get the hell out of dodge," Annabelle said, finishing her glass of wine.

"Why Alexandria? I would imagine you'd want to go to 1868, Oklahoma, with Malcolm and Hannah," Frank asked.

My thoughts drifted to my two friends in Oklahoma. Malcolm and Hannah were my biggest success story. When Ethan asked Frank to send Malcolm out of 1335, England, after our rescue when stranded there, we had no idea we would ever see him again. But when an acquaintance, Hannah Cole, begged me to help her exile away from her abusive and criminal husband, I immediately thought of sending her to Malcolm's care in 1868, Oklahoma. They fell in love, married, and adopted their son, Jacob after his grandmother died. Her husband sent an inmate after her who exiled to their time period, and we rescued her after the CCEA enforcement team exiled her to 1790 when she breached her restricted area. I rescued her with the help of two fellow agents, Stephen Gray and Nathaniel Adams, and brought her home to Malcolm and Jacob.

I wished going there to a familiar place with people I knew was an option.

"Of course, I would prefer to go there. But if we did, their history could, and likely would, change by adding all of us into the mix. Life turned out wonderfully for them, and I don't want to take the chance of disrupting that."

I leaned forward in my seat. "I've thought long and hard about this, and Ethan and I truly believe this is the answer."

"I agree with you," Annabelle said.

"Well, I don't. It sounds like suicide," Joe said.

"You're going to have to trust me, Joe," she said, reaching for his hand.

His gaze went to their girls as they ran across the lawn, chasing the dog. "I trust you, Annabelle, and I would do anything for our daughters. You know that. If you say we can stay alive there, then I'll go along with it—for now. I don't like it, and I want to go on record here and now, that I still have serious misgivings about this plan. But I like the odds of staying here even less. I would really like to talk more about this privately."

Annabelle kissed his cheek and followed his gaze to their daughters.

Linda peered at Frank. Her eyes searched his. "We should go, Frank."

"What? Really? You don't know what it's like, Linda. No running water, no bathrooms. Think about it. No electricity. Life is so difficult in the 1700s. There are no conveniences. The hygiene struggle alone is enough to make someone want to give up."

"I realize the sacrifices it would require. But what do we have here? A country on the brink of chemical, biological, and nuclear war, that's what. I'm frightened all the time that any minute could be our last. At least there, I wouldn't worry about that."

"Well, we'd stress about plenty of other things, trust me," he scoffed.

Michael and Maddie had their heads together, whispering, while Frank and Linda talked. Michael leaned forward, his expression unreadable. I waited for him to speak, perched nervously on the edge of my seat.

"Okay, if you guys think this is the way to go, then we're in."

I was so consoled by his answer I collapsed back in my chair and took a deep breath.

"We need to decide unanimously where and when we are exiling," Ethan said, glancing around the group.

When no one responded, I took the lead again. "I suggested Alexandria for a couple of reasons. As I mentioned earlier, it's populated. We could blend in more easily. They use silver and gold for money, but more commonly Spanish coins known as pieces of eight, which are easy to buy here in our timeline. There are plenty of coin dealers in LA and online. The late 1700s puts us there at a fairly uneventful time. The American Revolution is over. Old Town Alexandria becomes part of the District of Columbia in 1791, but that won't affect us. We'll buy land outside the city limits and keep to ourselves. It's settled on the banks of the Potomac River and is one of the original thirteen colonies. The river provides fish as a food source. Fresh water is a problem, but we can bring purification supplies. There is what they called a little ice age between 1550 and 1800, which brings wet spring flooding, hot summers, drought, and thick frost in winter. But since we are aware of it, we can prepare."

"Everyone here has transported except me, Linda, Maddie, and our girls," Joe said. "Why are you so sure we can make it there?"

"Because the rest of us know what to do," Michael said. "Ethan, my mom, and Annabelle all survived months with nothing. And I've been to the past with Frank. He knows what he's doing. I trust all of them, and you should too."

I smiled at Michael and turned to Joe. "This is doable, Joe. We just need a few weeks to gather supplies and make final plans."

"Let's have a show of hands in favor of Alexandria," Ethan suggested.

All hands went up except Joe's, and that mollified me. I knew Annabelle would convince him to go along with the plan.

"Should we say 1790? That would put us there seven years after the Revolution, plenty of time for that to have settled down."

Heads nodded all around, and I raised my glass of wine in a toast. "To relocating. And to staying alive."

We lifted our glasses, and I locked eyes with Annabelle. She gave me a small smirk and a look that I knew meant to say *here we go again.*

"There's just one more thing you should all consider. There is the possibility that we may never get home to our timeline. If the war affects our society the way I suspect it will, the CCEA exile program might not be operational. That would mean we are in the past permanently, no coming back when and if things ever return to normal," Frank said.

"That's a risk we have to take if we want to survive," I said.

"He's right. But so is Christine. I see no other choice for us at this point," Ethan said.

Ethan was right, we were running out of choices fast. And that same lack of options made me feel like a fly trapped in a spider web.

THREE

Los Angeles, California 2072

During dinner, I suggested we schedule a meeting in two days to assign tasks to each person. That would give them more time to think about the plan and come to terms with what we were about to do. Annabelle was the only one who maintained her normal level of chat at dinner. Everyone else was uncharacteristically quiet.

I guess I couldn't blame them—this was a lot to digest. But I truly believed our plan was the best option for survival. To stay would have been living in the unknown, waiting for disaster to strike at any moment. Living in the 1700s would be no picnic either. But if we prepared and were smart about it, we would be better off than most colonists and at least stood a fighting chance.

The next couple of days dragged by at work. Without transporting prisoners, there wasn't much to do, and most agents spent their workdays online or chatting to each other. A colossal waste of government payroll, but most of us were caught up on our backlogged reports, so what else could we do? I, of course, spent my time researching all I could about Colonial America in 1790, Alexandria. Most websites painted a bleak picture of life in that timeline, complete with mail-order brides and imported slaves. Disease was a major issue, and pirates sailed the Atlantic Ocean and the Potomac River. I already had some firsthand experience with pirates on my last excursion to the 1700s, and it was nothing I wanted to repeat.

My mind worked overtime throughout the next two days while I made list after list of things we should bring. Clearly, we were going to need to shave it down to something more reasonable, as I'd gone a bit overboard.

On the day of our meeting, Frank called me to his office. He didn't bother with small talk or even a greeting, just jumped right into what was on his mind.

"What if someone else wants to join us? How would that fit into the plan?"

"I guess it would depend on who they are. It would have to be someone we trust, obviously. And please don't take what I'm about to say wrong, but elderly people would not make it there. It's too tough, and with hygiene and disease being what they are there, you know that's a bad idea."

Frank exhaled and ran his hand over his short hair. "I know. I wasn't thinking about my parents. They would never agree to it anyway. I thought Adams and Gray would be excellent additions to our group."

The CCEA assigned Gray and Adams to the retrieval unit that rescued me in medieval England, and I already mentioned they were on my team when we went after Hannah in 1790, Alexandria. They were both top-notch agents, and Adams was a medic. He would be an enormous asset.

"I agree. They would certainly both be welcome additions. Do you think they would want to come along?" I asked, not realizing I was holding my breath, waiting for his answer.

"I feel they would both consider it. Adams has spoken to me about the current state of affairs in the world, and he's frightened for his wife and kid. Are you aware he reconciled with his wife?"

"No, he didn't mention it to me. That's good. I like her. What about Gray?"

"I haven't discussed it with him, but he's a pragmatic personality and he'll see the benefit of taking his family out of this situation."

"Well, I say ask them, and if they want to join us at tonight's meeting, that would be great."

"Okay, I'm going to call them both in. You can take off. I'd rather talk to them alone about this."

"Sure, no worries. I'll see you and Linda tonight then."

I made my way back to the orientation room to continue my research. There was literally nothing else to do at work now that my reports were all current. All the agents were in the same spot. They kept us on payroll in case the inmates staged an uprising and prisoner control needed extra bodies. Which terrified me because my son worked in that unit. I shook my head, forcing the image from my mind.

When the workday ended, I was ready to run screaming from the building. I studied the faces of my coworkers as I rode the elevator down to the first floor, and we all had similar expressions. An unlikely mixture of boredom and fear. We all worried about what would happen next. They wouldn't keep us around much longer with no transports on the schedule, and we knew it. The news reported the government was in talks to transport only the most serious cyber-criminals and bring back probation for the remaining offenders. Everyone knew what that meant. Only supervisors and agents with the most seniority would have jobs left.

I tried not to obsess about it as I left work. Bigger worries occupied my thoughts. If our group was to survive an exile to the 1700s, we had to prepare. Otherwise, Joe was right—it was a suicide mission.

I ticked off the list in my head on the trip home, working out who I thought should be in charge of gathering what supplies. Traffic was thick, so by the time I arrived, I only had minutes to change clothes and order food for the group on the ChefAid. I planned on making something homemade, as mediocre as that would have been, but thanks to the LA congestion, even that much was impossible.

I touched the screen on the computer built into my desk surface to wake it up and had just gotten settled when the doorbell rang. I opened the door to Linda and Frank, and they had Gray and his wife Kira, and Adams and his wife Gemma with them.

"Hi, everyone, glad you could make it," I said, giving the women hugs.

I left the door open, and the security screen unlocked so the others could come in when they got there.

"Anyone want a drink? Beer, wine? Something stronger, maybe?"

"I'll take a beer," Frank said, while Gray nodded in agreement.

"Beer sounds good," Adams said.

"Ladies, join me in a glass of wine?" I asked.

They all agreed, and I opened a couple of bottles of white zinfandel as Annabelle and Joe arrived with the girls in tow.

"Sorry, the babysitter bailed," Annabelle said. She opened the slider to allow the kids in the backyard with my dog.

"No problem. Max loves the attention." I made introductions as Annabelle and Joe had not met Gray and Adams or their wives. As we stood in the kitchen making small talk, Michael and Maddie arrived.

Maddie helped me take the appetizers into the family room where we found seats around the large sectional. Michael brought in a few extra chairs from the dining room, and once everyone settled, I directed the computer to bring up my notes and research on the television screen.

"So, have you both decided to come with us, or is this a fact-finding visit only?" I asked as I glanced between Gray and Adams.

"We are leaning toward going," Gray said.

"I'm just concerned about our son. He's only thirteen, and I'm uncertain this is the best thing for him," Gemma said, her brow furrowed.

"Our girls aren't much older—they're fifteen and seventeen now," Kira said. "I worry about how they will adjust too."

"I understand it's hard to imagine them living in the past, but it will be safer than staying here," Annabelle said as she took a sip of her wine. "My kids are young—only three and four—so they might adapt easier, but if you stay here, well, who knows what could happen. If this escalates like everyone is predicting, then it's going to affect everything. Hoarding has already begun, and if we go to war on American soil, it will cut off our food supply. Medical services will suffer and nowhere will be really safe."

Gemma turned to her husband and gave him a slight nod.

"I just want to go on record that if we get there and Gemma and Wyatt have too hard of a time adjusting, we are coming back," Adams said, draining his beer.

"Fair enough, but it might be more dangerous here. And if that's the case, I'm not sure how you would transport back again if you changed your mind about staying here. There might be no system to allow you back to 1790 again. Just another thing to consider. If they shut down the CCEA, then you would be here permanently," Ethan replied.

"We'll make that decision as a family and determine what's best for us, but I realize what that would mean."

"Okay, well, I made some preliminary notes on what we need and suggestions on who should get what," I said as my notes filled the large screen. "Of course, we set none of this in stone, and we can always change assignments if anyone wants to. All of this comes at a price, too. Michael and Maddie, I know you don't have a lot of extra money, so I can help you with the costs. Everyone else, if we all contribute, that's the fairest way of covering expenses."

Everyone agreed, and we came up with a figure that each of us would add to our fund.

"Mom, we have a little saved up, so we want to put that toward costs. We don't want to freeload."

"That would be great. And you're not freeloading. I realize you're just starting out, so money is tight."

"Another thing we should bring up is other family members," Ethan said. "Elderly people will not fare well in Colonial America. As crass as that sounds, it's the truth. The era we will live in is not for the faint of heart. Are you prepared to leave your families behind, perhaps forever?"

Heads lowered around the room as everyone considered the ramifications of what we were doing.

"My parents are gone, but Joe's mom won't consider coming with us," Annabelle said, glancing at Joe.

"Neither will mine," I said. I glanced at Michael, who lowered his eyes.

"I don't think any of them believe it will come to a full-on war," Gray said.

"Well, it had to be said. Of course, if someone's family member wants to come, we won't deny them, but it's just not somewhere older people would thrive," Ethan said.

"There are some general things we should talk about before we get to what supplies we want to take with us. Men shouldn't get haircuts from this point forward. Straight razors are in use then so you can shave, though. Women used straight razors then too, so it's okay for us to continue to do so. We should wear no jewelry or rings. Our stuff is too modern, and wedding rings aren't a necessity there. I will talk to Hoyt about sending us all back. If he will not cooperate, Maddie, can you preprogram it?"

"I don't know. I probably can, but I'm not sure I could keep it hidden like Hoyt can."

"Okay, so I have to convince Hoyt then."

Frank cleared his throat and glanced around the group. "Listen, I need to bring something up at this point. I've received word that furloughs are going into effect soon. Within the next two weeks. Once that happens, whoever they lay off will no longer have access to the building. We may need to accelerate this whole thing."

I sighed heavily. That was a fear of mine. Gray and Adams exchanged a look, and Annabelle put her wine glass down a little too hard on the coffee table.

"Crap. If it's happening here, then it's going on in Chicago too. I have a feeling we should step this up or we won't be able to leave."

"I agree," I said, looking at Ethan. Worry etched his face and I'm certain my expression mirrored his.

"All right, let's get to it then. We need lots of Spanish coins and silver. A combination of both. Ethan and I can get those. They will have substantial weight to them, so one person cannot carry them all. We should all leave room in our bags to each take some. We need to buy a lot of stuff when we get there. Things to build and furnish our homes, animals, gardening plows, and we need a boat. We are on the Potomac River, so transportation up and down the river is a must, and for fishing too. Oh, and a mule and cart."

"Will we be able to find all of those things?" Kira asked.

"Yes. I get this is overwhelming, but most of us have been back to the past many times, and a few of us have lived there. So we know what we are talking about. Trust me, if we prepare well enough, we will be fine," I said, trying to convince myself as much as them.

I scanned the group of people sitting in my living room, hinging the hope of their survival on this plan, and I prayed we could really pull this off. For all our sakes.

I knew this was the right thing to do. But sometimes the right thing also turns out to be the most frightening.

FOUR

Los Angeles, California 2072

I glanced over at Ethan while our guests refreshed their drinks and tried to guess how he thought the meeting was going.

"What do you think?" I asked him.

"Your son and Maddie are coming with, no matter what. So don't worry about what everyone else wants to do. If they join us, great, and if not, we will still be good."

I did not happen to agree with him. I thought it would take all of us to make this work. Safety in numbers really seemed to apply here. But Ethan was right—I couldn't stress over the others. I needed to concentrate on getting supplies ready. As everyone made their way back to the living room, I refreshed the television screen and referred to my notes again.

"Frank, can you handle the weapons and tools? Knives, axes, that kind of thing? Nothing modern, of course. We will need hammers, chisels, augers, and braces, but we will buy them once we arrive in Virginia, along with larger tools like saws and planes. And we need a compass. The oldest you can find so it doesn't draw attention."

"I worked construction for a lot of years before I started at the CCEA," Gray said.

We turned to gawk at him. "Really? I never knew that about you," I said, surprised to hear that from him.

"Well, that will come in handy," Frank said. "Maybe Gray and I should trade supply assignments?"

"I agree. Gray, can you do tools and weapons?" I asked.

"Sure, no problem," he said.

"I researched guns for the era, so I'll send that to you for reference. We might be better off waiting to buy them when we get to Virginia. If we locate flintlock muskets here, who knows in what shape we'll find them. I will leave that to you to decide."

"Michael and Maddie, I assigned wardrobe to you. Every person, including the kids, will need two full outfits. Everyday working clothes— what they refer to as undress clothing. I saved pictures and descriptions for men, women, and children. We can have them custom made. I found a website that will rush orders for a fee. Just be sure you are clear on materials. We cannot wear polyester or any artificial fabrics. Wool and cotton only. I'll send you the site information and my research. We need to get our measurements over to you no later than tomorrow. I assume everyone has a body scan on their scales at home?"

Heads bobbed around the room and Maddie grinned. "This is right up my alley. I will get started as soon as I get height and body measurements. Should I get something a couple sizes larger for the younger kids besides the two outfits we are already getting?" she asked.

"That's a fantastic idea," I said as I glanced at Annabelle and Gemma.

"Great idea," Annabelle agreed.

Maddie beamed and tapped her phone chip. She spoke low to dictate notes to herself.

"Annabelle, can you and Joe get seeds and fertilizer? Soil enhancers and grow packs? Also, we need water purification tablets, LifeStraws, and cheesecloth for filtering. Clean water is a huge issue there, so even powdered bleach would be good. We need MREs, protein bars, and meal replacement capsules. I don't want to rely on our hunting and fishing skills initially, and it will be thirty days before we see crops mature with the plant accelerator. We'll use the MREs for the interim, and to ease the kids into the new food. Does anyone here cook? I'm not really great at it," I admitted as I glanced around the room.

"I cook," Linda said as she raised her hand. "I bake too. I learned from my mother as a young girl. I've never really taken to the ChefAid, to be honest. It's convenient when I'm in a hurry, but I'd much rather prepare meals from scratch."

"Oh, good," I said. "We are going to need your skills there. You can teach the rest of us, if you wouldn't mind."

"I'd be happy to!" she said, smiling.

"Can you and Frank get our comfort and convenience supplies? Waterproof matches, soap, that type of stuff? We should be careful about what modern conveniences we bring back there. Bar soap only. We will have to wash bodies and hair with it. If you can find that old brand Ivory, get that. Or something else that's phosphate free, if possible. We will use a basin in fall and winter, but bathe in a stream in warm weather. We don't want to pollute the water for anyone else. Any hygiene products that we can take out of modern-day packaging and store are great, such as crystal deodorant we can wrap in cloth."

"If I get the small pack of one hundred wipes, the kind they fold really tiny, we won't be able to take them out of the package or they'll dry out. I can also get the dry brand where you wet them and activate the soap. Will that work?" she asked.

"Yes, those will work. The wipes will take the place of toilet paper, as there is none where we are going," I answered.

The civilian women gaped at me in shock. "No toilet paper at all? What do they use then?" Kira said.

"You don't want to know. Get as many wipe products as you can. We will have to keep them hidden, but they are a necessity," Annabelle said. "Thank God none of us have babies in diapers."

The women murmured in agreement, and I shuddered at the thought of using cloth diapers in Colonial America.

"Adams, since you're the medic, it makes sense you requisition the medical supplies. Keep in mind that tainted water is an issue and that brings stomach worms. So bring whatever combats those, in the event someone contracts them. Of course, we are more educated regarding sanitary water procedures, but just in case. We will need to get inoculations too. Malaria, yellow fever, and diphtheria are all very prevalent. Can you get us vaccines?"

"I think I can. I have access to them. If Frank will cover for me, I can swipe enough for us." His wife snapped her head in his direction.

"You mean steal them?" she asked.

"Yes, Gemma, I'm talking about stealing them. If it means saving Wyatt and you, then I'll do whatever is necessary. None of the children can go back there without vaccines. Neither can we. Our immune systems are no match for the illnesses from two hundred eighty-two years ago. Those diseases would take us all out in a matter of weeks."

Gemma blinked slowly. "It's just, that's not like you, to steal anything."

"I know, babe. But this is life or death. If we go back there, we need to take precautions. We need modern-day inoculations."

"Bring whatever you consider important, Adams. We'll hide all of it. Gray, can we build a hidden storage space in the floors or walls of our cabins for our transponders and medical stuff?" I asked as I turned to address him.

All heads swiveled to him, waiting for his answer. "Yeah, I can do that."

"Okay, it seems we are well on our way then," Ethan said.

"Ethan will come with me to see Hoyt. We usually do better when we double-team him."

"Sure, let's call him first thing from work and find out when he can see us," he said.

"Sounds good. In the meantime, I've ordered a ton of food on the ChefAid. Let's dig in, folks."

I stole a glimpse at Linda, who just shrugged at my lack of cooking. We spent the rest of the evening chatting, and everyone seemed to relax and warm up more to the idea of the move. Most of the group talked about what items they were going to get for their part of the supply storage, and they seemed eager to start the search. The couples all transferred money to a group account, and we decided how much to spend for our provision runs. The meeting was a success, and it reassured me things were in motion.

But the threat of impending war was a worry I could not get out of my head, no matter how hard I tried. I could not help but be uneasy, considering we might run out of precious time.

As the night wound down and people left, only Frank and Linda remained with me and Ethan.

"Frank, you should come with Ethan and me to talk to Hoyt. We stand a better chance of him cooperating if all three of us are there," I said, glancing at Ethan.

"What makes you think he won't preprogram the system for us? Besides, we don't really need him to, I can do that myself," Frank replied.

"Yeah, I realize you can, but it will go on the record if you do it. Ethan thinks, and I agree, that information on who is going, or where and when, should be confidential. It's just safer that way. And we are asking a lot of Hoyt. It's one thing for him to suspend the system now and again while I traipse through time doing humanitarian errands. It's quite another to ask him to hide travel for twelve adults and five children who want to go back over two hundred years. Especially when five of those adults don't even work for the CCEA."

"If things get as bad as we expect them to, I doubt anyone is going to be checking the system for activity. But if we can avoid any record of our trip, I agree it would be best to do so. Let me know when he can see us, and I'll be there," Frank said.

Linda took Frank's arm in hers and leaned into him. "There's a lot that could go wrong with this, but if we plan smart, we can pull it off," she said, smiling up at him.

I must admit, I was pleasantly surprised at how little resistance came from the agent's partners. As employees of the CCEA, our jobs adapted us to traveling to the past, so for us, we were just on extended transport. And for those who the CCEA already stranded with no notice, we understood the value of being prepared this time. I was grateful for the group of people going with us. It was a powerful mix of personalities and talents, and I was confident we stood a good chance of thriving in Colonial America.

Once Frank and Linda left, I called Jonathan Hoyt, eager to get that part of the plan out of the way. He picked up almost right away, his voice clipped and professional.

"Jonathan Hoyt."

"Jonathan, hello, it's Christine Stewart. How are you?"

"Christine, what a surprise. I'm very well, thanks for asking. Yourself?"

"Well, all things considered, I'm fine."

"Yes, it's quite a state of affairs across the globe at the moment. To what do I owe the pleasure this evening?"

"Well, Ethan and Frank and I wanted to see if we could meet with you tomorrow?"

"Oh? That will be tough to swing, but I can make time Tuesday morning, say ten o'clock."

"That will work. Thanks for squeezing us in."

"No problem at all. Of course, I'm always innately curious when you call to meet with me. Especially now that the CCEA is on hiatus, so to speak. Can I ask what this is about?"

"I'd really rather speak to you in person if that's all right? This isn't anything I want to discuss over the phone."

"Understood. I'll see you Tuesday morning at my office then. Have a pleasant evening, Christine, and give Ethan my best."

I ended the call and turned to Ethan. "Tuesday at ten."

"Okay, that's settled then. Let's get some shuteye. We have a lot to get done tomorrow."

"Yep, got a lot of Spanish coins to buy."

I snuggled close to Ethan on my ridiculously comfortable mattress, wondering what I would sleep on when I got to the 1700s. My mind raced with thoughts of things we needed to bring, and I finally dozed off somewhere around two in the morning.

Ethan was up early, having slept like the dead. I knew this because I listened to him snore for most of the night. I could have used a few more hours of sleep, but I dragged myself up like a trooper and stepped into the shower to wake up.

Once we got to work, the hours stretched before me, endless and boring. If I didn't have tasks to do for our trip to the past, I would have loathed showing up there every day to do nothing. I could not believe the CCEA had laid no one off yet, but I was also extremely glad, as it made what we were doing easier if they authorized us to be there.

Ethan and I both spent the hours at work speaking to coin dealers and purchasing Spanish silver. We kept coming up with more items we would need when we got there, and I wanted to make sure we had enough money. Tobacco was a huge cash crop then, and it was what helped Alexandria survive. Of course, we couldn't bring sacks of tobacco back with us, so silver it was. And we planned to stay at an inn before we built cabins, and that would cost money.

If we did this systemically, we would remain organized and hopefully miss nothing. My instinct to be a control freak served me well, and as I conjured up more necessities, I dictated messages to the rest of the group. By noon, I was certain they were all tired of hearing from me as I stopped getting responses. I sent a last message asking that we get together the following afternoon after work. That way I would have spoken to Hoyt by the time we met and hopefully have good news to share. If Hoyt didn't agree to cover for us, that would increase our exposure. And I, for one, did not want to take that chance. We were already risking so much. Any more gambling could be the end of our plan.

* * *

Ethan, Frank, and I exited the elevator at the top floor of Hoyt Enterprises. Jonathan Hoyt was bent over his assistant's shoulder, studying her desk screen when he turned at the sound of the lift opening.

He smiled and strode toward us with his hand extended. "Hello. Christine, Ethan, Frank, how good to see all of you. Let's go into my office and chat."

We followed him through the double doors, where he motioned to a group of upholstered chairs. I sank into seating that was more comfortable than my bed. Hoyt sat across from Frank and was still smiling as he glanced between us, waiting for someone to tell him why we asked for this meeting. I stole a glance at Ethan, willing him to start.

"Jonathan, we're here today to ask for your help," Ethan said. "The state of the world right now is tenuous. I'm sure you'd agree."

"Yes, it's certainly an unprecedented time in history," he responded.

Because patience was not one of my personality traits, I jumped into the conversation. "Jonathan, we don't wish to stay here any longer. We're frightened the situation is escalating and things are going to get even worse. We want to transport out of here. Can you help us by preprogramming the system for seventeen people? Say, two weeks from now?"

Hoyt stared at me with his mouth agape. "Send you to the past? Is that what you're asking me to do?"

"Well, yes. But not permanently. For several months, a year or two max. Just until things here are back to normal," Frank said.

Ethan and I nodded in agreement.

"Have you three lost your minds? There may not be any system to get you back once you're there. If the CCEA shuts down operations and the program is offline, you will be stuck there. You realize that, right?"

"We do, and it's a chance we will take," Ethan said.

"And just where do you propose to go?" Hoyt asked.

"1790, Alexandria, Virginia," I said, meeting his gaze.

"Again? You want to go back to Colonial America? Why on earth would you do that?" he said, chuckling. "I'm flying to my island home until all this blows over. I would suggest you find somewhere to hole up and wait it out. Transporting back to the 1700s seems extreme. I can't send you there in good faith. Honestly, this is the craziest idea I've heard all year. And believe me, I hear some fairly absurd suggestions from my staff."

I glanced over to where Frank and Ethan sat. I could tell Frank was going to say something stupid, so I shook my head at him, signaling him to be quiet. The best plans have flaws, and apparently Hoyt was the flaw in our plan. But I had no intention of aborting our project because he didn't agree with our strategy.

"Jonathan, we know it's a risk. But we don't have access to an isolated island retreat. Or a private jet to get there like you do. We are going through with this, with or without your help. It would just make things a lot easier if you helped. You can bury our transports, so no one follows or does a forced transport to bring us back. Chances are, no one will pay any attention to us leaving by the time we go, but I would feel safer if you covered for us. If you can't or won't, I guess we're on our own." I stood to leave, and Ethan and Frank did the same. "Thanks for seeing us, anyway. You take care and best of luck on your island."

Hoyt sighed and gestured for us to sit. "Fine. I'll do it. I owe you for helping me bring Wallingford's writing back from 1335 and keeping my involvement in that confidential. After this, we'll call it even, agreed?" We acknowledged with a brief nod. "Two weeks from today, then?"

"That would be great. 1790, Alexandria. Twelve adults and five minors. We'll only need fifteen pods programmed. There are two toddlers who will transport in their parents' cubicle," I said.

"You're taking children with you?" he asked, frowning.

"Three teenagers and two toddlers, yes," I answered.

I held his gaze, and my breath, afraid he was going to change his mind.

He lifted his shoulders after shaking his head, but didn't reply right away. "Alright then, consider it done. But I think you are insane for doing this."

I exhaled the air I'd been holding and rose. We shook his hand again and left, saying nothing else. I said goodbye to his assistant on the way out and we piled into the elevator. Once the door closed, I relaxed my shoulders and leaned into Ethan.

"I'm glad that's over," I said.

"He seemed none too pleased to help us," Frank said.

"No, but he agreed. So job well done. That gives us two weeks to get everything together and place the rest of our lives here on hold," Ethan said.

I looked at him, hoping for reassurance. But he stared straight ahead, lost in his own thoughts.

My entire world felt like a dynamite stick with a lit fuse. Then one day without notice, the dynamite exploded.

FIVE

Los Angeles, California 2072

Our group of deserters worked hard over the next week, ordering online and picking up supplies. We packed our stockpiles in large canvas rucksacks I found and stored them in the spare bedroom of my house. We had a few meetings to check on our progress, and everyone was pulling their weight, fulfilling the lists we assigned them.

Our spending almost depleted our getaway fund, so we all agreed to spend any extra money on more seeds and water purification tablets. Food and water were our priorities. Then again, so was shelter, medication, and defense. Everything was vital to our survival there. The nearer we got to departure day, the more I obsessed over supplies. I realized my nerves were getting the best of me, and I snapped at Ethan over minor things.

I tried to make it up to him and decided to fix us a nice dinner. Well, technically, the ChefAid would prepare us a meal.

I opened a bottle of wine and we talked about everything but our impending journey. It was good to relax for the first time in months, not worried about what was going on in the world. After we ate, I sent Ethan to the family room to find a movie. I heard the volume on the television rise and went to join him, standing behind the sectional. A special report flashed across the screen.

"*This is a special report from WZLA News, Los Angeles. There are reports of an airborne toxin released in several states along the Eastern Seaboard, including New York, Maine, New Jersey, Maryland, Virginia, Georgia, and Florida. At least two hundred people are reported dead with* hundreds more hospitalized. Victims continue to fill area emergency rooms with symptoms of exposure to the toxin. If you experience a severe headache with blurred or double vision, respiratory distress, or are coughing up blood, seek emergency medical attention immediately. Authorities have not officially identified the toxin, however, our sources at Homeland Security say it is a new variant of anthrax. We expect Homeland Security to go live with more information within the hour. A terrorist cell based in New Jersey has come forward and claimed responsibility. Sources say this group is under Algerian leadership. Algeria is one of the countries in direct conflict with the United States. The reports have not been confirmed by Homeland Security as of this hour.

"Authorities advise residents to stay indoors and barricade themselves inside as much as possible. If you have plastic tarps, seal windows and doors using that, or sturdy tape. If you do not have these supplies, shelter in place in a room in the interior of your home and secure as many layers of cloth as you can under the doorway."

The camera cut to a second newsperson who addressed the audience with furrowed brows. Her voice was low and somber as she spoke to her coanchor.

"Dan, if people do not have supplies to safeguard their homes, that could force them to shelter in an interior room, such as a bathroom or utility area. What should they have with them, and what can they do to protect themselves?"

"Carly, if you must barricade in an interior room, bring nonperishable food and extra water. You can use bath towels, for instance, to seal thresholds or other thickly blended fabrics. Experts do not recommend drinking from the tap for the time being. Of course, if you do not have an alternate water supply, this may compel you to do so."

"Dan, considering the events of the past several weeks, most of America has some stockpile of food and water. If you cannot get home and are at work, for instance, the same rules apply there. Move to an interior room as far from windows and outside exit doors as you can."

"Carly, this situation comes at the best possible time of the day, so we should be thankful for that. Many working-class on the East Coast have left their jobs now. It's well past the typical dinner hour for most people, as it is nine o'clock in the evening there."

"That's right, Dan. This would be far more critical if this stranded people at work, making them unable to get to loved ones or pick children up from school, for example. To recap for those of you just tuning in, we can confirm reports of a biotoxin released into the general population in major cities on the Eastern Seaboard. This is a quickly developing situation, and we will continue to give you updated information as it comes to us, but some states where authorities report deaths are. . ."

I stood frozen in place behind the couch, watching the screen. I tried to catch my breath. My world slowed down for a moment, and I bit my bottom lip. The ground shifted under my feet as I realized what the newscasters were saying, and I grasped the back of the sofa to steady myself.

It was really happening. I had hoped I was just being paranoid, or at best, overly cautious. A hundred thoughts raced through my mind, each worse than the one before, as a wave of helplessness surged through me.

"Ethan," I said, barely above a whisper.

He turned to see me clutching the furniture for support and rose to face me. His expression was not nearly as worried as I imagined mine was.

"It's going to be all right. Come and sit down with me."

"I need to contact Hoyt. We have to escalate the trip. We can't wait another seven days—we need to go now," I said, already voice-activating the cell chip implanted in my earlobe.

"Hold on, Christine. Disconnect the call. Maybe we should take a moment to think about this. We shouldn't do this while we're so emotional," he said.

"You mean when *I'm* so emotional?" I snapped back, although he was not wrong. My heart danced in my chest wildly, and I inhaled a deep breath, forcing myself to stay calm.

"No, that's not what I said. Let's just devise the best way to handle this before we call him. Perhaps we should talk to Frank and the others first and see what the consensus of the group is."

He was so maddeningly unflappable, making me sound more like a raging lunatic. I stared at the television screen, still in shock as they reported the number of deaths because of the as-of-yet-unknown toxin.

"How can you be so impassive?" I asked.

I was anything but calm. My head reeled with thoughts of how we could escape with such short notice, and I felt my self-control begin to crack like a thin layer of ice.

"I'm not impassive. I'm trying to maintain my composure. Let's be rational about this. We'll get a conference call together and see what everyone thinks about going earlier."

He was right, of course. I needed to think this through and not allow my nerves and stress to take over. I sat next to him while he conferenced our group on a call.

After we discussed it with the rest of the travelers, we collectively decided that leaving the day after tomorrow would be the best course of action. This calmed me slightly, but I was still anxious.

I called my parents, and they promised to leave for their mountain cabin in the morning with my sister and her family. They flat-out refused to come with us into the past, as did my sister and her husband. I knew they thought I was overreacting. I made sure they had enough supplies and tried my hardest to make sure they were safe. It was all I could do for them. I knew it was their decision, and I only hoped they followed my advice and retreated to their vacation home. I made plans to take Max to their house and say my goodbyes to my family.

We intended to spend the following day gathering any last-minute items we could find while they were still available. Panic buying and hoarding had already reached a peak, and this recent development would just make things worse. By tomorrow, we'd be lucky to find anything useful left on the shelves. Drones filled the sky day and night with people ordering supplies and stockpiling. I joined their ranks and arranged my own drone delivery for the following day.

I called Hoyt, and thankfully, he agreed to change our departure date. He sounded a lot more worried than he did at our last meeting. If they attacked the East Coast with biological warfare, it was only a matter of time before California was under siege.

I called Michael and Maddie and asked them to stay with us until we left, and it eased my mind when they agreed, promising to be there first thing in the morning.

I rinsed the dinner dishes and stared at the water flowing from the faucet, realizing with a start what a luxury that would be in a few days.

Are we really doing this? I thought.

The impact of what we were about to take on hit me hard in that moment, and I braced myself against the counter, dragging in deep gulps of air. Ethan was behind me within seconds and turned me toward him.

"It's going to be okay. We'll be fine. This is the right decision."

"Is it?" I desperately wanted his reassurance. "What if we can't ever get back?"

"Then that means there is nothing to come home to."

The reality of his words sank in, and I buried my head in his chest and sobbed until he led me out of the kitchen and to bed.

The stress of the past few days ate away at me and sleep eluded me. I tossed and turned most of the night, unable to relax enough to fall asleep. Ethan plunged into a deep slumber and didn't move once. It bewildered me how he remained so cool-headed, and I envied him that.

The next day was a flurry of activity. I shopped like a mad woman—anything we might use and could hide when we got there. I ordered more Spanish coins and constantly thought about all the supplies we needed to buy in Alexandria. We intended to build six cabins and furnish all of them. No small project. The process was overwhelming, and for the first time since proposing this idea, self-doubt crept in and settled in my stomach like a brick.

SIX

Los Angeles, California 2072

The day of our departure, everyone arrived early. We didn't expect many people to be in the CCEA building now; the staff was down to a skeleton crew. Most people were busy readying their own families for the certain disaster headed for the West Coast.

We were all subdued, each lost in our thoughts about what we were preparing for. Gray's daughters appeared sullen and ticked off and made no attempt to disguise it. I couldn't blame them, really. If I were a teenager and my parents were taking me to Colonial America, I would have fought them at every turn.

I glanced at Michael, who gave me a quick grin as he moved the rucksacks to the front entry with Adams. At the last minute, I stashed my flash drive of pictures and other memorabilia in the safe, hoping they would remain protected. Thirty minutes later we had everything packed in the SUVs and were ready to move out.

Our plan was for Ethan, Frank, Annabelle, and Adams to go in first to make sure it was clear to bring the civilians through. Gray, Michael, and I would escort the others in fifteen minutes later, unless we received a message to hold off from the advance group.

As the others settled in the SUVs, I turned to give my house a final glance. It was hard to fathom this might be the last time I would ever be here. What would become of all my belongings? Would someone else live here one day? Or would they destroy it in the upcoming war? This place had seen a lot of memories, good and bad. I lived here with my son Michael, and then with Ethan. The melancholy overtook me so suddenly

I grasped the doorframe for balance. The finality of it hit me harder than I expected, and my eyes filled.

This was not the time to fall apart, and I fought hard to maintain my composure. There would be plenty of opportunity to lose my self-control once we got where we were going.

I swiped the tears away with the back of my hand before I stepped over the threshold, clicking the door shut softly behind me. I took a deep breath and started down the walkway to the car, holding my head high and trying to appear calm for the sake of the others.

The drive to the CCEA building was quiet. Michael, Maddie, Annabelle, Joe, and their girls rode with us. The children were sleeping; it was much too early for them to be up yet. Joe appeared tense, staring out the window with his brows furrowed. Maddie was fidgeting, and I noticed Michael take her hand and put it in his lap to stop her. I wanted to tell her and Joe not to be nervous, that things would be okay. But honestly, I was just as anxious.

I glanced over at Ethan and he smiled at me and winked. I returned his smile and felt better. His confidence helped me stay calm.

As we pulled into the parking lot, followed by the rest of our caravan, I noticed it was nearly empty. There were only a few cars parked close to the building. That reassured me. We had no choice but to leave our vehicles here and hope no one connected that we'd fled using the CCEA system.

Ethan leaned over and planted a kiss on my cheek. "See you in the jump room in fifteen minutes."

"Okay, be careful," I said.

Annabelle gave her girls and Joe a quick peck and motioned to Ethan. We stayed in the car as they met Adams and Frank and disappeared through the back entrance of the building. I noted the time on the dash clock and began the countdown.

"We are going to be fine," I said, twisting in my seat to glance between Maddie and Joe.

They both nodded wordlessly. Maddie chewed on a nail, and Joe barely registered me.

"Joe, your girls need you to be strong and confident. So does Annabelle. Even though she has done this before, she needs to know her husband supports her and your children. She needs to lean on you."

"I know. I'll be fine. You're both used to doing this—we aren't. It's just going to take some time to let it all sink in, that's all."

"Well, time is one thing we don't have a lot of my friend. So suck it up and dig deep, for Annabelle's sake, okay?"

He smiled. "She's lucky to have you as a friend. She's such a strong woman, sometimes I forget she needs a soft place to fall now and then. Your advice is duly noted, and from this point forward, I will be that for her."

I grinned back at him and exhaled a deep breath. I glanced at Maddie snuggled against Michael.

"I'm okay, Christine, I promise. As long as Michael is here, I'm fine. I mean, this is scary, I'm not gonna lie. But I'm not going to have a full-blown panic attack or anything, so don't worry."

I smiled at her and reached back to squeeze her hand. "Okay, good."

I glanced at the clock. "We should unload our rucksacks. We have two minutes before we're clear to enter."

We exited the car and signaled to the rest of the group to unload. We all grabbed a pack, the men each taking two, and started toward the back door. I pushed the entry code on the pad and waited for it to click to the unlocked position.

I stepped into the building, glancing both ways down the expansive corridor. It was completely abandoned. I had never seen this place void of all people, and it was eerie. I was accustomed to wrestling through the throngs of employees hustling around the facility. We made our way to the bank of elevators without incident, and took two separate lifts to the tenth floor, which made me apprehensive. I would have felt much better if we all stuck together, but we arrived within seconds of each other. Ethan appeared in the hall and motioned us into the jump room.

"No problems?" he asked.

"None, I never even saw another person."

"We saw a couple of transporters, but they just ignored us and continued on their way. It's like a ghost town here."

"I know. Spooky. I've never seen it so deserted."

"Frank is getting everything ready. He confirmed that Hoyt preprogrammed the pods, so we're all set."

"Okay, good. Let's get these supplies in there and out of sight," I said.

* * *

Tony Alvarez was in a room at the end of the corridor packing his desk when he heard voices. He crept to his office door and peered through the crack, watching the group haul packs into the jump room. Interesting. He couldn't think of one legitimate reason for them to be in there. There were no transports scheduled. Rhoades was a supervisor, and he recognized Stewart and a couple of others as agents. But he was certain the others were civilians. They had kids with them, a dead giveaway. Besides, he would know them if they were transporters. Why would agents be in the jump room with civilians? It made no sense.

He waited quietly for close to an hour, and when they didn't come out again, he knew they had transported somewhere. *Not a bad idea,* he thought. He punched his code into the security system and stepped through the door to the jump room. It was empty, except for the pile of clothing in the corner, as was the adjoining holding area. He went to the computer screen and logged on, running the report for the last activity. It showed two agents transported out over thirty days ago. That couldn't be right. He tried again, but no other transports registered.

He paced the room for a minute, thinking. They had to have transported. That was the only explanation. But how did they hide the activity in the system? He was determined to find out and set to work on the computer. His supervisory position gave him almost unlimited access to the program.

Tony began his career with the CCEA fifteen years ago. After working as an agent for five years, he was on the fast track to becoming a supervisor. In his early days with the CCEA, he was gung ho. He wanted to do a good job and climb the ladder as a government employee. In the last year his enthusiasm waned, and he only did enough to get by. Now he was bone-weary and barely hanging on by a thread, tired of working for a government who couldn't even safeguard their own citizens from an attack on American soil.

It might take some time for him to find out where they went, but he was in no hurry. He ran report after report on the computer until he found what he needed.

Bingo. There it was. They went to 1790, Alexandria. He leaned back on the stool, thinking. They were good. Whoever hid their transport buried it well. Unless he was looking for it specifically, he never would have found them. Now he just had to figure out why all the secrecy. Why would the agents want to go back to Colonial America, obviously intending to stay awhile as evidenced from their packs? Well, now that his job was pretty much on the chopping block, he had nothing but time to solve the mystery.

* * *

We brought the packs into the jump room and Frank hauled them to the pods. I glanced both ways, up and down the hall. I had a strange sensation someone was watching us, but I saw no one, and attributed it to my nerves. Frank organized the packs in front of each station and called us all together.

"Let's get into our colonial clothing. We'll go change in the holding area. You ladies stay here."

The men grabbed their backpacks and filed through the door to the adjoining room. I rifled through my pack, pulling out clothing. Annabelle and I got dressed first, the others pausing when they realized they were not sure how to layer the clothing properly.

"You need to be sure to dress in the correct order. First, put on your shift. That's this long, white shirt type thing." I held up my extra shift to show them.

"Your stay goes over your shift. Next, put on your stockings, and at least two petticoats. Over that you wear your dress. The apron is the last layer. Put your new shoes and your cap on last. Be sure to pin your hair up under your cap." I held up each item as I spoke. They stared back at me blankly, and no one moved.

"Come on, ladies, get going. We don't have all day here," Annabelle said.

We moved through the group and helped the other women into their clothing. A knock on the door sounded moments after we finished and the men joined us, sporting their colonial outfits. They looked as uncomfortable as we did. The clothes weren't as bad as those I wore on my last excursion to Alexandria. I was in dress clothes then, and they were far more cumbersome.

Frank got our attention to go over last-minute details.

"Okay, it looks like we're almost ready to go. I'm going to strap all of you in pods with your supply packs. For those of you who have never transported before, put your backpacks on and secure them. Once I set the program, a couple of things happen. The room will go dark and sparks of light appear. Those pinpoints of light will increase and make you lightheaded and dizzy. This is normal, so don't let it frighten you. It's just your body reacting to the drop in air pressure. Once we arrive in Virginia, we'll wake up sporadically. If one of you wakes up before any of us transporters, please, get us up. Normally, the first few times you transport you tend to stay unconscious longer, so chances are we will be awake before you. Everyone good?"

Everyone acknowledged him, and Frank directed people to their pods. My nerves were like exposed wire ends twitching around, waiting to touch something and ignite. I'd done this same thing hundreds, maybe even thousands of times over the years, but this might be the last time I ever saw home, and that was daunting. And because I'd talked my family and friends into coming, that increased the ante tenfold.

I turned to Ethan and then Michael, two of the people I loved most in this world. They both appeared calm and collected. Annabelle leaned over and grinned at me. Her being here made me feel better. I watched as Frank finished at the laptop and strapped himself into his pod, securing the door from the inside. The rest of the group seemed slightly terrified as the room dimmed and sparks of light circled us. All but Gray's daughters, who did a three-hundred-sixty-degree turn, and now giggled like they were on a Disneyland ride.

If I had to guess on how long that would last, I wouldn't bet much past our first sixty seconds in 1790. Those girls were in for a rude awakening.

Joe jiggled Willow on his knee as she cried. Adam's wife had her eyes screwed shut in a grimace, and Linda stared at Frank for strength.

I felt myself fade and gripped the handle inside my pod. A small moment of panic seeped in as my confidence slipped away. We were doing the unthinkable. Taking our families and fleeing hundreds of years to the past with no guarantee of ever getting back. God help us all.

And so began the story of our journey.

SEVEN

Alexandria, Virginia, 1790

I was the first to wake up in 1790. Our group stretched out across the clearing, a hodgepodge of tangled limbs and scattered rucksacks. It was not a pretty picture. We looked exactly like what we were—a band of interlopers who landed here haphazardly and collapsed from exhaustion.

Gray and Adams stirred and sat up within minutes of each other, as did Ethan. We said nothing, just stared at one another wearily. Ethan rose to give me a quick embrace and collected the packs, stacking them in a pile. I got up to help, as Gray and Adams shook the others to wake them. I preferred to let them sleep. I didn't look forward to their reaction to being here. Linda was petrified and glanced around the clearing. Frank pulled her close, while she buried her face in his shoulder. He spoke to her softly, soothing her.

Adams searched for his pack, making security of the medical provisions his top priority. Our antibiotics were this era's entire stock of them as of this moment, and that was an unsettling thought. He was intent on protecting them at all costs.

Adams's wife, Gemma, stirred while he was securing the supplies, and I glanced over to see her sit up with a start. She was dangerously close to hyperventilating. She twisted around frantically, searching for their son, Wyatt, who was still out cold. Her chest heaved as she dragged in air between sobs.

I took a deep breath and moved in that direction so I could calm her before she escalated into a full-blown meltdown. I grabbed her shoulders and pushed her head down between her knees and instructed her to inhale slow, steady breaths. My movement caught Adams's attention, and I motioned him over to help her.

"Shit," he said as he jogged to her.

Gray's wife Kira and their two daughters, Rose and Emory, fought their way back into consciousness. The teenagers cried as their parents soothed them, their earlier excitement over transporting long gone. I felt bad about the bet I made with myself when they were giggling in the jump room, because now they were scared to death.

The commotion woke the rest of the group, and the more experienced agents were calming the civilians. Annabelle's girls sobbed when they saw others in our group crying. Their cries morphed into high-pitched wails within seconds, and before I could stop it, everything spun out of control. It seemed our immediate future would be more about regret management and not goal achievement, as I had hoped.

Thirty minutes later, we had the group calmed enough to speak to them. Frank stepped up and held his hands up to quiet everyone.

"We have makeshift canvas tents to set up as shelters for the next couple of days. After that, if we want to stay in town at an inn until we build the cabins, we can. But for now, we need to remain here while we acclimate and wrap our heads around where and when we are."

Ethan joined Frank and continued. "The day after tomorrow, a few of us will go into Alexandria and see about purchasing land and supplies. The sooner we get started, the better. We want to settle in before winter hits. I think me, Gray, Adams, and Christine should go to the city. That leaves Joe, Frank, Annabelle and Michael here at camp to watch things and get us organized."

No one objected, the civilians were happy to let us take the lead and make the decisions. I took a deep breath and made rounds, ensuring they were calm. The older kids babysat Annabelle's toddlers as the adults set up the shelters.

An hour later the tents were pitched, and we were ready to organize camp. I caught Michael's eye, and he smiled. He seemed to take this in stride, but a surge of guilt ran through me anyway. It was the right decision to come here, but I could not help but feel apprehensive that I talked my son into going two hundred eighty-two years to the past to call home.

We coordinated our supplies, storing them in the canvas shelters, and gave each adult a weapon as a precaution. We didn't have guns yet, so our knives would have to do. If we ran into anything other than close combat, or hostiles with guns, we could be in trouble. Even with our weapons, we could still be in trouble.

By late afternoon, we had organized as much as possible, given the circumstances and the group's energy level. Frank recruited Michael and Maddie to gather firewood with him while I sorted through the MREs for dinner. Once the fire was roaring, we gathered around, sitting on blankets. We were all unusually quiet, even the children. Transporting took a toll on us physically, and we all yawned repeatedly. Adams, Gray, and Ethan volunteered to take the first watch, and when darkness finally came, the rest of us headed to our tents, exhausted.

During the night rain soaked the woods, and we woke to a soggy, miserable, cold campsite. I prepared a breakfast of MRE powdered eggs and dehydrated bacon, not a popular choice with the younger set of travelers. Heather and Willow asked repeatedly for their favorite cereals, and Annabelle narrowly prevented a full-blown temper tantrum by adding a peach cobbler MRE to their breakfast plates.

The mood in camp was as sullen as the weather. A steady drizzle continued throughout the morning, further soaking anything outside the tents. Our new circumstances overwhelmed everyone. I found Annabelle on the far side of the clearing and sat next to her on a downed tree trunk.

"How does it, Goody Harris?"

"Huh?" she said, curling her lip. "The only thing I understood in that entire sentence was my last name."

"The local Puritans use Goody the way we do Missus. It's short for Goodwife. We have to graduate in social rank to use the Mistress title. Just trying to practice the local vernacular."

"I'm not virtuous enough for anyone to label me a Puritan. But I think I can pull off the Mistress gig."

I laughed and hooked my arm through hers. "How are the girls?"

"They'll be fine. Kids adjust, right? They're just tired and cranky this morning. I'm more worried about Joe, to be honest. He hasn't said more than a couple of sentences to me and seems a little shell-shocked."

"Yeah, they all do. What do you think we should do about that?"

"Not sure there's anything we *can* do, Christine. They need time to adapt. This is a huge readjustment for them. We take it in stride. Traveling around history is just work to us. Maybe if we busy them with chores, it will take their mind off their uncertainties."

"Well, they had better find some enthusiasm and learn to embrace their new lives, because we need a solid plan, and we need it soon. I hope to establish a base for a few good connections when we go into the city tomorrow. The sooner we buy land and start building, the faster we settle. That will keep us busy and make it feel more like this place is home. Even if it is temporary," I said.

"We have our work cut out, that's for sure. Come on, I'll help you get them up and going. We need to gather a ton more firewood, especially with this weather," she said, rising to stretch.

I followed her to the fire in the middle of camp, and we recruited the other women to help us gather wood. They were none too happy about it but didn't complain out loud. Annabelle and I tried to engage them, but it was obvious they weren't in the mood for a pep talk. I gave up and allowed them their solitary thoughts for the day, but vowed to myself that tomorrow, they were going to shape up and snap out of it. Or I would have to force them to find some interest. This was their one free pass, but after today, they needed to get motivated, because if they couldn't get to that point, we wouldn't make it here.

After two hours of dredging through the woods for anything dry enough to burn, we went back to the shelters. The civilians all wanted to nap, so the rest of us worked on stacking the wood and digging latrines. It was dusk before I knew it, and time to prepare dinner. Linda offered to help me with the MREs, and I was glad at least one woman was coming out of her funk. Maddie and Michael seemed to adjust easily and were carving stick figures out of the kindling to entertain themselves, much to the delight of Annabelle's daughters.

The rain finally stopped, so at least we had a fire. After we ate, the general mood hadn't improved, and I could tell it irritated Ethan too. He talked about all the things we were going to do to stay busy, then announced we should all get some sleep, as the following morning we started our new lives in Colonial Virginia. Joe, Gemma, and Kira met his motivational speech with blank stares. The teenagers rolled their eyes and sighed heavily. It was obvious they thought of this as a life sentence, and not a temporary escape.

I gazed around the muddy camp at the weary faces of our group, and I honestly didn't think our first full day here could get any worse.

I was wrong.

EIGHT

Alexandria, Virginia, 1790

My head turned at the sound of a horse neighing. At once, the entire camp was on alert. Gray motioned to Kira to take the children in the shelter. She grabbed her daughters' hands, practically dragging them into their tent. Gemma pushed Wyatt into their tent, while Linda picked up the toddlers and carried them in after him. Maddie twisted toward me, and I gestured for her to get inside as well.

A moment later, three men rode into view. One man steered his horse inside our camp and stopped at the firepit. The other two hung back at the edge of the clearing. The leader turned the animal in a circle, studying the tents. The six of us stood still and no one uttered a word.

"How does it this evening, good fellow? Who might ye be?" he said, directing his question to Frank, who stood closest to him.

"Frank Rhoades. Who are you? And why are you in our camp?" he said, eyes narrowing.

"I beg forgiveness. I should like to introduce myself. Horatio Travis. 'Tis my land where ye settle."

"We're just passing through. We plan to move on as soon as we buy property of our own to build."

"Search no further. I offer my land for sale."

"This isn't what we had in mind. We need a large area, big enough for six cabins and cleared to plant crops."

"Six cabins? Impressive. Save for cutting the trees, this should be all ye desire. I know naught of a better plot for miles."

"We aren't interested."

Ethan, Gray, and Adams took a step closer to Frank. The two men on horse each moved farther into the clearing. Now Michael and Joe moved forward too, while Annabelle and I remained where we were.

The pleasantries eroded with the shift, replaced by icy stares from each side. The fire flared in protest as a gust of wind found its way through camp, ending the tense moment.

"Be clear of my property by forenoon on the morrow, Mr. Rhoades."

"Or what? We need a day to break camp."

"I fear I cannot grant ye that request."

"Oh, for God's sake, give us until the day after tomorrow, and you will never see us again," Gray said, taking another step forward.

"Mayhap a religious man? Praise God, but tarry not, my fellow. Foul deeds committed in the name of the Lord run deep."

He pulled on the reins, turning his horse toward the woods. "I shan't wish to raise the topic on a second occasion. Ye shall have till the morrow."

They disappeared into the cover of darkness, leaving us with their ultimatum. The women scrambled out of the tent to join us at the fire.

"So what do we do?" Linda asked.

"Unfortunately, I don't think we have much choice," Ethan said.

"We can't start a feud with a local. We don't have guns or fortified homes for protection," Gray added.

"We're sitting ducks if we stay here," Adams said, kicking a rock across the clearing in frustration.

"We move in the morning. It is more critical than ever that we secure land and begin the build on the housing. We'll go into the city tomorrow and rent rooms while we search for someone to help us get established. But mark my words, I will not forget Horatio Travis's name," Frank said.

"Neither will I. He is going to be trouble," Michael said.

"I think his name and face will stay with all of us for a very long time." I said, staring after him into the murky woods.

* * *

The following morning, we were awake early, breaking down the camp we set up only the day before. We had planned to buy a cart and horse to transport our provisions when we moved to more permanent housing. Horatio Travis now forced us to haul the heavy packs into the city, two miles through the woods. I resented him more with each labored step, and I funneled my frustrations into devising ways he could pay for my misery.

We crossed over a narrow bridge and soon after, we passed the house where Hannah stayed while stranded here last year. Gray, Adams, and I exchanged a glance as we passed it. My thoughts drifted to Cecelia, the slave girl who lived on the plantation until we took her to 1868, Oklahoma, with Hannah. I wondered what the plantation master thought of her sudden disappearance. I pondered that for a while as we trudged through the forest. At least it steered my mind elsewhere, away from villainous thoughts about Horatio Travis.

An hour later, I recognized the landscape and smelled the brackish water of the Potomac. We stopped to let the kids rest and drink. Annabelle and Joe chased Heather and Willow as they ran off their pent-up energy.

Once the children settled down, they joined us to sit on the forest floor to cool off.

"Should we go to Mason's Original again?" I asked, glancing at Gray and Adams.

"That's as good as anywhere if they have room," Gray said.

Adams nodded in agreement. "The innkeeper seemed like a decent guy."

"When we get to the edge of town, everyone sticks close together. It's crowded and the streets are muddy. Stay on the sidewalks and don't fall behind the rest of the group. There is a lot to see, and it's easy to become distracted. If you separate from us somehow, we are going to Mason's Original Tavern and Inn on Royal Street," I said.

"We should warn you about the odor too. It takes some getting used to," Adams said, looking at Gemma. "Wyatt, stay close to your mom. Don't wander off."

"I'm not a little kid. Seriously, like where would I even go? I didn't want to come here at all. I sure don't plan on sightseeing," he said, rolling his eyes at his dad.

"Watch your attitude, Son," Adams said, flashing him a look.

"Okay, I know we are all hot, tired, and sick of hiking. Let's just get to the inn, and we can unpack and rest. It's been a rough couple of days," Frank said.

"Amen," Maddie sighed.

I picked up my pack, the weight pulling my shoulder low. Twenty minutes later, I saw the first signs of the city. The sound of the busy port drifted into the forest. The knock of small boat bows hammering into the wooden dock kept rhythm to men barking orders to crewmen as they loaded and unloaded cargo. The boards of the wharf creaked and moaned as the waves lapped at them. We paused at the edge of the trees and gave the group a minute to collect themselves before we blended into the crowds.

"This way," Gray said, stepping clear of the tree cover.

We followed him as he led us through Alexandria. It was as populous as it was the previous time I was there. People crowded the sidewalks, carts and carriages maneuvered the muddy streets. Gemma and Linda had their hands over their noses, unused to the stench. The odor of live animals in pens, the animal carcasses behind the meat market, and smoke all blended, giving the city a pungent, almost sour aroma. Young boys roamed the streets, selling goods and trying to entice shoppers to the market on the next street over. When I saw Mason's up ahead, I sighed with relief. My pack had dug a groove into my shoulder.

Gray turned to glance at me, and I gave him the go-ahead as I smoothed my dress and apron. He swung open the door to the inn, and we stepped into the tavern, signaling the others to remain outside. Just as I remembered, the lack of any climate control hit me all at once, the air stale. The back entrance was ajar to the alley, but no breeze found its way through, and it did nothing to improve the current situation. Laughter and spirited conversation swept through the room while barmaids carrying plates of food and tankards of ale stepped around us. Adams walked forward and stood beside Gray, where I joined them. We approached the bar, and the innkeeper glanced up at us, the recognition registering on his face.

"How does it, good sirs, madame? Come to cast away more good pieces of eight, have ye?" he said, chuckling.

"You remember us?" Adams asked.

"Aye. 'Tis not ofttimes I am paid for a room with no lodgers."

"Ah, yes. Business called us out of town suddenly last time we were here," Gray said.

"Do you have rooms available?" I asked. "We have a large party, and we need all you have. We aren't sure how long we will stay."

"All bedchambers are empty now, so 'tis yer good fortune. Four rooms and use of the privy. No victuals with the price of lodging."

I studied the guys and shrugged. That meant four or five people per room. Remembering the size of the one we rented here last year, the thought of cramming that many bodies into each room was not a pleasant image. But we had no other choice.

"We'll take them," Gray said, pulling out a bag of coins.

"Can you tell us who to talk to about buying land and building? We want to purchase plots," he asked.

"Aye, Samuel Johnson has the ear of many with property for sale."

"Where do we locate Mr. Johnson?" Adams asked.

"He praises us with his company every forenoon. After supper, ye shall find him here. Benjamin Mason, at yer service," he said, with a slight bow.

Gray made the introductions and paid for the lodging a week in advance, while Adams peered outside and gestured for the others to follow us upstairs. I saw Frank's eyes narrow as he studied the owner's flintlock pistol tucked in his waistband.

The second floor had two rooms on each side of the hall. Benjamin unlocked the doors and brought extra quilts before leaving us alone in our temporary housing. The faces of our group reflected their disappointment in the accommodations.

Gemma stepped into the bedroom Ethan and I were sharing with Michael and Maddie.

"We are supposed to live here until we build houses?" she asked.

Adams appeared behind her. "Yep, we are. And Frank and Linda are in with us too. Gray and his family in one, and Annabelle, Joe and the babies in another."

"But they're so small."

"It's this or the forest. We can't take a chance out there again. We're safer here, Gemma. Wyatt is safer here. It won't be forever."

He wrapped his arms around her and pulled her close. I understood this was an enormous change for them, and these crowded rooms were going to trigger tempers quickly. I prayed Samuel Johnson showed up today. We needed to buy land and start work on the shelters before one of us snapped.

I dropped my pack on the floor and collapsed into the only chair in the room. As I peered around our new lodgings, I couldn't help but feel apprehensive for the work to come. We had a long road ahead of us and no end in sight.

NINE

Alexandria, Virginia 1790

As I predicted, the lack of personal space and privacy wore thin quickly. I saw members of our group begin to sink under the weight of the pressure. This was bad news, considering it was day one of our temporary living arrangements. The babies were cranky and the older kids restless, but I was thankful we had the entire second floor to ourselves. If we had to share the area with strangers, I shuddered to think how much worse things would be.

It relieved me when Benjamin announced supper. We collectively decided to send agents only downstairs to speak with Samuel. We found a table in the tavern and waited for Benjamin to tell us when he arrived. We ordered hard pear cider, and after two tankards, my head spun. The bar filled up quickly, dock workers and businessmen ordering food and drink. Frank asked the barmaid for bread and cheese, but I passed on the meal. A stomach issue thrown into the mix was the last thing I needed.

I grew impatient waiting for Samuel, and I was about ready to suggest we try again tomorrow when the innkeeper approached us.

"Mr. Johnson and his associates are o'er yonder."

He pointed to the corner where three men roared heartily at something the barmaid just said.

"Thank you, Benjamin," Frank said, handing the innkeeper two coins.

He grinned and dropped the money into the pocket of his apron.

"Okay, let's see if Samuel Johnson can be any help," Ethan said, rising.

We crossed the room to Johnson's table. The men peered at us curiously and rose as Annabelle and I approached.

"Please, sit down," Ethan said. "Do you mind if we join you? We have business to discuss and hope you will help."

"Ye and yer fellows are welcome as our guests. Please, sit," Samuel said, smiling.

He motioned for the server to bring a round of drinks. Ethan made our introductions to Samuel and his friends.

"What business have ye in our fair city?" Samuel asked.

"We wish to buy guns and land. We also need to hire builders to erect six cabins. We have traveled from the west with several families and are lodging here temporarily."

"Have ye guns for trade?" asked one of Samuel's associates.

"I'm afraid not. Highwaymen robbed us while traveling. They took all our weapons. Our silver was well hidden, and we escaped with all of it. We can pay in pieces of eight or silver."

"Praise God. 'Tis a common fate, I fear. Traveling becomes more perilous with each day," Samuel said.

"Jonathan Wayfair sells arms," said the other friend.

"Unless ye care naught for yer silver," Samuel said. "The man is no more than a thieving scoundrel. 'Twould be much safer to buy from Martin Collins. I can make an inquiry if ye desire."

"We would appreciate that, Mr. Johnson. We are happy to pay a finder's fee for any introductions," Frank said.

"Aye, 'tis unnecessary for arms. If I am to locate land for ye, we shall work out a fee for the purchase then. And please, call me Samuel."

"That is more than fair, Samuel," Frank said.

"I shall begin the inquiries at once. 'Twill be two days afore I return with news."

We rose to leave, and Frank placed coins on the table for the drinks. The men bid us good evening while I did a clumsy curtsy with Annabelle.

"Good day, sirs, 'twas my pleasure to make yer acquaintance," Samuel said.

Ten minutes with Samuel was all we needed to be certain he would be not only a valuable asset, but a friend. We began the climb upstairs, reassured we would make progress over the next few days, but our good mood quickly faded halfway up the staircase. Shouts carried into the stairway before we reached the hall. Gray took the stairs two at a time to the top as we hurried after him.

"What the hell?" Gray said, recognizing the voices of his wife and oldest daughter.

He rushed toward their room just as Emory flung the door open, running right into him.

"Emory, what's going on?"

Kira appeared in the doorway holding a mini tablet, her lips pinched together tightly.

"Go ahead, tell your dad."

Before the girl could answer, Kira thrust the tablet to Gray. "Your daughter snuck this in with her things," she said.

Gray took the device from Kira and turned to Emory. "Are you serious? You brought a modern-day computer here? How did you think this would work, Emory? With magical wi-fi? We talked about this. Nothing but the things on your list were to come to this timeline. Are you trying to get us all killed?"

"I just wanted to have pictures of Brian, Dad! It's not fair! You drag me away from my life with no choice, and when I want a picture of my boyfriend, *she* has a total breakdown about it," she said, glaring at her mother.

"Your boyfriend? What the hell, Emory? Our lives are at stake, here. The lives of sixteen other people besides yourself. This was a selfish, stupid thing to do. You tell me right now if you have anything else like this. Anything at all that wasn't on the list of items to bring with you."

"Tell us, right now!" yelled Kira.

Emory dropped her head and reached into her apron pocket. She lifted out a silver chain with a heart pendant and dangled it over her father's palm. He snatched it from her grip and turned to Adams.

"Can you destroy these for me, please?" he asked, handing them to Adams.

Adams mumbled a quick response and stepped next door to his room without another word. By that time, the other three doors were open, and everyone watched the scene unfold. Gemma and Wyatt followed Adams and closed the door softly behind them.

Gray turned to the rest of us. "I'm sorry. We'll go through their stuff to make sure there is nothing else."

Kira grabbed Emory's arm and pulled her into the room. It was going to be a long night for that teenager. And rightfully so. If anyone were to find that device, we could never explain it. I didn't think witchcraft was a concern this late in the eighteenth century, but the discovery of a device like that could undo everything. And going on trial for witchcraft was definitely not the way to ingratiate ourselves into the community.

We exchanged glances and went to our respective rooms for dinner. We had planned to eat together, but Stephen Gray and his wife had bigger things to deal with, and it didn't feel right for the rest of us to get together without them.

Ethan and I settled in with Michael and Maddie to eat our MREs.

"I'm glad her mom found that, and not someone here," Maddie said.

"Yeah. That was not very smart," Michael said.

"Gray will take care of it, trust me," I said.

"I'd wager Adams and Gemma are searching Wyatt's things too, as we speak," Ethan said.

"I hope so. We cannot risk another chance like that," I said, between bites of spaghetti.

I pushed the incident out of my mind and focused on Samuel finding us weapons and land. It was somewhat disheartening that after only two days here, we had a run-in with a local and discovered a teenager snuck in a computer. Not exactly the untroubled beginning I had imagined.

I went to check out the privy before bed and bundled up for the trip down the back stairs. It was located several yards from the inn. I held up my candle to peer inside and quickly decided the chamber pot would have to do if I couldn't make it until morning. There was no way I was stepping foot into that privy. Especially in the dark. A vision of my newly remodeled bathroom back home flashed into my mind, and I cursed under my breath. I climbed the stairway back to our room, convinced my bladder could make it through the night.

Michael and Maddie volunteered to sleep on the floor, and we accepted the offer. I told myself they were younger and probably wouldn't wake up with a stiff back. I made Ethan check the bed with me for any signs of fleas or bedbugs. A thorough inspection satisfied him there were none, but I still climbed in on top of the extra blanket. *Why take a chance?* I thought.

Michael and Maddie were still awake and giggled softly as I ran through all the things to do in my mind. I heard nothing more from Gray's room but imagined it was tense in there. I lay there in bed, my mind refusing to shut down as the sounds of conversation and laughter floated up from the bar below us. Our window was ajar, and the streets outside were quiet but for the occasional noise of horse hooves or the clack of buggy wheels going by. People bid each other goodnight as they left the tavern, while the lamplighters lit the oil lamps on the street.

The smell of smoke from chimneys was strong. I snuggled closer to Ethan, who was already fast asleep and snoring. When I finally fell asleep, I dreamt of war and Horatio Travis and got a fitful night's rest.

But morning brought a new day, and with it, new hope. I was ready to get out of that inn and explore the city.

TEN

Alexandria, Virginia 1790

It took the group an hour before we were ready to leave the tavern. The teenagers were unusually quiet, no doubt a result of last night's scene. We broke off into three groups. Michael and Maddie went with Adams and his family to check out the local apothecary to find anything we might use. Frank and Linda joined Gray and his wife to locate construction tools and a carpenter. Annabelle and Joe stayed with Ethan and me to search for household items.

We stashed our most important supplies under beds and in drawers and locked the rooms up tight. Our transponders remained with us always until we could hide them in our permanent lodgings. I was wary of leaving our things alone, though. We were Benjamin's only guests, so I hoped he had the sense to stop anyone headed up to the lodgers' floor. We could not haul our heavy packs all over town, so we had no choice. That was becoming a commonplace theme for us—no choices.

It was late summer, and the heat wasn't as bad as yesterday, but still hotter than Los Angeles. Or more likely, it was the many layers of clothing this era required women to wear for public dress. Either way, I longed to be in shorts and a sleeveless top with flip-flops.

"This place has dishes, let's see if we can find something in here," Annabelle said, interrupting my daydream.

She pulled the door open and a small bell jingled, bringing the clerk to the front.

"Good day. Welcome to my shop. Horace Fitch," he said, smiling.

"Good afternoon. We need household items. Dishes, cooking utensils, pots," I said.

"Ye have come to the right place then. I sell everything a modern lady shall require for a new residence."

"We need supplies for six homes. Can you accommodate an order that size?" Annabelle asked.

"Six, you say? Oh, gracious me. Well, fear not. I have stock enough for three and shall have the remaining items in a fortnight."

"That will be fine," I said, admiring a display. I picked up the dainty teacup and showed it to Annabelle.

"They're beautiful," she said, running her finger across the top of it.

"That is the finest porcelain imported from France." I examined the cup a moment too long before replacing it on the shelf. The shopkeeper saw his chance and pounced. "Let's discuss what ye will need, shall we? I'll take this for pricing," he said, reaching past me for the cup.

We spent thirty minutes making a list of dishes, pots and pans, utensils, oil lamps, and food storage barrels. I resisted buying the beautiful set in the window, even though the shopkeeper did his best to talk Annabelle and me into it. We were tempted, but they weren't practical, and we had no plans to entertain the upper echelon of Virginia society.

Ethan and Joe took the children outside while we completed the sale. We left a deposit for the purchase and arranged to come back in two weeks to pick up everything.

We strolled through the city, browsing shops. We passed silversmiths and blacksmiths, bakers and seamstresses. Merchants hawked their wares to passersby. Animals cried from inside their pens, and the children wanted to pet each one. We stopped at a furniture maker, and Ethan and Joe ordered beds, chairs, chests, and tables. I was glad I insisted we get more silver before leaving 2072. Goods were inexpensive by our timeline's standards, but we needed so much. The carpenter could make a cart, so we commissioned that too. It was a productive day for the four of us. We met our group, as planned, at the tavern at midday to check our progress.

Adams carried a large package wrapped in paper.

"They had a ton of dried herbs. Some we may only use for cooking, despite their medicinal claims, but others really have some benefit. The less I must use our modern-day medicine, the better. We should save that for emergencies and when we truly cannot use anything else."

"We found tools, and I ordered custom gadgets from the blacksmith. We also left a deposit on a plow and several flintlock pistols," Gray said.

"He didn't have rifles, so we have to count on Samuel for those. Short guns are fine for protection, but we need rifles to hunt. But he is checking with a local builder who has crews to see when they can start a build. I should warn you, when he said workers, he probably meant slaves," Frank said.

"We'll have to cross that bridge when we get there. So, all in all, a very productive day," Michael said.

"Yes, so it seems. I hope our new friend Samuel found us property," Gray said.

"I'm not sure how much longer I can tolerate living in a room with two teenagers," Kira said, glancing over to her daughters. They sat with folded arms, looking as bored as possible.

"We should spend the rest of the afternoon out of the city, somewhere in the country. Maybe we can find a stream and swim or something? We could have a picnic," Maddie suggested.

"I like the sound of that," Linda said.

"That might be just what we need. We can relax without prying eyes, worrying that we may give ourselves away somehow. The kids can have fun and chill for a while," Gemma said.

"Let me go see if Benjamin knows of someone who has a buggy or a cart or something. We can hire them to take us and pick us up later," Gray said.

He and Frank rose to find the innkeeper and were back to the table within ten minutes.

"It's all settled. The driver will meet us outside shortly. We'll pay him to wait a couple of hours for us."

Linda and Maddie packed MREs and water pouches for the group, and we all stood on the sidewalk to watch for our transportation.

A moment later our ride arrived. An elderly man grinned and tipped his hat as he stopped in front of the tavern. I stared at the rickety cart and old horse, ribs poking through skin stretched thin across its torso. If I were a betting woman, it would be difficult to make a call on which of them might collapse first—the cart, the old man, or the horse. Despite my misgivings, we piled into the wagon.

Frank and Gray sat in front on the buckboard with the driver, while the rest of us rode in the back. The toddlers squealed with delight as he snapped the reins.

"Giddup, ye ancient wretch!" he called out to the animal. The mare neighed and plodded ahead, barely able to pull the weight.

Maddie gasped and clutched the rail for support as the wagon lurched forward. I turned to Annabelle and shrugged. We exchanged a look and burst into laughter. Soon, the rest of the group joined in, even the teenagers. We rode out of the city along a dirt road into the country. Wildflowers bloomed on the trail, and birds sang in the trees. I swatted at the cluster of gnats that followed us and hoped Adams had packed insect repellent with his supply of medical items. Lavender and honeysuckle scented the breeze, and I closed my eyes and leaned my head against the back of the wagon, breathing in the unpolluted air.

We arrived at a fork in the road, and the driver veered right to a dusty path full of potholes. We bounced over the ruts, each pit flinging us farther airborne than the one before. My tailbone thanked me when he stopped the cart next to a clearing.

"Creek is just o'er yonder," he said, pointing.

I jumped out of the back, stretching my limbs to rub what I was sure would be an enormous bruise on my back from the jarring ride. Michael grabbed the pack, and we left the old man as he unhitched the horse to let it graze.

After a short distance, we heard the rush of the creek. It was a beautiful spot with shade trees lining the bank. The men stripped down to their shorts, the women tying our sleeveless shifts up to create bloomers. I dipped a toe into the stream, the icy water nearly numbing me. Everyone else had braved the cold water, and Ethan threatened to pull me over the side if I wouldn't come in on my own. I gathered my courage and stepped in. The sun beat down on my shoulders, warming me.

For the next hour we forgot our troubles. We weren't displaced time-travelers who fled a world war. We were friends and family enjoying a lazy afternoon together. Emory and Rose found wild blackberries and strawberries, and they were like nothing I had eaten in our timeline.

"My God, these berries are fantastic," Linda said.

"They really are. Not like the hot house stuff we get back in our time," Gemma agreed.

Some of us stretched out on rocks in the sun, the kids splashing in the shallow water. After lunch we packed up, reluctant to leave. We found the old man dozing under a magnolia tree, the horse grazing nearby. He jumped up when he heard us approach.

"At yer service, my good fellows," he said, saluting.

He hitched the mare to the cart, and we climbed in again. The younger kids fell asleep the moment they were in the wagon. We meandered along the path in silence when I heard the old man speak.

"Whoa, girl," he said, stopping in the middle of the road. "Highwaymen," he said to no one in particular.

I saw Ethan reach down for the knife in his boot, and Adams, Michael, and Joe did the same. They sat up straight and inched down to the end of the cart.

"Don't want no trouble. We 'ave no silver or goods. On our way to the city proper aft a day of swimming, 'tis all. Womenfolk and children aboard," yelled our driver.

Frank and Gray jumped down from the buckboard, and the other men joined them. We had six men against five of them, yet they dismounted and started toward us, unfazed.

"Walk away now, before you no longer can," Frank said.

The men laughed. One took a step closer.

"Ye intend to do that, old man? Ye endeavor to instruct me in the art of fight?" he asked.

"I intend to kick your ass unless you leave peacefully. If you do that, I see no reason to harm you. If you don't, you'll leave us no choice," Frank said.

There was that no choice matter again. I was quickly tiring of that popping up.

He laughed again, glancing at the other men he came with. He held his blade in front of him and suddenly lunged for Frank.

By this time, the kids were crying, and it was chaos in the cart. Linda gasped and jumped to the ground, but Annabelle grabbed her before she could go anywhere.

Frank kicked the knife out of the assailant's hand and twisted his arm behind his back. The snap of a bone caused the man to cry out in pain. The other three rushed forward, but Ethan, Gray, and Adams disarmed them before they knew what hit them. The would-be robbers were in a heap on the road, writhing in agony. The entire incident was over in minutes.

"Let's go," Frank said, climbing onto the seat.

"I ain't ne'er seen scoundrels go down so fast afore," said the old man. "No, sir."

"Back to Mason's before we run into any more trouble," Gray said, dusting his breeches off before taking his place beside Frank.

Everyone was now on alert as we made our way to the city. Tears rolled down Linda and Kira's cheeks, the impact of what just happened hitting them full force.

It was unsettling, but I realized it had to happen, eventually. Violence was part of life here. I reached over and squeezed Linda's hand in mine. Things were going to get worse before they got better. I only hoped the women could toughen up and fight their way through it.

ELEVEN

Alexandria, Virginia 1790

I woke up early, before Ethan. Michael, and Maddie were both asleep in front of the fireplace. Yesterday ended on a frightening note, but today was a new day, and we hoped to acquire land.

I eyed the chamber pot in the corner. As horrible as it was, I liked the idea of that better than using the outdoor privy. But some things were necessary, and I had no privacy sharing a room with three other people.

I threw my wrap around my shoulders and headed down the back stairs. The sun was just rising, but I could already hear the farmers in the marketplace. We would buy fresh fruits and vegetables from them until we grew our own. After that we might sell our own crops there. With any luck, our money would last us until we left for home again and it wouldn't come to that.

Home.

The thought made my heart quicken. I wondered what was happening in 2072. Was my family safe? I finished in the privy and took the stairs two at a time up to the room. Ethan stirred and sat up.

"You're up early," he whispered.

"Couldn't sleep."

"Fancy breakfast with me downstairs?"

"Here? Made in their kitchen?" I asked, wrinkling my nose.

"It's bread and butter, maybe some cheese. How badly can they muck that up?"

"Well, I guess Frank ate some of it the other day, and he's still alive. What the hell. I'm feeling adventurous today. You're on."

"Great. I'll be ready in two ticks."

Michael and Maddie rolled over to face us. "What's going on?" Michael asked.

"Nothing. Sorry if we woke you. Ethan is taking me downstairs for breakfast. If we aren't back in an hour, send Adams down with his medkit."

"You got it. Have fun," Michael said, rolling over and pulling the blanket over his head.

The tavern only had a few customers this time of morning, but Benjamin was behind the bar wiping down the counter. I wasn't sure the man ever slept.

"Good morn. What news from our friend, Samuel?" he said smiling.

"Good morning. Nothing yet. He was asking about, and we expect to have word from him today," Ethan said, pulling out a chair for me.

"What shall ye have this morn?"

"Coffee and bread with butter," I said.

"No cream this morn."

"Sugar will do," Ethan said.

He brought a platter of bread and homemade butter, along with mugs of steaming coffee and a small plate of block sugar.

The coffee was as bitter as medicine. I shaved a hunk off the sugar loaf equal to two lumps and dissolved it in my cup. Ethan didn't seem to mind the bitterness and sipped his black. We chatted and ate, and to an outsider we looked like any other colonial couple sharing breakfast.

A young man entered the tavern and took a table near us. Benjamin waved and shouted to him.

"Jeremiah, are ye working for Samuel Johnson this morn?"

"Aye, 'tis a long day ahead in the fields. A man needs a hearty meal afore such labor. Not the cakes and coffee they serve yonder," he said, tilting his head toward the door.

"Has Samuel taken to the coffeehouse then?"

"Aye. With the others."

"Take a message to him whilst I prepare your victuals. Mister and Missus Ward await word on his enquires on their behalf."

I didn't bother to correct him, to tell him I wasn't actually Mrs. Ward, but Ms. Stewart. I decided it was probably best he assumed I was married to Ethan.

"I shan't be reduced to an errand boy."

"Ye shall. Do not be quarrelsome, lad. Off with ye! Mutton stew and bread wait upon yer return. Mayhap a slice of pepper cake if ye bring good news."

He stood and glanced over at us, clearly not happy Benjamin was sending him to the coffeehouse in search of Samuel.

Footsteps on the stairs drew my attention, as I watched Gray, Kira, and their daughters make their way down to join us. The door closed behind Jeremiah as they sat.

"Hey, decided to brave breakfast too?" I asked.

"I need coffee. And the bread does smell delicious," Kira said.

"Use the sugar with the coffee. Trust me on this," I said.

The men engrossed themselves in a conversation about farming, while Kira and I made small talk. The girls ate their bread and cheese in silence. The tavern door swung open, allowing a stream of hot air in with it. Samuel Johnson strode in with Jeremiah right behind him.

"Good morn. I have much to discuss with ye," he said when he reached our table.

Jeremiah stood there with his mouth agape, spellbound. I followed his gaze to Emory. She smiled at him shyly and batted her eyelashes. Gray's eyes darted to his daughter, then back to the tall young man.

"Hey. That's my daughter you're ogling, Son."

"Jeremiah, have ye taken leave of yer manners? Close yer mouth afore ye catch a fly with it."

He snapped his jaw shut, but his stare never wavered. Emory glared at her dad before returning her gaze to the young man standing in front of her.

"Pleased to make yer acquaintance, Miss. Jeremiah Stanton, at yer service," he said, taking his hat off and giving a little bow.

"Emory Gray," she said, offering her hand. He took it in his and planted a kiss on the back of her hand.

"Okay. Enough of that," Kira said, grabbing her daughter's arm.

"Jeremiah, were ye not here for victuals? Carry on then. I expect ye in the field within the hour if ye wish me to pay a full wage for the day," Samuel scolded.

He went to the bar to eat, glancing back at Emory and smiling.

"I beg yer apologies. I employ Jeremiah. He is young, but a good worker for nineteen years. He is faster than an experienced man twice his age. He lost both parents to a summer grippe fever when he was but seventeen. They were our neighbors. Mrs. Johnson 'twould not allow Jeremiah and his sister to go to the orphanage house, so they both work for us now."

"He's nineteen?" Emory asked.

"Enough, Emory," Gray said.

She rolled her eyes and folded her arms in exasperation.

"I have news of property. Widow Blanchard has ten acres she is considering for sale in the country outside the city. The land is empty for building and planting. A hearty stream runs through with fish. Turkey, deer, duck, and rabbit are bountiful in the surrounding woods."

"That sounds ideal if we can work out a reasonable price," Ethan said as we all responded in agreement.

"The land 'tis very near my homestead. Mayhap ye will all visit my home this forenoon and we ride to Widow Blanchard's property together? Benjamin can direct ye there. I advise ye to have yer fellows along. Should ye wish to place an offer with Widow Blanchard, do it before the sun sets today. Horatio Travis seeks this land, and when he hears of my inquiry of a potential sale, he will stop at naught to claim it as his own."

"Horatio Travis. Unfortunately, we have had the displeasure of meeting him," I said.

"Then you know of his unscrupulous manner, Madame."

"We do, and we are prepared to make an offer today if the land fits our needs," Gray said.

"'Tis settled then. I shall expect ye at my farm, forenoon. I bid ye good day."

Jeremiah shoved a last bite of food into his mouth and jogged to catch up to Samuel as he left, but not before glancing Emory's way. I watched her smile at him as he passed our table. She caught my eye and looked away quickly, but I had seen enough. I was a teenaged girl once myself and recognized the beginning of a crush when I saw it.

"Well, that is good news. And to be honest, I really hope this is a good fit. I'd love nothing more than to swoop this land right out from under Horatio Travis's nose," Gray said.

We finished our meals and went upstairs to update the rest of the group. They were as excited as we were to see the land. We discussed our top price for the property and agreed we would offer a down payment and bi-yearly payments, to pay it off in the first year, with a provision that if we missed a payment, the deed would revert to Mrs. Blanchard's ownership. That would leave us silver for emergencies until we were self-sufficient, and if we could go home before the year was up, it would once again belong to Mrs. Blanchard or her heirs. That seemed the fairest way to handle it. We did not intend to cheat the widow, but we also did not want to go broke buying land. We had to save enough for the build, materials, animals, and furnishings.

We asked Benjamin to schedule the same driver we had yesterday for the trip to the Johnson's farm.

After lunch, we waited on the walkway in front of Mason's again. The old man showed up with the same rickety cart and tired horse, and my back spasmed just thinking about riding in the wagon. We settled in as the mare faltered before pulling us away from the inn.

Samuel's farm took a thirty-minute ride to reach but may as well have been in the middle of nowhere. If I hadn't known better, I would not have believed there was a major city only a few miles away. The rolling hills backed up to wooded forest, and the house was a classic two-story farmhouse with a barn, several outbuildings, and a water well in front. A wooden fence surrounded the property where horses and cows roamed.

Samuel Johnson had done nicely for himself. The cart stopped at the gate, and the old man hopped down to stretch. I stepped onto the porch with Ethan, Frank, and Linda. The others stayed behind with the children. A woman about my age answered the door, wiping her hands on her apron.

"Ye must be Samuel's new fellows. Prudence Johnson," she said, "Please, come in. I'll send word to Samuel that ye have arrived."

We made our introductions and stepped into the house. The modest room was large, but not elaborately decorated. Simple, functional furniture filled every available space. Despite the warm weather, the fire flared and crackled, with a pot hung over the flame. There was a military sword mounted over the fireplace, and a sheathed knife lay on the mantel.

"Nellie, come down here please," Prudence shouted.

A young girl in her teens bounced down the stairs and stopped short when she saw us.

"Nellie, go find yer brother and have him send word to Mister Johnson his guests have arrived."

She didn't move but continued to stare at us.

"I am to prepare the midday meal, Mistress Johnson, not scour the fields for my brother."

"Nellie! Child, tarry not. What has possessed ye? Must ye be so quarrelsome?"

She darted down the stairs, pushing past us and out the front door.

"That poor girl. I fear she is not fit to prepare a meal for the animals. Orphaned when she was but fifteen. Still, that gives her no cause for ill manners and no call to be rude. Lord only knows why no one taught her to cook before then. Her mother, although our neighbor, was not a well-bred woman. God rest her soul. That girl sees darkness in every corner, and ne'er a jolly mood is upon her. A smile has yet to grace her in my presence. Betwixt that and her lack of any useful household skills, she is sure to be a spinster. It will require great effort to secure her future. I suspect it lies in the almshouse. I have too little time to prepare her to be a proper Goodwife, I fear."

I cleared my throat, not sure how to respond to her statement. "I'm sure she will come around," was the best I could manage.

I glanced at Linda, who was as equally at a loss for words.

"Her older brother, Jeremiah, is a young gentleman. I know naught how the same blood runs through their veins."

Thankfully, the young gentleman Jeremiah bounded through the back door at that moment, sparing me from further responding to Prudence.

"Ma'am. Mister Johnson 'twill be ready shortly. He asked that I escort his guests to the north field to depart for Widow Blanchard's property from there."

"Well, then off ye go."

Jeremiah opened the front door and motioned us outside, where he mounted a horse. We piled into the wagon again, much to the dismay of my tormented tailbone. The cart bumped along the path to where Samuel waited on horseback. He led the way off his property, and after a ten-minute ride, we stopped. A narrow trail descended into the most beautiful valley I had ever seen. The stream was visible from that vantage point, as was the lie of the land. The water cut through the grass, clearings on either side, which backed up to wooded areas. The valleys were large enough to build shelters on and plant crops. A smile spread across my face as I studied it.

It was perfect. I believed our luck was turning.

TWELVE

Alexandria, Virginia 1790

Widow Blanchard appeared upward of eighty years old with eyes as sharp as a pin. Her bony fingers dipped the quill into the inkwell a second time as she completed filling in the blank spaces on the deed. She passed it to Samuel, who read over it. Ethan and Frank sat perched on the edge of wingback chairs across from our hostess, while Annabelle and I shared the settee on the other side of the room. The men read over the paper and Samuel handed them the quill for their signatures. A real estate transaction took only a signature with the promise of payment and silver coins to complete the sale. We certainly complicated things over the next two hundred eighty-two years.

Frank lifted the heavy bag onto the desk. "Would you like Mr. Johnson to count this, Mrs. Blanchard?"

"Unnecessary, young man. 'Tis anything missing, Samuel shall forfend ye from taking root. I wish to be a fly on the wall when Horatio Travis learns he is not to have my land. That scoundrel has naught but ill intentions."

"I agree with you, Mrs. Blanchard. It's been a pleasure doing business with you. Thank you again. We will build as soon as the carpenters are available. We will try not to disturb you, but if you need anything, you send one of your staff to get us," Ethan said.

"Ye are a charming Englishman, Mister Ward. Unlike the British scoundrels who seek to steal our colony. Ye take care of him," she said, flashing me a glare.

"I shall do that, Mrs. Blanchard," I said, smiling.

We found the others outside and announced we were the proud owners of ten acres of Virginia countryside. We asked our driver to take us back to town. We had much to do. The most pressing order of business was to contract with the builders for labor and materials. We arranged a price with the old man to transport us to the property every day, once construction began. We did not want to buy our own horses until they finished our cart and fencing and an outbuilding was complete.

Until then, the decrepit wagon and aged horse would have to do. We thrilled him with the prospect of steady work for the next few weeks, and he finally told us his name.

"I s'pose we should properly introduce ourselves. Abraham Fitzgerald, formerly of the Twelfth Virginia Regiment. Everyone calls me Fitzgerald," he said, lifting his chin.

We introduced ourselves and I climbed into the back, settling into the corner for the ride to the city. We stopped at the carpenter's shop where Frank and Gray worked out the details of the build. Ethan and Adams went to the blacksmiths, where Samuel said his brother could sell us horses. Michael and Maddie browsed the marketplace and showed up with apples and pears. Annabelle and I stayed close to the wagon with the kids and the other women.

"I wish there was something else we could wear besides these dresses," Gemma said, tugging to adjust her apron.

"Seriously," Kira said. "It takes master yoga moves just to get in and out of this nonsense every day."

"Once we are alone in the country, we will enjoy more privacy and freedom," I say. "But right now, we need to blend in with everyone else here. I know it's not ideal, but it shouldn't be much longer."

"I'll deal with it," Kira said.

Frank and Gray were back first. "We arranged everything. We hired builders, and they will secure hardwood and materials. They start tomorrow," Gray said.

"Wow, that was fast," I said.

"We need to move quickly. Having our own places will improve our quality of life. I know everyone is tired of the inn and it's only been a few days," Frank said.

Ethan and Adams arrived, and we filled them in on the build.

"Brilliant. We have horses procured. We didn't inspect them. None of us knows how to determine a good horse from a bad one anyway. Even Fitzgerald's old nag gets us around, so anything is better than nothing at this point," Ethan said.

"Let's get back and take it easy for the rest of the afternoon. Tomorrow we start the real work," Adams said.

* * *

The following morning, we were up with the sun. Excitement was in the air as we prepared for the first day of construction. I was downstairs before everyone else, even the bitter coffee Benjamin served, a welcome jolt of caffeine. One by one, the others joined me for breakfast. We finished quickly and gathered in front of the inn to wait for Fitzgerald.

The lamplighters used their long staffs to extinguish the oil lamps as we huddled together in the early morning chill. Fall was just around the corner, and I felt it coming. There was probably another month of warm weather before it turned cool, and once winter was upon us, we would need to be in our own homes.

Farmers guided their carts by, full of fresh produce for the market, as doors along the sidewalk opened for business. I pulled my shawl tighter around my shoulders as a shiver made its way down my arms. Fitzgerald and his ancient mare rounded the corner onto Royal Street, and he waved his hat in a greeting.

We said our good mornings and climbed into the all-too-familiar cart for the ride to our new land. We arrived thirty minutes later, the builders already chopping and sawing wood. The foreman directed several workers, some of them colored. I hoped they were not slaves. I could not condone that, but I realized we would need to be careful regarding our revulsion to slavery. We would only draw unwanted attention to ourselves if we objected too loudly. The only thing we could do was make certain the foremen treated them fairly and did not abuse them while working on our cabins. How I intended to do that was still unknown. I only knew I must.

Gray took charge of construction for our group, so he assigned tasks to each of us, from clearing bushes and weeds, to sawing wood. The younger travelers brought water to workers and acted as runners. If anyone needed a tool or wanted to talk to a foreman, it was their job to fetch them. It was an efficient system that cut down waste and allowed the framing to happen in record time.

At noon we broke for a lunch of bread, cheese, and fruit. The children asked for spaghetti, but of course, we could not eat MREs in front of the workers. Annabelle slipped the toddlers each a piece of candy to quiet them. They ran in the grass chasing a butterfly, happy for the moment.

"God, it's like they are holding me hostage, these kids. I have to give in and bribe them with candy," she said.

"Don't feel bad. They're too young to comprehend what's happening, and the need to be discreet. They have been surprisingly well behaved, considering the circumstances they are in," I said.

"Really? I was thinking you probably thought I was a terrible mother, giving in to them all the time. I feel like a crappy mom."

I placed my hand over hers. "Annabelle, nothing could be further from the truth. You are so brave to bring them here. They are toddlers, who behave as every other toddler does. They are learning to test the limits with you. Michael once had a tantrum in the bank because I wouldn't let him touch the electronic brochure the teller had at her cubicle. I'm talking complete meltdown. Over a frigging piece of plastic," I rolled my eyes at the memory.

"The girl gave me the stink eye and totally judged me and my mothering skills. Clearly, she had no children, or she would have just ignored his ear-drum-piercing screech, given me my cash, and sent me on my way. On a do-over, I would let him touch the stupid thing. Pick your battles and all that stuff."

Annabelle laughed and squeezed my hand. "Thanks for having my back, Christine."

"Always. You know that."

"Yes, I do. It looks like it's time to get back to work," she said as Samuel approached us.

"Back to work, my good fellows," called Samuel.

"We are at your service," Ethan said, rising.

"Aye, I have some doubt regarding yer skills. Stephen will be of help, however, the rest of ye have much to learn," Samuel said, chuckling.

I rose and shook the grass from my petticoats, grabbed my axe and started to the wood pile. Samuel Johnson had an enthusiastic spirit. One I wished would rub off on me, as I could have used some of that energy right about then.

As the afternoon gave way to dusk, Samuel and Jeremiah inspected the construction site. The men showed him all we had accomplished on our first day, and they seemed impressed with our progress. Framing on one cabin was almost complete.

I noticed Jeremiah gaze around the clearing, trying to be subtle. But once he spotted Emory, his face couldn't hide his excitement. This was sure to be trouble. I felt it in my bones. A teenage romance while under strict instructions to keep quiet about our origins would not be a good mix. Emory met his stare and grinned at him. He trotted his horse over to her, all smiles and starry eyes.

I caught Kira's eye and motioned my head toward them. She dropped the log she was holding and stalked over to them, pulling the teenager away. She said something to her unhappy daughter, who turned back to wave at Jeremiah. Kira glared at her mom as she tugged on her hand.

The foreman announced the end of work for the day, and we gathered up tools and stacked wood for tomorrow. The ride to the city seemed especially rocky after a full day of physical labor as we bumped along the uneven roads. We moved at a glacial pace as I breathed in the dust that settled in my chest. Dirt streaked the faces of my fellow travelers. The kids were subdued, the smaller ones unable to keep their eyes open.

When we reached the inn, we were too tired to do anything but wash in our room basins and eat an MRE for dinner. My entire body ached, all my muscles overworked and sore. Our lives in 2072 had prepared none of us to work this hard, physically, and the fatigue was overwhelming.

"An honest day's labor is rewarding, isn't it?" Ethan asked as we climbed into bed.

Michael and Maddie both moaned and pulled the covers over their heads. I curled my lip at him before I turned off the oil lamp.

"This has done nothing but highlight every single one of my inadequacies. I am not in as good as shape as I thought I was, because I'm hurting," I groaned.

"You'll be in better condition before you know it. A couple of weeks of this and we'll have you tip-top," he said, kissing my forehead.

"Shut up and go to sleep, Ethan," I said, turning to face the window and resisting the urge to smack him.

"Yeah, shut up and go to sleep, you damn sadist," Maddie said from under the covers.

Ethan chuckled and settled deeper into the bed, asleep in minutes. I lay awake thinking about what might be happening in Los Angeles in our timeline. I made a mental note to talk to Frank tomorrow, wondering if we should send someone back in a month or so to see if things had improved. My intuition told me the hardships of colonial life were just beginning, and the sooner we could go home, the better.

THIRTEEN

Alexandria, Virginia 1790

I forgot my plan to ask Frank about a reconnaissance trip home in the morning. I was too tired to focus on anything but building our houses. I remained in this state of exhaustion, as we all did, for the next week.

Halfway through our second week, Gray called a meeting to review the footprint for the cabins with us.

He unrolled a piece of parchment paper with the renderings drawn on it.

"All the houses are alike. An open living and kitchen area, fireplace, and two bedrooms. I know not everyone needs both bedrooms, but it's just easier to work from one set of plans. Plus, the spare room is extra storage if you don't need the sleeping space. Frank and I are building the fireplaces ourselves. The mantels will have a notch system. They are removable, and behind them is a hidden compartment. That's where we'll keep our transponders, medical supplies, and anything we don't want prying eyes to see."

The houses were nothing fancy, a little under eight hundred square feet, but they would offer us much-needed shelter. We had commissioned basic furniture that included beds, a table and chairs, and a dresser for each room. The food preparation areas contained a long counter height shelf. Just the necessities. Annabelle and I insisted they build two outdoor shower stalls. We positioned barrels to catch rainwater, and a spigot released the water. In the summer, we wouldn't mind showering with cold water, but in winter we couldn't tolerate it. So Gray added a tub. It was a large barrel cut shorter for easy access. While not ideal, it gave us a means to keep ourselves clean. But there was only one straightforward method of heating it. We had to pour boiled water into the barrel, a pot at a time. The locals only bathed once a year, but there was no way we were following that custom. Their personal hygiene standards were abysmal.

One crew framed the housing while another constructed the outbuildings and fencing. Michael and Joe cleared a field of stray bushes for a garden, and Ethan and Adams dug a shallow trench to divert stream water to the new plot. The build was progressing smoothly, but it wore us thin. Our room rent at the inn was putting a dent in our silver, and we were almost out of MREs. We would run out of pre-packaged food within thirty days. Which meant we either bought it from the marketplace, hunted and grew our own, or starved.

We decided that a bonus to the contractors to rush the work would be money well spent. We wanted to get our houses furnished and livable, bring our livestock home, and plant our vegetables. Our accelerators matured the crops quickly, so we planned to tell anyone who asked that we bought fully grown produce and transplanted it. I was uncertain that would convince someone observant enough to notice, but that was the most believable story we could concoct.

Wild berries were abundant near the stream, so we didn't plant any more. Our modern-day enhancers allowed otherwise seasonal fruits and vegetables to grow year-round. We had seeds for squash, pumpkin, corn, lettuce, potatoes, carrots, celery, and onions, along with herbs to seed in small pots. Linda insisted that a mirepoix base would allow her to make a variety of hearty soups. I was glad she was here, because I didn't even know what that was until she explained it. Left to my skills, we would have eaten boiled corn and raw carrots for every meal.

We planned to buy chickens for eggs, a few cows for milk, butter, and cheese, and maybe a couple of pigs. I couldn't imagine butchering a swine or plucking a chicken for a meal again, but Ethan, Annabelle, and I all did it when the CCEA stranded us in the past two years ago. I knew when the time came, I would do what I had to, to stay alive and protect the rest of our group.

Lost in thought, I was working next to Kira and Rose, her youngest girl, when Emory approached.

"Mom, I'm gonna have lunch with Jeremiah today," Emory said.

Kira didn't stop stacking wood. "Uh, I don't think so," she replied.

I kept chopping but stole a glance at her.

"Oh my God, Mom. This is so stupid! Like, what do you think is going to happen? It's only lunch. He's the only person close to my age I have met here."

"Can I go?" asked Rose.

"No!" Emory said, sneering at her sister. Kira paused her work and glanced between her daughters. "You know what, actually yes, you can go. Rose, you go too. There's no reason your sister can't come with you since it's so innocent. Wyatt can tag along too. And you'll eat on the grass where we can see you. That's the deal, take it or leave it."

Emory stood with her hands on her hips, lips pursed. "Fine! It's like I'm in prison here."

"Oh, stop. Don't get your petticoats in a ruffle. You're still having lunch with him."

Emory rolled her eyes. Her signature look during those days. "You're not funny, Mom," she said.

"Sure she is," Gray said, sauntering up to give Kira a high five. "You're lucky she agreed to it at all. I wouldn't have. Wanna try your luck with me?"

"Dad, I'm seventeen years old!"

"You're seventeen in the year 1790, not 2072. Young ladies conduct themselves differently in this timeline. And while you are here, you will do the same and act accordingly."

Emory grabbed the hem of her skirts and stalked away, back to the pile of logs we assigned her to de-branch. Rose smiled and hugged Kira.

"Thanks, Mom."

"Just came over to tell you Samuel got word the furniture maker will complete our furnishings next week. The pay bonus sure helped production. The builder brought on another crew, and we should be ready to move in within a few weeks," Gray said.

"Good. Not a day too soon. Getting settled in and having a routine will help the girls," Kira said.

I stopped to wipe my face on my apron. "Do you think we will have guns and livestock by then too?"

"Yes. Samuel is seeing to the animals, and he has a seller for long guns too."

"Okay, good. Better get to work on those bathtubs. I suspect there is going to be a line of us for those," I said.

"Amen, sister," Kira said, resuming her work.

* * *

After four weeks of hard manual labor and a few setbacks, we finished the houses. There were three crews and our group working from sunup to dusk every day. We completed the barn, erected the fencing, and cleared a plot for planting. A chicken coop and pig pen were on the far edge of the property. We dammed the water diverted from the stream, but it was ready to release when needed. The bathhouses awaited the first bathers, constructed of solid black oak. Each cabin had an outdoor privy, and Annabelle and Joe fenced their place so the girls could play in a yard. Joe even made them a swing on a large tree that entertained them for hours at a time. If I hadn't known better, I would have thought this was a permanent settlement.

We moved our things from the inn to the cabins, and the furniture maker delivered our furnishings. Samuel brought us chickens, cows, and two pigs. We bought six horses; we didn't want to spend money on one for each adult. We gained a mule to pull the plow, and six flintlocks. Ethan, Adams, Frank, and Gray gave daily shooting lessons, teenagers included. We planted the garden and got anything else we needed from the market. We hauled goods back in our cart, and life settled into a routine of weeding, watering, and caring for the animals.

Linda made the women her sous chefs, and we all learned the basics of cooking. Even me. I had done very rudimentary food preparation while stranded in Oklahoma and England. Linda took our dining to the next level. Her chicken soup was seriously the best I have ever had, and I had to force myself not to overindulge on her pumpkin pie. Frank built a brick oven in their cabin, our only one. But since she did most of our meals, it just made sense to have it at their place. It was a lot of work, and we decided that not every house needed one as we usually ate our meals communal style.

We fished the Potomac for shad and herring, and the men hunted venison, turkey, and geese. We steered clear of some of the more colorful local favorites. Beaver tail, boiled ox liver, ambergris, and savory eel pie, to name a few. Turtle soup and pepper cake were two other popular dishes we passed on making. Linda baked our bread herself as many bakers used sawdust as a filler to make it stretch further. We decided we should not trust the bread at the market.

Time passed without incident, until one dreary winter morning, when the thing I feared the most came to rear its ugly head.

An epidemic.

FOURTEEN

Alexandria, Virginia 1790

I had hoped to make it through the end of the year with no one close to us falling ill. Although we inoculated our group against a few diseases for this era, I was nervous about sickness here. Antibiotics couldn't cure everything, and we could only get so many vaccines. There was no way to protect ourselves from all illnesses. What scared me the most was that so many ailments were dormant in our timeline, so we had no tolerance built against them. We wiped out the common cold and the flu in 2040. Adams administered us N1H1 inoculations, but there were several variants of influenza. We took every precaution to stay healthy. We practiced safe food preparation, maintained our personal hygiene, and washed our hands often. We had little contact with outsiders, except Samuel and his family, but one flu bug could undo all of that.

So when the urgent knock on the door came that morning, intuition caused my stomach to drop.

"Goody Ward! Come quick, please!" The voice was tinged with desperation.

Ethan flung the door open to a breathless Jeremiah.

"Praise God ye are here. Mistress Johnson needs ye. Samuel and their son have taken ill. Naught relieves their suffering, and they are delirious with fever."

I exchanged a worried glance with Ethan. He threw his coat on and tucked his flintlock into his waistband. "Nathan Adams is the person we need. He is a physician, of sorts."

"Mister Adams is a doctor?"

"Not officially. He has medical training more advanced than the doctors here. He trained in France," I said, wondering where I came up with that story so quickly. It was far enough away that no one here would be familiar with the practices of a French physician. At least I hoped not.

Ethan studied me with a puzzled expression. I shrugged and turned my attention back to Jeremiah while Ethan left to find Adams.

Jeremiah paced the room nervously. "The Johnsons sacrificed a daughter to disease. They mustn't lose another child. I fear they cannot bear the grief."

"I didn't know they had lost a child."

"Aye. Two winters ago. She was but a mite, only here one year. Shook with fever for three days. 'Twas God's will, but she did not go to her final resting place peacefully. I witnessed what lay in their hearts with that loss."

I blinked away tears as I listened to him. The image of Prudence and Samuel watching their baby die, helpless to do anything to prevent it, was heart wrenching.

Ethan arrived with Adams, Gemma trailing closely behind him. Others started toward our cabin when they realized something was wrong.

"Tell me their symptoms," Adams said.

"Burning fever, delirium, coughing, and some vomiting."

"How long?"

"Two days. Mistress Johnson tried to cure what ails them. She thought it was a lingering summer grippe. But 'tis becoming worse, and she has no more fever drink."

"All right. Let's see if I can help them."

"Mistress Johnson asked for Missus Ward," Jeremiah said.

"No. Until I know what we are dealing with, we can't risk infecting anyone else."

"I'll go, Adams. I'll wear a mask and gloves," I said. "You might need help with something."

Ethan protested, but I held my hand up to stop him. "I'll be careful. I'll take every precaution I can. The last thing I want to do is bring it back to anyone here."

"Then I'll go too. Samuel will need someone to tend the animals while he is sick." Adams shook his head. "The fewer people there, the better."

"I am minding the farm," Jeremiah said.

"Okay, it's settled then. We'll be back as soon as we can," I said.

Adams grabbed his satchel with the medical supplies and followed me outside where we mounted our horses. Jeremiah wasted no time reaching the edge of our property, eager to get to the Johnsons.

* * *

We entered the house to a deathly still. The only sound was coughing from somewhere upstairs. As we climbed the stairs to the bedrooms, I heard soft weeping. Jeremiah opened the door and stepped aside. Prudence was crying and dabbing a damp rag on the forehead of her youngest son. The boy's skin shone with perspiration and his head rolled back and forth as he moaned. She raised her head to look at us, her expression a mixture of relief and fear.

"We have no more fever drink," she said, tears rolling down her cheeks.

Adams picked up the bowl on the nightstand and sniffed the inside. "Quinine flowers. We are way past that point."

"I have given him every poultice I know. Nothing works. Nellie was to fetch the doctor, but he is overwhelmed with the many ill, and she left word. He sent a messenger last eve. If he does not awaken by the morrow, the doctor will call. He is to bleed him to remove the pestilence and fever."

"Absolutely not! That will kill him," Adams said.

We already had our masks on and slid our hands into the gloves. He guided Prudence out of the chair next to the bed. He waved the thermometer over the boy's forehead and turned to me.

"104.2. I need to get the fever down first thing."

He pulled the boy's eyelids up and used his penlight to inspect his pupils. He listened to his heart and chest with his stethoscope and examined the lymph nodes in his neck. He held an oxy saturation tab to his fingertip pulse and shook his head.

"Well, it's not yellow fever. It's either diphtheria or a severe case of influenza that has turned into a respiratory infection. His ox-sat is only sixty. Way too low for normal brain function. That's why he's delirious and in such distress. Without oxygen, I need to knock out the septicity as quickly as possible to return his breathing to an acceptable level."

Prudence stood in the corner watching him work on her son. She hadn't said a word until then.

"What are ye doing to him? What are those tools ye use?" she cried, stepping forward.

"We are trying to help him, Prudence," I said, grabbing her arm.

She must have seen something in my eyes because she stepped aside and let us continue.

"Mister Adams is a trained medical doctor. He received his education in France," Jeremiah said, stepping farther into the room.

Adams turned to Jeremiah with raised eyebrows, then back to me. I lifted my shoulders in a slight shrug and looked away.

"Prudence, without my treatment, your son will die within twenty-four hours. Let me help him, please," Adams said. "Christine, pull out the liquid fever reducer, one of the adult dosage antibiotics, and the children's decongestant. Crush the antibiotic in water."

I rummaged through the satchel and pulled out the items. "I need a clean cup," I said, turning to Jeremiah.

He ran down the stairs and returned with a tin cup in hand. I used it to crush the pill into powder then sweep it off the dresser, pouring water from the pitcher over it.

Adams motioned me to come closer. He poured the medications into the boy's mouth while I held it open, then held it shut to make sure he swallowed everything. Next, he snapped the tab off the decongestant blister pack and held it under the boy's nose so he would inhale the medication.

"He'll show improvement by tomorrow." He measured more fever reducer into the empty cup and set it on the bedside table. "He gets the rest of this in the morning. Give him as much fluid as he'll take. Broth or water only. Where is Samuel?"

"This way," Jeremiah said, stepping into the hallway.

We followed him to the room at the end of the corridor. Samuel lay curled up on the bed. A cough racked his body. Sweat soaked his shirt. Adams repeated the same examination and dosed him with the fever reducer, antibiotic, and decongestant. His hacking quieted within ten minutes and he slept.

"Everyone in the house needs to take these," he said, holding out the small white pill. "Starting with you, Prudence."

"But I am not ill."

"We're trying to make sure you stay that way," I said.

"Let me see the other children so I can adjust their dosage properly. Samuel and your son are to remain in quarantine until they show no symptoms for twenty-four hours. When you sit with them, or bring them food, wear a mask for protection. Is there anyone else living in the house?"

"Our oldest son, and Jeremiah and his sister, Nellie," Prudence said.

"They each need to take one too," he said, handing her three more pills.

"No dairy products for a few days. No milk, butter, cheese. It helps the congestion clear if you lay off those for a bit."

"What about Mother Johnson?" Jeremiah asked.

We turned to Prudence. "Samuel's mother won't perish until the good Lord himself comes to deliver her a personal invitation to heaven. She is stubborn and muleheaded as a person can be. And just as mean when she sees fit. She is bedridden with age and has not left her room in months. She shows no sign of feeling unwell," Prudence said.

"Nevertheless, she must take the medicine if she wants to stay that way," Adams said, shaking another pill out of the bottle. "And whatever you do, do not let the doctor give them anything else. And under no circumstance is he to bleed anyone in this house. Do you understand? I'll be back sometime tomorrow."

Prudence nodded wordlessly. She was clearly unsure whether our efforts would help her son and her husband, but she thanked us anyway. We rode home talking about what we saw.

"What if they aren't the only one with a sick family?" I asked.

"I don't know. That could be disastrous. Given the hygiene standards here and that they don't practice sterile *anything*, it will spread like wildfire."

"How can we stop it?"

"Simply put, we can't. We must be very selective about who we share our pharmaceuticals with, not to mention our methods and modern-day medical tools. I think we can trust Samuel and Prudence, but I still intend to talk to him about not sharing that information with anyone else."

"It's everyone for themselves, here," I said. I knew we must keep our medication to ourselves, but that didn't make me feel any less guilty about it.

We rode the rest of the way home in silence. As we approached our settlement, there seemed to be a flurry of activity. A sense of dread traveled through me as I wondered what was going on. As we got closer, I saw Ethan and Michael carrying a body across the clearing toward my cabin. I couldn't make out anything about the person they carried. My view was blocked. But whoever it was, they were in trouble. I saw the sense of urgency in their movements. I tapped my horse with my heel, and he broke into a trot. I inhaled a deep breath and prepared to deal with the next crisis.

FIFTEEN

Alexandria, Virginia 1790

Ethan and Michael had whoever they were carrying inside the cabin by the time I got there. I dismounted and quickly tied my horse to the porch post, then reached for the door handle just as Michael opened it.

"Oh good, you're back. We need Adams in here, now."

"He's right behind me," I said, twisting to see him secure his stallion next to mine.

"What's going on?" he asked.

"Wyatt and Rose found an Indian in the woods near here. He's unconscious and looks pretty bad," Michael said.

Adams brushed past me, and I followed him inside the cabin. I stopped at the doorway to the spare bedroom where an indigenous man lay on the bed. He was wearing nothing but a hide that covered him from waist to thigh. If they found him like that, or they took his clothes off because of his fever, I did not know. But it was cold enough now that wandering bare-chested in the woods would be foolish. Sweat gleamed on his torso and face. He coughed, and his head lolled to one side as Adams donned his mask to examine him. He turned to the group of us gathered outside the room.

"High fever, swollen lymph nodes, and a cough. His oxygen level is low, and he is very congested. Same symptoms we just saw at the Johnsons."

"What does he have?" Ethan asked.

"I can't be sure without tests. It's either diphtheria or influenza. If it's flu, this is a severe strain that attacks the respiratory system."

I heard the native struggling to breathe from where I stood. He shivered, and chills shook him so violently, Adams held the man's arms in place.

"Can you get me a light blanket for him, Christine? I need the same meds you pulled for me at the Johnsons."

He turned to us again. "Assuming we want to use our antibiotics to help him. If we don't, we'll bury him in forty-eight hours."

"We have to save him. We can't pick and choose like that," I said.

"Give him the medicine, and we'll meet later to make a firm plan as far as helping anyone in the future goes," Frank said.

I put my mask on and dug through the satchel. I handed Adams the bottles and pulled another chair to the bedside, where I helped him get the medicine down the man's throat.

"Now we wait," he said, rising.

We stepped out of the room, closing the door softly.

"Let's gather everyone. We need to talk about things before this illness forces us to make impossible choices," Adams said.

Twenty minutes later, we assembled in the living space of our cabin. The teenagers were watching the toddlers run in the yard, as we didn't want to alarm them with worry of disease and death.

"This strain of flu, or whatever it is, is serious. If we did not have fever reducer and antibiotics to clear their lungs, all the sick I saw today would be dead in a matter of days," Adams said.

"How can we not help people if they are dying?" Gemma asked.

"With every dose I give someone else, that means one less for our group. We do not have an infinite number of antibiotics, and eventually we will run out. And our vaccines may not protect against this. The only flu shot we took was N1H1. This could be diphtheria. I can't be sure. Even another strain of influenza would make us susceptible."

"Why don't you know for sure what it is?" Kira asked.

"I'm not a doctor. Despite what Christine tells people." He glanced at me when he said it. "I don't have viral tests or blood testing equipment. My training is in emergency medical procedures. Field trauma and sustaining life until further help is available. My diagnosis is all supposition at this point."

"So I guess we decide if we are willing to share," Linda said.

"How likely is this to turn into an epidemic, Adams?" Gray asked.

"Very likely. The lack of sanitary procedures and ignorance about how bacteria and viruses spread will only help ignite the expansion," Adams replied.

"One more thing we need to consider. The minute word gets out we have a cure, and it *will* leak out, people are going to beat down our doors for it," Frank said.

"And I doubt they'll stop at just asking politely," Ethan said.

"Alexandria is a very large port. Ships dock here from all over. And exports leave daily. This has the potential to be out of control quickly," I said. "The only thing we can do is send someone to our timeline to get more antibiotics."

"What? Are you crazy? No way. They might never get back here. You said it yourself before we left," Joe said.

"Christine, that's too big a risk. I don't want to sound insensitive, but this really needs to play out here as it was meant to be. If an epidemic is in their history, then so be it. We cannot chance one of us getting stuck there for the sake of strangers," Annabelle said.

"She's right. We need to protect ourselves from the disease and leave well enough alone," Michael said.

"I realize that. It just doesn't feel right knowing we could save people, but aren't going to," I said.

Ethan reached over for my hand. "No, it won't sit properly with any of us, I'm sure. But our group should be our first and main priority. It has to be. Maybe we can educate the locals as much as possible to squelch it, but that's all we should do."

"It's decided then. This guy," Frank lifted his chin in the Indian's direction, "he's the final one outside of our group who gets meds. Show of hands to confirm?"

All hands rose, and mine reluctantly did the same.

I checked on our native guest throughout the day. He wasn't improving much, and I worried about the Johnsons even more. Adams and I planned to go see them in the morning, but that didn't ease my concern much.

Michael and Frank inspected the area where the kids found the Indian. There was no sign that anyone else was with him. It would probably stay a mystery forever. If and when he recovered, I was uncertain he could reveal what happened. I suspected he spoke Algonquian, which meant communication between us would be nonexistent.

The following morning, he showed signs of improvement, opening his eyes for a few seconds at a time. His fever was down considerably, and his chills subsided. But he slept through breakfast, and Adams and I decided to check on Samuel and his family.

The journey to the Johnsons' farm took longer than usual. Rain had muddied the woods, and the horses plowed through it slowly. The place appeared deserted as we rode through the gate. As we stepped onto the porch, Jeremiah opened the door before we knocked.

"Good day," he said.

"Hey, Jeremiah, how is everyone doing?" I asked.

"Samuel and Samuel Junior fare well this morn. However, I fear Mistress Johnson is unwell."

I exchanged a glance with Adams. "Jeremiah, can you give me a moment alone with Nathan, please?"

He stepped off the porch to allow us privacy.

"Look, I understand we said no one else would get medicine, but we can't save the rest of the family and let her die," I said.

"She shouldn't have symptoms if she took her antibiotic."

"I agree. Let's go see her and find out what happened."

I opened the door and motioned to Jeremiah. "Show us to Prudence."

The moment we entered the room, I could tell she was in terrible shape.

"Did she take her pill yesterday?" Adams asked.

"I know naught of that. She gave my sister and me the medicine."

Adams listened to her chest and shook his head. "There is no way she took it. I cannot believe she is this bad overnight. Give me two more, Christine."

"Two? Are you sure?"

"She won't make it through the day otherwise. Did the doctor come here yesterday?"

"Aye. He checked in with the ill and proclaimed his cures were working. 'Twas nothing more than a lingering summer grippe."

"Bullshit. What an idiot. His comments probably convinced her she didn't need to take the meds."

I crushed the pills into the cup on the bedside table.

We got the water down Prudence, along with a fever reducer and the decongestant inhalant, and I relaxed a bit once we finished. We checked on her son next, who was cool and sleeping peacefully. Samuel was awake when we reached his room. He sat up quickly, falling back onto the bed when he was too weak to remain upright.

"Whoa, take it easy, Samuel," Adams said, pulling a chair up beside him. "Let me listen to your chest."

While he did his exam, I instructed Jeremiah to bring warm water for him. Dry vomit caked his arm, and once he noticed it, I was sure he would want to wash himself.

"How does my son? Where is Prudence?"

"He is doing well. Your wife is ill, but we gave her medication, and she should be better by tomorrow." I told him.

"Jeremiah tells me ye have poultice that cures the fever and cough."

"You cannot share that with anyone. We do not have more to hand out," Adams said.

"Is my son the first to receive a cure from this poultice?"

"No, many people benefit from it where we come from. But don't worry about that now. You will all be fine, and that's all that matters," I said.

"Jeremiah hears talk of fever and illness in Alexandria and as far away as Jamestown," Samuel said.

"Aye. 'Tis more alarming with each passing day. Men who stand fearless against savages and the British run from this sickness. 'Tis a foul pestilence," Jeremiah said.

"Many more will perish afore it ends, I promise ye. We are most fortunate to have yer medicine, but I fear others shall not fare as well. I'll not forget yer help," Samuel said.

They were truly frightened. I saw it in their eyes and heard it in their voices. I was afraid too.

If there were cases of this in the city, it was probably already too late for us to quash it. I realized what was coming, and it chilled me to the bone. Alexandria would be the epicenter of this epidemic unless we found a way to control it immediately.

"Jeremiah, we need your help to get the word out to as many people as possible. They must wear masks around everyone and quarantine the sick away from healthy people. They should isolate anyone with symptoms."

"I can take the news to Mister Brighton at the papers. He will send an announcement throughout Alexandria within a day."

"Good. Tell him if they don't follow this advice, the disease will spread quickly and there will be terrible loss of life because of it. This could overwhelm the city," I whispered, my voice cracking.

SIXTEEN

Alexandria, Virginia 1790

For the next week we kept to ourselves, sheltered on our property, too fearful to have contact with anyone. Adams and I quarantined ourselves from the others as much as possible until we were past a reasonable incubation period. When we showed no signs of illness after seven days, we allowed ourselves to integrate back into the group. Adams had everyone take an antibiotic as a precaution, and we were fairly certain we would all stay well.

The Indian recovered and slipped away three nights after his arrival without a word. Ethan didn't attempt to hide his disappointment when he left, but I was just thankful he didn't kill us while we slept.

Our more immediate worry was heavy on all our minds. Our store of fresh fruits and vegetables was running low, as was our meat. We were not skilled hunters, and our crops would not be mature for another couple of weeks. Mastering the flintlock was difficult and did nothing to improve our track record, as we were all slow loading the guns no matter how much we practiced. The deer and turkey in our woods were safe, and they knew it. They taunted us by appearing and then disappearing before we even aimed our muskets. Ethan set rabbit traps, but we caught more squirrel than rabbit, and the little meat they offered made it difficult, if not impossible, to feed seventeen people.

Someone had to go to market—that was the solution. With the start of winter, game promised to become even scarcer, so our already subpar hunting skills were about to take a tremendous hit. We depleted our supply of MREs weeks ago, and while it was possible to live on our protein bars and supplement capsules, those did little to fill our stomachs. Plus, we planned to save them for dire emergencies only. Adams and I were the first exposed to the epidemic and had taken two rounds of antibiotics by then. We decided it was safest if we were the ones to venture into Alexandria for food.

We packed silver coins and wrapped scarves around our faces to conceal our modern-day masks. They were the safest way to filter bacteria but would stand out in 1790.

We planned to stop and check on Widow Blanchard on the way home. She and her staff were alone, and if anyone was sick, chances were, they had no help.

We made good time and arrived at the edge of the city in under thirty minutes. The port was eerily quiet. The normally busy dock was barren but for a few men. The berths held only a few ships, not the usual full wharf space.

"This is not a good sign," Adams said.

I didn't respond, so shocked was I at the lack of activity. We rode past the water, farther into town, the clomp of our horses' hooves echoing through the vacant streets. Most storefronts were closed, some boarded up, with only a couple of essential businesses open. Most of the city was shuttered. The apothecary and the blacksmith were still available, but void of customers. A man pushing a dilapidated cart rounded the corner headed toward us, wavering under the weight of his load.

"Dead! Bring out your dead!" he cried out.

As he drew closer, I saw the bodies. He was collecting the deceased. He stared at us sadly as he wheeled the cart past, continuing his shouts for the departed.

I gasped and turned to Adams. "Are they serious? They collect the expired in a death gurney? Like trash service?"

"I guess so. I don't have a good feeling about this at all, Christine. This place is a ghost town."

"Yeah, I can't say I hold out much hope for the marketplace," I said.

We guided our horses onto Brookshire Street on the outskirts of town toward the market. The stalls were empty, nothing more than dead leaves blew across the deserted road. The quiet was unearthly. The city was bereft of all signs of life. A fouler stench replaced the usual fetor of animal carcasses. Death.

We stopped the horses as we realized how significant the emptiness of our surroundings was. I don't know how long we were there. Time seemed to slow to a crawl. As the day surrendered itself to dusk, no lamplighters came to light the oil lamps, and soon the darkness would be claustrophobic in the abandoned city.

"Let's try to get some news. Maybe the blacksmith can tell us what's going on," I said.

We stayed on our horses and called out. The man approached the entry but stayed inside the stall of his shop.

"Where is everyone?" Adams asked.

"The fever has driven most to the countryside."

"What about the market?"

"Aye. Farmers fear traveling into the city whilst the pestilence ravages. Who will buy their goods?"

"Right. When did this all start?"

"Sunday, last. It spreads quickly. They bury the dead at the edge of town. The list grows with each sunrise. If ye search for family, Mister Brighton carries the names."

"The gentleman who runs the paper?" I asked.

"Aye."

"Thank you for speaking to us," Adams said.

He retreated into the stall. I worked to get a grip on my emotions as we started for home. We did not venture farther into the city. We had both seen enough.

We took a different route back, around the dock and through the residential area of the city. Some homes had bodies wrapped in blankets on doorsteps, while others appeared completely deserted. I noticed a few curtains pull aside when I glanced up, but they quickly closed. No one wanted to talk to strangers. Those who remained in the city hid in their houses, waiting for the outbreak to pass.

We passed the potter's field where men dug trenches while others removed bodies wrapped in cloth and piled them at the edge of the mass graves. It was a grim sight. One I hoped to never see again.

I turned away and pushed the image from my mind as my thoughts drifted back to our conversation with the blacksmith. With people going underground to the country, the chance of strangers wandering onto our land increased, and I felt an urgent need to protect against that possibility. We rode in silence, still stunned by what we saw. We did not go to Widow Blanchard's. Our desire to protect our own overpowered all else. It wasn't until we crossed the stream to our property that Adams spoke.

"So, I guess we should prepare for the onslaught of city folk visiting us, huh? We need to set up a perimeter and stand watch."

"I was thinking the same thing. And this time we should include the teenagers. They have to be aware not to get near anyone we don't know."

When we reached our property, we went our separate ways but planned to gather everyone within the hour at Adams's place. I led the mare into the barn and guided her to the stall. I stroked her mane while I collected my thoughts and calmed my rattled nerves. My mind drifted once again to Los Angeles and our former timeline. I wondered if things were better there—because this era just became far more problematic than I had expected. I crossed the field and entered my cabin. The flickering candlelight played across the looking glass hung on the wall, casting an eerie light around the room. Under different circumstances, I might have considered the ambiance romantic. But in that moment, all I could think of was how much the gloom mimicked my uneasiness.

* * *

"I understand it will be a challenge to maintain a twenty-four-seven perimeter, hunt and forage, and still take care of the livestock. But we really all need to pitch in and make it work," Adams said.

I glanced around the room and the expressions on some faces of our group were not encouraging.

"Look, you didn't witness what we did today. This is more than a minor flu outbreak. People are hiding in the country. We heard it from the blacksmith, this isn't guesswork. They are pushing wheelbarrows full of their dead through the city. Before long, those who fled to less populated places are going to run out of resources, especially with the weather changing. And they will come looking for food and shelter. That means our settlement will be right in their crosshairs. We aren't in 2072, Los Angeles, anymore. We can't just call the police for help. It's all down to us," I said.

The CCEA agents all agreed, while the civilians stared at me blankly.

"They're right. Let's get a schedule made up and start the first shift tonight. If people have been sheltering for a week, it won't be much longer before they search for alternate accommodations," Frank said.

"There are twelve adults, so six on and six off at all times until the threat passes. We all know how to shoot. We keep our penlights on us at night and signal if we see something. Everyone checks in once an hour. One flash for all clear, two for activity," Gray said. "Frank has the timepiece, so he can check in first. Once you get his sign, answer back with yours. During the day we will have to use sound."

I was on the second shift, which started in the morning. We assigned the teenagers most of the animal duties. We did not designate the three couples with children under eighteen simultaneous shifts, so one parent was always available.

Emory insisted she was no longer a child, her eighteenth birthday only four months away. I must admit she had a point. But I knew that Gray and Kira didn't agree. Plus, they were wary of her friendship with Jeremiah and wanted to keep an eye on her. The two of them spent a lot of time together whenever he was here. I sensed a budding romance had already begun, but I shut my mouth and let her parents handle it as they chose.

I fell into bed exhausted three hours later. It felt strange, sleeping alone while Ethan was on border duty. I tossed and turned for an hour, as usual, before I finally slept. I was awake before dawn and got up to make myself a breakfast of plain oatmeal and powdered milk. We were saving the eggs for protein, assuming our hunting skills wouldn't improve.

One of us really needs to bag a turkey, I thought as I ate the flavorless cereal.

I washed and dressed and was outside as Ethan finished his watch. The air was chilled, and I drew my wrap tighter around my shoulders. A shiver ran through me as I determined it couldn't be over forty-five degrees. Michael passed by on his way home and waved to me, and I smiled and waved back, watching him pull Maddie into a hug when he got to his porch. Ethan and I embraced before I left, with only a few minutes to spare before my shift started.

"Like ships passing in the night," he sighed.

I chuckled. "The story of our lives, huh?"

"Sadly, it is. Be safe out there."

"I will, promise."

I gave him a quick kiss and headed out to the edge of the woods. Our posts spaced us out every half mile around the perimeter. With only six people on watch at a time, it was the best we could manage.

The day went smoothly, with nothing unusual to draw my attention. Then, halfway through my shift, a branch snapped somewhere nearby. My senses went on high alert as my heart slammed into my rib cage. I crouched down and sent out the activity signal—an owl hoot. It came out more like an alley cat being kicked, but I got a response, so it did the trick. I didn't hear Annabelle sneak up, and I jumped when she tapped me on the back. Voices carried through the trees as we ducked behind a bush, muskets aimed. A minute later Samuel, Jeremiah, and Prudence rode into view. I stood up and heaved a sigh of relief.

"How does it, Missus Ward?" Samuel said, hopping off his horse.

Annabelle rose, shaking leaves from the hem of her petticoats. "Goody Harris, how lovely to meet ye again," Prudence said.

Her young son sat in front of her on the horse, fidgeting with the reins. Jeremiah reached up and plunked him on the ground beside him.

"Prudence, Samuel, you're feeling better, I see. I'm so glad," Annabelle said.

"Aye, we are fit as a fiddle. We pray the fever has not reached ye?" asked Samuel.

"No, everyone here is fine," I said.

"Praise God. We brought victuals, as the market 'tis empty. Yer crops are not ready, and we owe ye a great thanks for our cure," he said.

"Cranberry tarts, meat pottage, and clabber," Prudence said, holding out a basket. "The apples and pears shan't last long. I fear they are near to spoilt."

I reached for the food. "Thank you so much. We can certainly use this."

We accompanied them through the woods and into the clearing next to the houses. Jeremiah trotted his horse straight to Emory, who was weeding in the garden.

"Those two get on like a house on fire. Jeremiah believes her a finer catch than the largest shad from the river," Prudence said. "Is she betrothed to another?"

"Betrothed? No, no, she isn't. Her parents think she is too young to consider marriage or an engagement," I replied.

I immediately worried that I should have said nothing either way.

"Too young? Oh, fribble. She is near to a spinster at her age."

Her statement confirmed I needed to keep my mouth shut.

"Not where we come from, Prudence. Women wait until they are older to choose a husband," Annabelle said.

"What of child rearing? Should she tarry much longer, she may have a babe in a clout whilst she is too old to care for one properly."

Annabelle glanced over at me and frowned. She mouthed *clout* to me with a questioning look.

"Diaper," I whispered to her.

She turned away from Prudence and rolled her eyes at me.

"Well, I'm sure she will be just fine," I said.

Frank and Gray came out to talk to the Johnsons while Annabelle and I started back to our positions in the forest.

"She's a spinster at seventeen? Good grief," she said, shaking her head in disbelief.

"I know, right? Don't let Kira or Gray hear that. They will have her on lockdown faster than you can say shotgun wedding."

"See you later at dinner. At least we get out of cooking tonight because we're out here freezing our asses off," she said.

"You have a way of seeing the silver lining in every dark cloud, Annabelle. One of your many outstanding traits."

She smiled and turned to leave for her post. I found my spot and settled in against the cold, hard ground to stave off the boredom for the next four hours of my watch.

SEVENTEEN

Los Angeles, California 2072

Nick Goebel rode the elevator to the tenth floor of the CCEA building. His wife Suzanne grasped his arm.

"Hey, it's going to be okay," he said.

She peered at him but didn't respond. He could tell she still wasn't fully on board with his plan. But he was certain this was the safest thing to do. Los Angeles was fast becoming a war zone. There weren't many civilians left in the city, most people had headed for the hills when the government still allowed travel. Or wherever else they could escape.

Terrorist sleeper cells had popped up in almost every state, and chemical warfare was becoming a daily occurrence. There were travel restrictions in place now that prevented anyone from leaving their city of residence. They grounded all flights, and public transportation was nonexistent. People everywhere were panicked, and rightfully so. No one knew what was coming next. Those left in the city were running out of resources, and gang looting and home invasions were the norm. If they didn't leave today, right now, they wouldn't get another opportunity. He was sure of that. But that did nothing to prevent his stomach from twisting at the thought of what they were going to do.

When his buddy, Tony Alvarez, told him about his plan, he considered him crazy for even entertaining such a dangerous idea. Tony had always been a dreamer. He was the type of guy who was sure his big break was right around the corner. The lottery win would be his if he could just buy enough scratchers. And when nothing ever happened, it was everyone else's fault.

Suzanne never liked him, and Nick understood why. Most people regarded him as little more than an overgrown, blustering loudmouth. But they were friends since they met in high school, and he had grown accustomed to Tony's fantasies. The more Nick thought about what his friend planned to do, the more sense it made. Maybe this one time he was onto something. When it mattered most. Nick wasn't entirely convinced it would work, but he kept that to himself.

He planned to transport to eighteenth century America for a couple of reasons. First, to escape Los Angeles and the war. He also hoped this would reconnect him and his wife, and the experience would bond them and rekindle the closeness they once shared. After fifteen years of marriage, they needed a kick start.

Tony was a supervisor at the CCEA before it all went belly up. The agency was still operational, but barely. There were no transports for weeks. The overcrowding reached its limit, but they'd exiled no new prisoners since then. Nick wasn't sure if the agents had made no arrests and just given up or if they took detainees elsewhere. And to be honest, he didn't care anymore. Protecting his wife was his priority. So, because Tony could transport them back, they were going to 1791 with him.

When Tony found out Rhoades and Stewart transported to the past, he came to Nick at once. At first, Nick was angry to discover they had left for 1790. But after some thought, he could not blame them for trying to save themselves. He was only sorry he had not thought of the plan himself. He intended to find the other transporters when they got to Alexandria, and hopefully, they would allow him and Suzanne and, of course, Tony to join their group until they all came home together. He just hoped Tony would keep himself in check and not make waves once they found the others.

The elevator doors hissed open, and he grabbed the two packs while motioning for his wife to follow. She stepped off the lift and glanced around the deserted corridor before trailing him into the jump room. He opened the door to see Tony working at the computer.

"Hey, buddy! You made it! I had my doubts you were going to show up. My dude grew some cojones," he said, laughing and slapping Nick on the back.

He moved to hug Suzanne, but she sidestepped his embrace. Unruffled, he shrugged and returned to what he was doing.

"This is almost ready. You can both get in your boxes, and I'll have us out of here in a few minutes."

Nick led Suzanne to her pod and reviewed last-minute instructions with her. He handed her a pack and gave her a kiss, strapping her into the cubicle.

Tony rubbed his palms together with a huge grin. "We're ready, *mi amigo*. Let's do this."

Nick strapped himself in and glanced over to Suzanne. He realized she was frightened, and he loved her for not fighting him on this. But he felt guilty about it too. Something in the way she stared back at him made his chest constrict, and he turned away. He could not look her in the eye in that moment. Guilt and fear swept over him as they transported out of Los Angeles to an uncertain future.

* * *

Alexandria, Virginia 1791

Nick awakened before his wife and Tony. He shivered in the cold and grabbed his long coat from his pack. Tony stirred and rolled onto his side. He found his wife's coat and covered her, then went to Tony's bag, intending to do the same for him. He rifled through his friend's belongings, finding the coat on the bottom of the satchel. When he pulled it out, he froze, not believing what he saw. A 9 mm Glock semiautomatic handgun. Reaching in, he lifted the gun. What was Tony thinking, bringing a contemporary weapon to this timeline? He stood up, running his hand through his hair and pacing in front of the pack. He glanced down at the handgun again, then crouched next to his friend.

"Tony, wake up," he whispered.

Tony groaned and turned to face away. "Go away," he mumbled.

"Tony, wake up! I'm not playing. Get up, right now," he hissed.

Alvarez rolled back over, groaning. "What the hell, Nick? What's wrong?"

"What's wrong? You brought a gun with you, that's what."

"Yeah, so what? And what are you doing in my pack, anyway?" he said, sitting up and twisting to find his bag.

"I was gonna cover you with your coat. And what do you mean, so what? Have you lost your mind? What if someone sees it? You said we were just going to hook up with the other transporters and wait out the action back home."

Tony scoffed as he stuffed his things into the backpack. "Well, you know what? I'm tired of always playing by the rules. I saw an opportunity, and I'm taking it. Calm down, Nick. I don't know why you're so upset. It's not even a new gun. It's like forty years old. It was my pop's."

"What? Who cares how old it is? It is a semiautomatic handgun, for God's sake. They carry muskets here. Flintlock mechanism guns. Not automatics. And what about the others? They will lose their minds when they find out you brought a handgun from home to wave around colonial times."

"Those losers are on their own. I don't give two shits what they think, and you shouldn't either. You need to come with me. I have a plan—one that will make me rich. And if you're smart, you'll do the same."

"What are you talking about, Tony? What plan? Our plan is to find the others and stay with them until it's safe to go home."

"I'm not looking for them. They're probably camping somewhere, freezing their asses off and wondering where their next meal is coming from."

"What are you planning, Tony? What happened to your safety in numbers theory? And what do you mean, you're going to get rich?"

"I have a perfect plan. I'm taking some stuff back to 2072 with me, and then I'll sell it."

"Sell what?" Nick asked.

"Valuable stuff. Like a copy of the Declaration of Independence, autographs, maybe some rare coins. Whatever historical documents I can get my hands on here. It shouldn't be hard. They won't mean much to the people in this timeline. I brought a camera too. I can take pictures that will be worth a ton to collectors."

"You can't be serious."

"You bet I am. Why not? I am just meeting a demand for goods. Nothing wrong with that, buddy."

"It's dishonest! We shouldn't even be here, let alone remove things from the timeline. What if it changes something in history? What if someone takes the gun? This can't happen, Tony."

"It can and it is happening. With or without you," he said, standing and pulling his arms through the straps of his backpack.

"Please don't do this. You don't know what effect this might have. You could cause irreparable damage to our history. Do you not get that?"

"So, what if I do? What's the difference? It's not to going to matter if a document is missing from here or there. A few missing coins or a personal effect from one of the founding fathers? That's not going to change the course of humankind, Nick. Stop being such a wuss."

"Screw you, Alvarez. I won't let you do this."

Tony sneered and turned to leave.

"Good luck stopping me. You always were a mamma's boy, even in school. Grow up and start thinking about yourself, for once. Suzanne might be more interested if you did."

He jogged off as Nick stared after him in disbelief. All their years of friendship crumbled in that moment. He had never felt so betrayed by anyone in his life. Suzanne stirred behind him and sat up.

"What's wrong?"

"Get up, Suzanne. Tony has gone off the rails. We need to find the other agents and stop him before he destroys history and decimates this timeline."

EIGHTEEN

Alexandria, Virginia, 1791

We made it through the end of the year without incident. Willow developed a low-grade fever and cough, but Adams squelched it before it became anything more. An occasional family wandered onto our land, and we gave them whatever food we could spare and sent them on their way.

The most memorable of those visits was from a young boy and his mother while I was on perimeter duty. He was dirty with torn clothing and crashed through the woods toward me, stopping short when he saw me. My heart went out to him instantly. Something about him reminded me of Michael when he was young. But the boy was so thin. His mother found us a moment after, still staring at each other. She ran to him, pushing him behind her, while she called for her husband. I had my mask on and stepped closer to hand them a basket of food.

"I'm sorry, you can't stay here. The fever. We don't want anyone near us," I said.

She peered in the basket and then at me.

"God bless ye," she whispered as tears sprang to her eyes.

She took the boy's hand and retreated into the woods the way they came, before her husband arrived. The boy turned to glance back at me, and I smiled, although he couldn't see that with my mask over my mouth. Maybe the smile reached my eyes and he could tell. I hoped so.

I sat on the forest floor and cried for a long time after they left. I thought of them often after that day and prayed they were still alive. It was one thing to read about history in a book or watch a documentary. It was altogether something else to witness the suffering for yourself.

Soon after that, as spring bloomed, the influenza outbreak slowly receded, although Alexandria was not back to its normal level of activity yet. More shops opened, but only a few brave farmers came to the market. Our crops were mature now, and Samuel and Prudence asked more than once how our vegetables grew in the winter weather. We claimed beginner's luck, but I knew they were suspicious. We became more skilled at hunting and bagged an occasional deer or turkey, but sustained ourselves mainly on fish from the creek and larger catches from the Potomac. Eggs were another of our primary sources of protein.

The kids took to farm life better than I expected them to. They pitched in with the care of the livestock and named all the animals. I really hoped we maintained our food supply. None of us wanted to put one of our egg-producing chickens on the dinner table. I was not sure how we would explain to the children that Repecka or Hennifer was our evening meal.

I cannot say our lives were trouble free, or even slightly easy. We worked hard from dawn till dusk every day to sustain our way of life. But we were still better off than many other people. We had tubs, healthy crops, and warm fireplaces and beds. And we had each other. A group of friends and family we could trust and count on.

We continued to post three people around the cabins at night, even after the fever scare. It just seemed the safest thing to do. We had not seen Horatio Travis again, the one enemy we'd made. But we were not naïve enough to think he wouldn't show up eventually.

Life was fairly quiet for us, and that complacency made me let my guard down and relax. I was picking berries with Linda one afternoon when she grabbed my arm. I was bent over and glanced up to see her staring ahead, mesmerized. I followed her gaze to a group of Indians about twenty feet away. I pushed myself up slowly and stood next to her. There were three men and two women, one of whom held a baby strapped into a front-facing papoose. The men wore breechcloths and pelts slung over their shoulders. The women wore long deer hide dresses with pelt cloaks. All of them had on moccasins. They stared at us without speaking. Unsure of what to do, we both remained silent, staring back at them. I held out my basket of blueberries. None of them made a move to grab it, so I withdrew it, keeping it at my side. One man stepped out from behind the others, stopping to stand beside the woman with the infant. It took me a moment to realize it was the same native Adams took care of, the one we found in the woods and who vanished from the cabin in the middle of the night. He said something in their language to the woman, and she reached into her deer hide satchel to hand him a bundle wrapped in corn husks. He stepped forward and held it out to me. I reached out, and my fingers brushed his as I accepted it. He said a few words I could not understand, but I nodded to him in acknowledgment anyway. The woman spoke and gestured toward the cabins. Then they all turned and disappeared into the woods. Neither Linda nor I spoke during the encounter. I studied the corn husk package in my hand.

"Must be a thank-you for taking care of him."

"I'm sure. Should we unwrap it and see what it is?" she asked.

"I guess so."

I peeled back the husks carefully to a block of square meat. It reminded me of the old-fashioned Spam that used to be around years ago.

"Looks like pemmican or scrapple," Linda said.

"What?"

"Scrapple is usually pork trim and parts molded with corn meal, and pemmican is typically deer with fat and berries. You slice it and fry the scrapple, but they eat the pemmican as is. My grandmother used to cook scrapple. She learned to make it from the Amish in Pennsylvania, where she grew up. American Indians have eaten both for hundreds of years."

"Pig scraps, huh? Well, one of the guys will eat it, whichever it is," I said.

"My Frank will love it. He'll try anything, especially if they make it with pork."

I wrapped it back up and placed it in the basket with the berries. "Should we go to the stream and get any fish in the traps since we are halfway there anyway?"

"We may as well."

We trekked through the woods silently but for the crunch of leaves under our feet. Right before we reached the creek, muffled voices and laughter echoed through the forest. Linda must have heard it too because she stopped and motioned to me. We snuck closer to the sound and hid behind a tree. I peeked around the massive trunk just in time to catch Emory and Jeremiah's kiss. They stayed in an embrace, speaking softly to each other. I stepped into view, and Emory pushed him away quickly.

"Don't bother, Emory, we've already seen you," Linda said.

"Are you going to tell my mom and dad?"

"I beg your forgiveness, 'tis highly improper of me. But one must only gaze upon Emory to know she is an angel," Jeremiah said, stepping backward.

"I love him. I am old enough to make my own decisions," she said.

"I loathe hiding to see her. The lies and deceit shame me. It taints our time together. Yet I fear I cannot stop myself. I wish to spend every moment with her. I shall never love another," he said, bowing his head.

I hadn't said a word yet, but I sighed heavily.

"I'm not your mom or dad, so I can't tell you what to do, but I will not keep something from them either. Save your explanations for them, Emory. My suggestion is you both go to them together and talk it out. They're not unreasonable."

"Are we talking about the same people? They think I'm a child," she scoffed, folding her arms across her chest.

"Well, you are certainly acting like one, sneaking around and pouting when you get caught," Linda said. "If you want them to treat you as an adult, then act accordingly. Go tell them how you feel about each other and talk it out."

"They won't listen," she said.

"We'll not learn until we have a private audience with them, Emory. I shall cast off my fears and face your father with an open heart. I pray ye do the same," Jeremiah said, taking her hand in his.

I motioned for them to follow. "Let's go. No sense in postponing this."

When we were halfway across the clearing, Stephen and Kira Gray strode toward us, looking ten different kinds of ticked off. I understood none of this was my doing—I had no part in their daughter's escapades—but Gray's expression intimidated even me. Emory released Jeremiah's hand with one glimpse at her father. I cringed inwardly and hoped I could make my exit before Emory dragged me into this any further.

Her parents stopped when we met in the middle of the field. Emory and Jeremiah stood beside Linda and me. Gray's shoulders sagged with relief, but his face told another story. I knew him well enough to realize how angry he was.

"Where have you been?" he asked his daughter.

"Everyone is out searching for you. We thought something happened, and you got lost or kidnapped!" Kira said. "You can't just wander off here."

"I didn't wander off," she said, making air quotation marks at the last two words. "I was with Jeremiah."

"Get back to the cabin, we will talk about this in private, young lady," Stephen said.

"I told you they wouldn't listen to me," Emory said, turning to me and Linda.

I opened my mouth to protest, but Stephen shot me a glance that made me think better of voicing an opinion.

"I'm not going with you. I'm staying with Jeremiah."

"Excuse me?" Kira said, placing her hands on her hips.

"You do not have any choice in the matter," Stephen said.

Emory grabbed Jeremiah's hand in hers. "I'm staying because I belong with him. With my husband."

I held my breath. I did not see that coming.

Kira gasped and her hand flew to her mouth.

"What?" Gray bellowed.

"We're married, Dad." She reached into the crossbody satchel she wore and pulled out a piece of folded parchment paper. Time moved in slow motion as she unfolded it. A breeze lifted it from her grasp, and we watched it flutter in the air for a moment before it settled at Stephen's feet. He picked it up by the corner as if it were contaminated and studied it, mouth agape. My gaze darted between the young couple and Emory's parents. He raised his head slowly and met her stare.

"Jesus, Mary, and Joseph. What have you done?"

"I love him," Emory said.

"Aye, and I her, sir," Jeremiah said.

Kira jabbed her finger in Jeremiah's direction. "No. Not another word from you, do you understand me?"

Jeremiah wisely shut his mouth and let his chin fall to his chest.

She snapped her head back to her daughter. "You *love* him? You are seventeen years old! You know nothing about life or love or the level of commitment it takes to make a marriage work. Absolutely nothing! Oh, you might think you do, but trust me, you don't," she shrieked.

Stephen nodded furiously at his wife's words. Emory opened her mouth to retort, and I stepped between them.

I held my hands up in a time-out gesture. "Okay, everyone, let's calm down for a minute. Stephen, Kira, can I have a word with you please?" I motioned for Linda to take Emory and Jeremiah a few feet in the other direction.

Kira looked like she could spit nails. Stephen stood with arms folded across his chest and glared in the couple's direction.

"Listen, before you say anything, I know. I'm a parent. I get it. But if you forbid this, they are only going to keep sneaking around, and pretty soon, they'll just run away together. She's almost eighteen, and you can't tell her what to do forever. Isn't it better if she's here? Build them a cabin. In the meantime, they can stay in our spare room with me and Ethan."

"Did you know about this? Before today?" Stephen asked, twisting to face me.

I felt like a mouse caught in a trap with the cat poised to jump. My head swiveled between them with my best incredulous expression plastered on my face.

"What? No, of course not! Linda and I found them in the woods today and were bringing them back here to confess to you. I told them I would hide nothing from you."

He gave me a curt nod and relaxed his face a fraction.

Kira dropped her head to her chest. "What do we do now?"

"At least if she's here, you can keep an eye on her. I understand it's not ideal. But remember when you were her age, Kira? If your parents restricted you from seeing a boy, what did you do? The same thing I did, I'm guessing. Run straight into his waiting arms."

Kira bit the inside of her cheek as Gray scrutinized the sky for answers and exhaled loudly. I stepped aside and let them talk privately for a few minutes.

Stephen stalked back to the couple, who stared at him with wide eyes.

"You two are going to stay with Christine and Ethan in their spare room until I can build you your own cabin here. The two of you can't very well share a room with your sister in there. You will live here. With us. On our settlement. That is non-negotiable. Understood? And when we leave here, you are coming with us, Emory."

"But what about Jer—"

"You are going with us. By any means I must deploy to make that happen."

She pursed her lips but didn't respond. I was thankful she was smart enough not to push it any further today. I was also surprised her parents were allowing this. I expected them to march her to the courthouse for an immediate annulment.

"I'll help you gather your things and get settled at our place," I said, glancing at Emory.

Emory grabbed her husband's hand, and they followed me across the field, as I mentally braced myself for the next round of punishment the eighteenth century had in store for me—moving a newlywed teenaged couple into my home.

NINETEEN

Alexandria, Virginia 1791

Nick doused the fire with the water from the basin and glanced over to the bed, where Suzanne was asleep. The inn was nowhere close to the standard their timeline accustomed them to, but at least it kept them out of the elements. They had been there for a little over two weeks and had no luck finding the agents from their timeline. Until last night. They overheard the blacksmith from town mention a group of travelers who purchased land outside the city. It must be them. It was the closest to a lead they'd had since arriving. And he needed to find them soon, because their meager supply of silver coins was dwindling quickly.

Suzanne stirred as he sat on the bed to brush the hair off her face. She opened her eyes and smiled up at him. The trip had brought them closer, as he hoped it would. He looked at the woman he had spent almost half his life married to and couldn't imagine losing her. He came close recently, and he vowed never to take her for granted again.

His thoughts drifted to Tony and he wondered where he was. His stomach twisted at the thought of him. He could easily change history, and the worst part was, he really didn't care. But Nick did. And he had every intention of preventing that.

He rose from the bed to pack. "Are you ready to search for the others today?"

"Sure. I'm looking forward to seeing people from our own timeline. Maybe they have news from home. Do you expect they've gone back to check on things?"

"I don't know, Suzanne. I guess it's a possibility," he said, but he didn't believe his own words. "There's only one way to find out, right? Let's go find them and figure out our next move."

Suzanne dressed, and they ate the stale bread and warm cheese left from last night's dinner. He grabbed their packs and slung both over his shoulders.

"I can carry my pack," she said, reaching for the bag.

"No, you're hiking a few hours in all that garb," he said, motioning to her skirt and petticoats. "We have a long stretch ahead, and only general directions on where this settlement is. Save your strength for the hike."

She tensed at the thought of tramping through the Virginia wilderness with nothing but their meager supplies. But she realized her husband was right. They must find the other transporters or take a risk and go home to 2072. They had no chance of survival here alone. Tony had left with all the meal replacement capsules and antibiotics in his backpack. Luckily, they had their own silver. If not for that, who knows where they might be now.

"Ready?" Nick asked, his hand on the doorknob.

"Yep. Lead the way," she said.

They strolled through the middle of Alexandria, past the marketplace, where they bought apples and more bread. The market stalls were only half full. They heard talk of a fever and realized they arrived in 1791 at the tail end of an outbreak. They exchanged a knowing glance, now more eager than ever to get away from the city and other people. Without antibiotics, they were at high risk for every illness. They were both more comfortable when they reached the outskirts of town and headed into the woods.

Nick checked his compass. "If we continue on a steady course northeast through the forest, we should run into their settlement. We're still several miles off, but it's safer if we stay off the roads. Without weapons, we are fair game for robbers. Besides, it will be like a romantic hike, just the two of us. Don't you agree?"

"I'd feel much better if we were in our RV."

"Try not to worry. We'll be okay. Once we find them, it'll be smooth sailing from there."

He smiled and tried to convey confidence. But it worried him. What if they couldn't locate the others? Or got lost in the woods? Or ran into Indians or outlaws? They wouldn't last long out here alone, and he realized it. She knew it too, but neither of them dared to voice that out loud. If things got too bad, they could always transport back home. He still had his transponder. But he knew that would be their last resort. Home would be no better than being lost in the woods in 1791.

They made small talk for the first couple of hours while they trudged through the landscape. By the third hour, they were both quiet. They stopped at a stream where they used their Lifestraws for a much-needed drink. Eating their bread and apples, they rested on a bed of leaves, using their packs as pillows.

"How much farther do we have to go?"

"A couple miles, I think. When I saw the map at the tavern, the woods thinned out a bit and the land became somewhat hilly. That's where they should be, just beyond the edge of the woodlands."

"We should keep going then and not stay here too long. I don't want to get caught out here at night."

"Neither do I. Suzanne, I'm so sorry I got us mixed up in this. We should have stayed in Los Angeles. I didn't know what Tony was planning."

"It's not your fault. I agreed to this, remember? And as far as Tony goes, well, nothing that man does surprises me. It's no secret I'm no fan of his, but this was pretty shitty, even for him. Do you think he really plans to steal historical documents and valuables?"

"I do, yes. I'm not so worried about him taking a few antiques back to 2072. He's right when he says no one will miss them here. It's dishonest, but I doubt that has any effect on history. But his gun, that's what worries me. If his weapon falls into the wrong hands, that could devastate this timeline. What if it was used to kill someone who shouldn't die now? Like an important historical figure? That could alter history in a matter of seconds. And who knows what that could do to the future."

Saying it out loud made it more real for Nick. There were a hundred scenarios running through his mind, none of them good. He was more determined than ever to find the other agents. He needed their help. More importantly, history needed their help.

They finished their lunch in silence, then packed up and started out again. After forty minutes, they crossed a clearing. They reached the edge of a hill and peered down into a green canyon. Six small log cabins, a barn and animal pens filled part of the valley. Nick smiled and grabbed Suzanne's hand.

"That must be them. It has to be. See how they built the houses in a semi-circle, like a cul-de-sac from our timeline? And the garden? Full stalks of corn. It's too cold to grow corn here now. But not if you use an accelerator and hybrid laboratory seeds."

Suzanne grinned back at her husband and squeezed his hand. They started the trek to the lowland with a renewed energy.

* * *

I sat in the open space of our cabin next to Ethan. Stephen, Kira, Emory, Jeremiah, Samuel, and Prudence all crowded into seats around the room. Somehow Emory appointed me her spokesperson and insisted I be there for the meeting to discuss her marriage to Jeremiah. I would rather have been almost anywhere else. But Kira wanted me to stay too, so I remained still, listening to the conversation.

"I think they are just too young to get married. Besides, they have only known each other a few months," Kira said.

"I agree. What happened to Brian, Emory?" Gray said, staring down his daughter.

She looked at him incredulously as he referenced the boy whose pictures were on the tablet she snuck into the timeline.

"Dad! Stop it! Brian and I weren't even a thing when we left Los— when we left home," she said, glaring back at him.

Jeremiah turned to Emory. "I know naught of this Brian fellow."

"That's because he is no one important. My father just doesn't know any better, because he knows *nothing* about my life," she said, casting her mom a look for help.

"Okay, we are getting off track here. You are only seventeen years old, Emory. Too young to marry *anyone*," Kira said.

Prudence turned to Kira. "I fear 'tis too late for regret. I was but one and twenty with a babe in my arms, whilst another was in clouts at my feet, and I was with child again. We are scripture-abiding people. If the Lord wills it, 'twill be so. They vowed their promises, courted, and wed. 'Tis naught left to do but praise God."

"My wife speaks the truth. Ye need not agree, but I pray ye put all to rights and forgive young Jeremiah. Sup with us on the morrow, whilst we celebrate the marriage."

"You took advantage of her," Stephen said, glowering at Jeremiah.

"What need have I for that? I give ye my solemn vow, I have done naught but to disclose my true intentions toward yer daughter. Sarah Clark has oft asked me to court her, yet I shun her in favor of Emory. So bestirred am I by her beauty, my love for yer daughter is too great to ignore. I fear the lure of her heart weakens my resolve. I beg yer forgiveness, sir. Ye have my pledge and my word of honor as a gentleman. My feelings for Emory are genuine."

Gray grunted and folded his arms across his chest. Kira sighed in exasperation. "Will you all excuse us, please? We would like to speak to our daughter alone."

I rose to follow the others out, but Kira grabbed my arm. "Christine, you stay. Emory seems to listen to you."

I sat back down, and watched Ethan go outside with Jeremiah and the Johnsons, feeling like a trapped mouse again and wishing I were part of the group who escaped.

"If you two think you can force me into leaving him, you can't. I'm almost eighteen. Even in our time, that's old enough to do what I want," Emory said, raising her chin defiantly.

I took a deep breath and steeled myself. "Emory, since you asked me to be here, I'm going to say my piece. Your attitude stinks. Instead of talking to your parents and explaining why you wed Jeremiah, and your feelings for him, you are acting like a spoiled, rebellious kid. I don't blame them for being pissed at you. And you are doing nothing to change that. *I'm* pissed at you right now. I understand. I married very young too. Yet you have done nothing more than irritate them today. Why don't you grow up and speak to them in a civilized tone, as an adult? You will get no respect from them or me while you act like this."

I saw Stephen's smirk out of the corner of my eye.

Emory stared at me with her mouth agape. "Well, I, I . . ."

I tilted my head at her and raised my eyebrows in a question.

"You what? Tell them how you feel. This is your opportunity to convince them you're mature enough to be a wife."

She inhaled a deep breath and moved her chair closer to her parents, leaning forward, her elbows on her knees.

"I love you both, I really do. But I love Jeremiah too. This move hasn't been easy for me and Rose. You ripped us from our lives to take us back in time to this colonial *hell* with no say in the matter. The one shred of happiness I found here is him. I realize I'm young. I'll give you that. And at home, I would never dream of getting married at this age. But I am no longer home, am I? I'm here. Where I have no friends and no social life at all. And I'm scared. Everything is different, and hard, and I can't handle it all. Until he came along and was nice to me. And after a while, I realized what a great guy he is. If I have to stay here, then I need someone to get me through it. He's my someone."

She sat back in her chair and studied them. I smiled to myself and glanced over at her. Her gaze darted to me for a second and she gave me a slight bow of her head. I was glad I was right and she found the words to mend the relationship with her parents.

Kira turned to Stephen, who let his chin drop to his chest. "I'm sorry, honey. I guess I wasn't considering all you were going through here. I understand this change is hard. We only did this to save you and your sister. But getting married? That was unexpected, Emory."

"I know, Dad. But I'm asking you to trust me now. And be happy for me, because I found someone I love and who loves me back. That's incredible no matter where or when we live."

"I think I just watched you grow up before my eyes," Kira said, wiping away tears.

Emory rose to hug each of them.

"I'll go tell Samuel we'll *sup* with them here tomorrow, to celebrate the marriage of my oldest daughter," Gray said, swiping at the corner of his eyes.

She beamed at her father, and pulled her chair next to her mom, where they talked and giggled, heads together. I left them there and went outside in search of Ethan, crisis averted. I found him playing a game of football with Adams, Wyatt, Michael, and Joe, using a huge pinecone as a ball. The prickly ends of the scales caused them to juggle the cone whenever one of them caught it. I joined Annabelle and her girls on the sidelines, where we laughed at the sight of them pricking their hands for the love of the game. I thought life here had its enjoyable moments. If only they stuck around longer than a day.

TWENTY

Alexandria, Virginia 1791

I trudged across the field toward the animal pens. The frost on the grass crunched under my boots like delicate glass, while my breath blew out in frigid wisps. I longed for the spring thaw Prudence assured me was coming soon. The minute I stepped away from the fireplace in my cabin, I was cold. Day or night, it made no difference.

I watched Frank and Ethan gather eggs while the chickens pecked at the ground around their feet. If we did not get a deer or turkey in the next few days, we would have to butcher them or one of our pigs. The pigs were really piglets, not large enough yet, but we must eat, so it could come to that. Our fishing skills plummeted with the winter weather since a thin layer of ice covered the stream. Which meant it was harder to catch enough to sustain all seventeen of us.

"Hey, you guys need help?" I asked as I approached.

"Sure, do you want to spread some more feed for them?" Frank asked.

I grabbed the bucket of dried corn and sprinkled it around my feet. Ethan stepped closer and planted a kiss on my cheek.

"We are going to try our hand at hunting again this morning," he said. "Those bloody deer have seen their last days. I'm determined to get one for the celebration later."

"Well, if not, we have fish Linda will fry. And of course, corncakes are abundant. I'm sure the Johnsons will bring food too."

"We are bagging a damn deer today if I have to stay out there all day," Frank said, not bothering to look up.

"I almost feel sorry for the deer," I said.

Movement to my right drew my attention. Joe ran from the woods across the clearing toward us, waving.

He stopped at the fence to catch his breath. "There are a man and woman who breached the south perimeter," he said, sucking in air. "The guy claims he knows you and Christine," he said, looking at Frank. "His name's Goebel. Michael is guarding them until we get back."

I twisted toward Frank. "Goebel? It can't be," I said.

"Let's go find out," he said, wiping his hands on his breeches.

"I'll gather the others in case there's trouble. Who is Goebel?" Ethan asked.

"A transporter from home," Frank said, already starting out of the pen.

I tossed the empty bucket to the ground and followed Frank. Joe led us to Michael, who held a musket aimed at Nick Goebel and a woman I didn't recognize.

"It's okay, Michael," Frank said.

My son relaxed the gun at his side.

"What are you doing here?" I asked Nick.

"The same thing you are. Trying to live through World War III back home. This is my wife, Suzanne."

She lifted her head in my direction. "Hey. Nick's told me a lot about your group."

"How did you find out we were here?" Frank asked.

"I'll tell you everything, but can we get out of the cold, please? We've been walking all day, and we could use some water," Goebel said.

"Follow us," Frank said, reaching out to help him up. I did the same for Suzanne.

The others gathered at the communal fire pit in the middle of the settlement and watched us lead the pair across the field. Annabelle threw logs on the flame, while I got water for our guests. Maddie brought blankets, and they bundled up in front of the campfire. Frank made introductions all around and then focused on Nick.

"So what's the story?"

Nick put his tin cup on the ground at his feet and laid his hand over his wife's. "We came here with Alvarez. He found out you all transported here, and things were getting worse in Los Angeles. We thought following you here was a good suggestion. The idea was to find you and, hopefully, hook up with you and survive here until it's safe to transport home again."

"So where is Alvarez?" I asked.

"I don't know. He ditched us after he told me his alternate plan and I refused to go along with it."

"Which was?" Adams asked.

"He plans to get historical documents and bring them back to our timeline to sell later."

I glanced around the campfire, and most of us wore the same expression of disbelief.

"He cannot be serious," Gray said.

"Well, let him traipse through 1791 like an idiot. I don't care," Frank said, waving his hand in a dismissive motion.

"If it were just that, I'd agree with you. But there's more. I found a gun in his pack."

"We have guns too," Ethan said. "It's a given in this timeline."

"No, he has a weapon he brought from home. An old semiautomatic handgun."

Frank rose quickly. "What? Are you sure?"

"Yes, I saw it and held it myself. It's a 9 mm Glock."

I felt my earlier peace of mind begin to slip away.

"So he's out there somewhere running around half-cocked with a gun that won't be available until the late twentieth century? And a sketchy plan to steal national treasures? Great. Do you have any idea what this could do to the timeline?" I asked.

"Of course I do. Why do you think I'm here? We could have transported back home and just taken our chances there. And to be honest, with what we've experienced so far from this era, we might be better off at home."

"I'm sorry. I didn't mean to imply you had anything to do with his stupidity," I said.

"All right. So obviously, we need to find him and at the very least, disarm him," Gray said.

"How do we do that? He could be anywhere," Michael said.

"We don't know this area at all. But we have a friend who does," Adams said, pointing toward the bluff behind the houses.

I turned to see Samuel and Prudence winding down the trail in their buckboard wagon. At that moment, Emory and Jeremiah stepped from the cabin and joined us at the firepit. They looked around the group, their gaze stopping at Nick and Suzanne.

"What's going on?" Emory asked.

"These friends of ours from home made it here," Kira said.

"Oh, hi. I'm Emory and this is my husband Jeremiah."

"I'm pleased to make your acquaintance," Jeremiah said.

"Hi," Nick said, while Suzanne raised her hand in a wave.

"Here come our guests. We are celebrating their recent marriage," Kira nodded toward her daughter and new son-in-law. "You two must be hungry."

"We are starving," Suzanne said.

"Follow me and you can wash up and help us get the food ready," Linda said.

They followed the women into Linda's cabin.

I sat next to Frank. "So how are we going to convince Samuel to leave his family and guide us around Virginia after a rogue agent?"

"*We* aren't. No offense, Christine, but they do not treat women the same way here as at home. It's not safe for you to come with us—not this time. I need you here. I'll take Ethan and Goebel with me. The rest of you can stay here and protect the settlement. Alvarez won't be hard to track. He's a blowhard, and I guarantee he will shoot his mouth off everywhere he goes. He'll leave us a nice trail by which to locate him."

I started to object, but he stopped me. "I know what you're thinking. But this is an untenable situation. We find him and quietly get him here with his gun. Then both he and his weapon need to go back to 2072."

I bit my tongue, even though I realized he wasn't wrong. I hated this century for considering women the weaker sex, but I could do nothing to change that in the next few hours. Which meant I was stuck here on the settlement playing the role of the dutiful Goodwife, while the men chased after Alvarez.

I helped Maddie set the long table near the firepit. Even though it was cold we had to eat outside. Our cabins were not big enough to seat the twenty-two people there. We were sure not counting on two more mouths to feed, so I was glad to see that Samuel brought venison. Linda made corncakes, green beans, fried potatoes with onion, and fried fish, so we had plenty to choose from. I added the pemmican the Indians gave us and breathed in the scent of the mincemeat pie Prudence baked. My stomach rumbled as I glanced up at the clouds in the sky, hoping the weather held for our al fresco dining.

Annabelle brought a pot of sassafras tea out and poured me a cup. "It sucks we can't go with them. I'd love to get a shot at this Alvarez character. What on earth was he thinking, bringing a weapon back here from our timeline?"

"Who knows? Frank is right about him though. He's a loudmouth who won't be able to resist showing off his toy. I just hope someone hasn't already offed him and stolen the gun. It will be lost to the wind if that's the case."

"Well, with any luck he's stayed alive and out of trouble. I envy him a bit, if he's really trying to get historical documents. It would be nice to meet even one of the fifty-six men who signed the Declaration of Independence."

"The honor of meeting any of our forefathers would probably sail right over his ridiculous head," I said, sipping my tea and rolling my eyes.

Linda headed toward us, ending our conversation, followed by the other women, who each carried dishes of food. We settled onto benches at either side of the table and bowed our heads while Samuel said grace. I saw Prudence studying the pemmican.

"Would you care to try it, Prudence?" Linda asked.

"It looks like no scrapple I have seen before. How did ye prepare it?"

"Oh, I didn't. Christine and I received it from the local Indians. I think it actually might be pemmican."

"Ye trade with the savages?"

"No, it was a gift," I said. "It was a thank-you for medicine we gave them for one of their sick. He was burning with the fever so many had recently. They are friendly natives."

Prudence's eyes widened. "I know naught of any friendly savages. I hear tell of many raids against forts and settlements hereabouts. A great many settlers perish at their hands. Scalped and taken captive, ne'er to release them. I know of only one captive returned to her white kin. Poor girl, her face bespoke of the terror and torture she suffered. Nary a word did she ever speak of her captivity. Her family learned naught of her time with the savages."

My fork paused midair. Although we were all aware of the strife between colonists and indigenous tribes, this was the first actual account I'd heard of violence near our settlement. Washington had driven most Indians west after the French and Indian war ended in 1763, but there were still pockets of natives living in Virginia. I didn't imagine they were fans of the people who forced them from their land and into hiding.

"You say there were raids close to our settlements?"

"I fear ye shall find it so," Samuel said. "I plan to build a garrison house when the spring thaw comes. Ye would be wise to do the same."

I exchanged a glance with Annabelle. We had prior experience with Indians in another timeline, and we both recognized the need to take this seriously. I made a mental note to discuss it with her tomorrow.

Frank cleared his throat and rested his fork on his plate. "Samuel, I have a favor to ask of you. A huge one. We need your help."

TWENTY-ONE

Alexandria, Virginia 1791

Samuel studied Frank. "I know naught what more I can do for ye. I negotiated land and materials fairly."

"You certainly did, and we have no right to ask you for anything else, but we really need your help," Frank said.

Samuel laughed and glanced at Jeremiah, who grinned. "I jest with ye, sir. How may I be of service?"

"You had me going for a minute there, pal. There is a man who traveled from the west with our guests," Frank said, motioning to Nick and Suzanne. "He deserted them, but not before taking something that doesn't belong to him. An item of great value we must recover. We need help to track him. Once we find him, we intend to bring him here, then send him on his way back home."

"This gentleman, he does not wish to be found?"

"No. He brought our guests here under false motives and only told them his true intentions once he arrived."

"Aye, so his perfidy reveals him as more foe than friend."

"Yes."

"Mayhap 'twas never a fellow at all."

"I believe you are right, Samuel," Frank said. "Ethan, Nick, and I can go with you, if you will help track him. You know people here and are familiar with the area, as we are not."

"And the others shall stay? I only ask they forfend my homestead and family in my absence, so no harm becomes them."

"Of course. We can have someone stay there. Or Prudence, you may come here," I offered.

"Nay, 'twould be highly improper for a gentleman to live at our home with my husband away."

"Ethan will be gone too. Why don't you come here temporarily, with me then?"

"What of the animals?"

"I will mind the livestock. I shall remain at yer homestead with Missus Johnson and my sister. Emory may stay there," Jeremiah said.

"Aye, 'tis settled then. We depart at the next forenoon as soon as Prudence provisions us," Samuel said.

"We go tomorrow?" Ethan asked.

"I hope to find yer fellow by day's end at the morrow. Tarry too long and Prudence shall make me sleep with the cows."

We finished our early supper, and as dusk set in, the Johnsons left for home.

Jeremiah and Emory were still in the spare room at our cabin until Gray built them their own, so we made space for Nick and Suzanne next to the fireplace. Once the newlyweds went to stay with Prudence for a couple of days, our new guests could bunk in the extra bedroom temporarily. After that, they would have to move to someone else's cabin. There simply wouldn't be enough room.

"Sorry we don't have a bed or anything nicer for you," I said.

"Please, this is fine. It's far better than sleeping in the woods," Suzanne said. "Thank you for letting us stay. I realize it was probably a shock and obviously completely unexpected to have visitors from our time."

"What is it like there now?" Ethan asked, sitting across from them.

Nick cast his eyes downward. He looked weary and sad. "Not good, that's for sure. They hit the West Coast with water contamination. People scrambling for bottled water and supplies. You can no longer order groceries through your ChefAid—they suspended deliveries. The trucks were being hijacked by gangs and looters. Now you wait hours in line at the warehouses for food. Medical services are so overwhelmed, they don't even try to save patients in the field anymore. If someone flatlines, there is an automatic do not resuscitate order in place. It's only going to get worse. They shut down most of the eastern United States and the Midwest. And I mean *shut them down.* No services. It's everyone for themselves."

Every sentence was like fingers closing around my throat, cutting off my oxygen and gripping me tighter with each word, until I could no longer breathe. I stood and excused myself, dragging in deep breaths of cold air on the porch. Ethan followed to check on me.

"You okay?"

"Not really. What about our families? We should have insisted they come with us. How are they going to survive?"

"We could not force them to do something they weren't interested in doing, Christine. You know that. They made their decision, and we must respect that."

"What if they regret it now? And they're stuck there with no way out?"

"Your family is very resourceful. They are tucked away in their cabin with a massive supply of goods, remember? They have a well for their own water. Your brother-in-law is a police officer. He has weapons and knows how to use them. I wouldn't worry about them."

"What about your parents in England? And your daughter?"

"They are on a farm in the countryside with livestock, a stream, and a garden. Not unlike our situation here. My ex-wife would know to take Sian there. My parents are die-hard, stiff-upper-lip Brits. It will take more than a food shortage to bring them down, believe me."

He took my hand to lead me back inside, out of the biting cold of the night.

"I'm sorry. It was difficult to hear that. I just needed a moment to digest it, I guess," I said.

"No need to apologize. I only wish I brought better news," Nick said.

We talked for the next two hours, before I suggested the guys get to sleep early. Tomorrow began their hunt for Alvarez, and they would need to be on point. I lay in bed long after Ethan fell asleep thinking about my family in 2072.

We awoke to snow covering the ground as far as we could see. Ethan packed a light bag for himself and loaned Nick a flintlock.

Ethan gave our guest a crash course in loading and firing the flintlock, as Nick had no experience with the weapon. It was a tedious process, pouring the gunpowder down the muzzle to the bore, placing a cloth wad on the muzzle, and then the lead ball on top of the wad. The wad wasn't always necessary, but it ensured the ball was airtight in the barrel. Then you withdrew the ramrod and reinserted it into its holder. Finally, you lifted the frizzen and filled the pan with priming powder before relocking it. Once you pulled the cock back, you could aim and fire. Historical records said musketeers could reload a muzzle loader four times in one minute. None of us could imagine how. It took us considerably longer than the more experienced colonists and therefore wasn't a very efficient weapon in terms of protection. Or hunting. But it was all we had, unlike our fast, convenient, modern-day weapons that loaded quickly and carried plenty of ammunition. Our respect for the colonists increased every day.

The men each hid a knife in their boots and announced themselves ready to go. Frank came over to wait at our cabin, and Samuel arrived soon after, with a large pack full of provisions from Prudence. I stood on the porch with Suzanne to watch them leave. Ethan turned once to wave before they rode out of view, and I got teary-eyed. I swiped at the tears angrily. It was so unlike me to break down like that. Although it had become a habit by that time. Anyone who met me during those months would have thought I was in a constant state of emotional collapse. I worked hard at convincing myself I wasn't.

I kept busy, trying to focus on anything but Los Angeles or tracking Alvarez. But my mind wandered back to both, and I finally gave up trying. I spent the rest of the afternoon with Suzanne and Annabelle, and when evening came, I had calmed enough to sleep. I climbed into bed alone, wondering how the first day went for Ethan.

* * *

Samuel walked out of the coffeehouse toward the three men on horseback.

"Seems yer fellow has found himself in trouble."

"What did you find out?" Ethan asked.

"Talk circulates of a stranger with an unfamiliar accent and a foreign weapon who the sheriff arrested for public drunkenness and held in the watch-house."

"Can we get him back?" Frank asked.

"Mayhap after a trial, 'twere he still there."

"He's not there? Where then?" Nick asked.

"Hear tell the pirate Edward Blake broke him from the watch-house. Killed the guards whilst escaping last eve, and 'tis nowhere to be found."

"Can't they arrest Blake?" Ethan said.

"Aye, 'twould if they found him. 'Tis all rumors. Yer fellow is gone, two sentries are dead, and Edward Blake's name 'twas raised. Save for the local gossip, 'twould not fare that much information."

"We cannot give up yet. It is vital that we find him. If he even still has the gun," Frank said.

A man stepped from the shadows of the tavern, blinking against the bright sunlight.

"I have knowledge of where Edward Blake anchors his sloop. Yer fellow lives."

The voice startled them, and they twisted on their horses to confront a disheveled man. He was dirty and reeked of rum and body odor. He swayed on his feet and steadied himself against the building.

"Is that a fact?" Ethan asked.

"Aye. Yer fellow showed Blake's man his weapon. Most unusual, 'twas. He came outside for a pipe and the necessary. Too much ale. I was hidden at this very building. Then saw him hide the gun well down in his boots. 'Tis a small weapon. The pirate searched for it, afore the brawl, but he found naught. Aft the watchmen searched him, still they did not find the weapon, so well hidden 'twas. Blake and his mates took him from the watch-house last eve. 'Twas determined to make him tell them where he hid it. Took him on the ship. I followed them to the cove where they anchor."

"Aft ye sober yourself, mayhap ye recall where ye last saw the King of England as well. 'Tis naught but a drunkard," Samuel said, dismissing the man with a wave.

Frank held up his hand in a gesture to wait. "Can you take us there?"

"Aye. 'Twould cost ye. I am but a poor gentleman."

"A fool's errand," Samuel said.

Ethan removed coins from his pack. "I have pieces of eight. Two coins now, and two more when you show us to them. If we find it is actually them, I will add two pieces of silver to the bounty. If you try to cheat me, I will have no mercy on you."

His eyes sparkled at the prospect of money, and he cupped his hands. Ethan dropped the two coins into his palm, and he danced a little jig.

"Lead the way," Frank said.

The man led them through Alexandria as the four men followed on horseback, hooves clopping loudly on the hard ground. They rode past the docks and the merchants who crowded the wharf on the Potomac until the noise of the city was long behind them.

"Just o'er yonder. She's anchored offshore there," said the man, pointing toward the river.

"Wait here with him. I'm going to go have a look," Ethan said.

"I'll come with you," Frank said, sliding off his horse.

They made their way along the shoreline, under the cover of vegetation, until the landscape opened to the beach. Masts were visible above the bushes, but they crouched to stay hidden. The sloop sat about a half mile out. They could not tell who was on the ship from their vantage point, but a British flag waved prominently in the wind above the gunwale. They hurried back on the path, camouflaged by the brush.

"There's a sloop moored out there, but we can't see anything from this far away. It flies a British flag. It doesn't appear to be a pirate vessel," Ethan said.

"Pirates ofttimes fly British flags. They run their own colors only before ravaging another ship," Samuel said.

"Then it could be the right one," Nick said.

"Aye, 'tis Blake's sloop, I give ye my word," said the man. "For two more pieces of eight 'twill sneak upon it tonight with ye to capture the man ye seek. I know where they hide their jolly boat."

"Nay, I shouldn't want to face Edward Blake with only the four of us. Could be twenty or more men under his service. 'Tis best if we wait for them to come ashore," Samuel said.

"I hear tell they are to cast off on the morrow. 'Twill be but one chance to seize yer man," said the man. "Two coins, and I shall have ye aboard the sloop this nightfall."

"Deal," Frank said. "Samuel, we'll go alone. You stay here. I promised Prudence I would bring you home safely. This is our man and our duty to get him back. We will work faster alone."

"As ye wish. I pray in the name of our Lord ye shan't perish by the sword of Edward Blake and his crew."

They settled down for a meal and to wait for nightfall. Ethan glanced at Frank and then Nick. The three of them against who knows how many pirates. The odds were not in their favor. The men on that ship were known for their brutality and fighting under close combat. He took the knife from his boot, running the blade against a rock to sharpen it.

They needed Tony Alvarez to be on that ship and his gun to be with him. Ethan shuddered at the thought of that weapon in the hands of eighteenth-century pirates.

TWENTY-TWO

Alexandria, Virginia 1791

The men waited on the shore until well after dark. The sound of the marauders celebrating eventually died out, and the man dragged the jolly boat from its hiding place. Frank insisted the man stay on shore with Samuel, and he didn't argue against that decision.

"Take care whilst there. The pirates fight like the devil," Samuel said.

"If the grim look on your face is any indication of what we're going up against, I'd rather not hear the details," Frank said with more asperity than intended.

"We'll be back as soon as we can," Ethan said as he, Frank, and Nick climbed into the small canoe.

"Remember, whistle if you see anything or are in trouble," Frank said.

They cast off into the cold water of the Potomac headed for the pirate ship. The night offered them little light, but it silhouetted the large outline of the sloop against the moonlight. They rowed in silence toward their target. It took longer than expected, as they were careful not to splash the oars loudly and warn someone of their arrival. Because the pirates were drinking and celebrating earlier, they hoped most of them were either passed out or asleep by now. But when they were a few hundred feet from the ship, the unmistakable sound of automatic gunfire pierced the stillness. Nick stopped rowing, and they sat frozen, waiting. It wasn't long before voices carried over the water.

"Be rid of him, Mr. Coates. Ready us to sail to New York at first light."

"Yessir, Cap'n Blake."

Two shadows moved closer to the side where they hoisted something large overboard. Seconds later a loud splash broke the silence, the waves causing the small boat to rock. The figures maneuvered away, and Nick glanced over to Frank, who motioned for him to row them forward. He paddled them onward when suddenly they collided with an object in the water.

"What is that?" Ethan whispered. Nick craned his neck to see past him but was too far away to make out anything in the dark and fog that settled over the water.

"I'm not sure," Frank said, reaching out to touch the surface of the frigid river. He explored the murky water until he hit something solid. He felt around, then recoiled, snapping his hands back to his side. "Shit. It's a body."

"Do you think it's Tony?" Nick asked.

Frank reached into the cold water again. "Who knows? We'll have to bring him aboard to find out anything more."

Anger tempted Frank to let the river swallow him if it was Alvarez. But his sense of duty would not allow him to watch a fellow agent die, or even leave him for the fish if he were already dead. He leaned farther out of the boat and pulled the limp body from the water. Ethan helped him drag the man over the edge and into the canoe. They flipped him over to see Alvarez, bloody chest, and bruised face. Frank felt for a pulse.

"He's still alive, but barely." He opened the agent's shirt to a clear bullet hole in his chest. "This isn't good. Adams might do something for him, but we're a day's ride from home." He searched Tony's pants and vest, pulling out his small camera. "No gun. They must have it on the ship. Goebel take us closer and anchor us to them. We'll leave him here and go for the gun. I'm certain Blake is keeping it safe and to himself."

Frank disassembled the camera and threw the pieces overboard.

"He looks pretty beat up," Goebel said, staring at Alvarez's bruising.

"I'm sure they had to convince him to give up the gun. Let's just hope they didn't persuade him to show them how to load and fire it. With any luck, that gunfire was him getting off a shot before they dumped him," Frank said.

Ethan grabbed the knife from his boot and crouched, ready to disembark. They tied the jolly boat to the ship's bow line and scaled up the side. They dropped onto the deck silently, one at a time, and then crouched low, staying still to make sure they alerted no one. When they were satisfied none of the crew were aware of their breach, they snuck along the edge of the gunwale. Several men snored loudly, sprawled out haphazardly. The ship rocked gently with the current, lulling them deeper into a slumber. The only man awake was pacing slowly at the port side bridge.

"We may not have much time if that guy decides to have a stretch," Ethan whispered.

Frank motioned to a door that led below deck. Nick and Ethan followed him through and down a steep, narrow staircase. The stench of rotting food and urine was strong, but the body odor was overbearing. Nick covered his mouth to stifle a cough. Frank snapped his head back to signal him to be quiet. An oil lamp gave off enough light to illuminate bodies in every available space, curled on the floor, asleep. They picked their way across the ship's hold, over the sleeping men and around barrels of cargo and supplies. The ship creaked and moaned, and pirates stirred under the trespass. Frank pointed to double doors, and the two men nodded in acknowledgment. They expected Edward Blake to have a captain's quarters to himself. Frank pushed the entry open slowly, the creak making the hairs on his neck stand on end. They entered the stateroom and pushed the door closed. Another oil lamp burned on a small table next to the bunk, where a bearded man in a navy doublet coat and dirty white breeches snored. Boots were strewn in the corner, and a blue hat with gold trim sat on top of them. He clutched Tony's gun against his chest in a death grip. The box of ammo lay at the foot of the bed, and Ethan immediately pocketed it. Frank motioned for Ethan to silence Blake. Ethan approached and slammed his hands down over the man's face. His arms flew out instinctively, letting the weapon go. Frank grabbed it and stuffed it into his waistband, but not before using the butt to knock the pirate unconscious. They made their way back through the same path they came, creeping through the mine field of bodies as quickly as possible.

They approached the edge of the vessel and Nick climbed down first. He hung from the side of the ship, trying to get his footing on any part of the hull. Shouting from below deck startled him, and he dropped into the frigid water below with a loud splash. Frank and Ethan scrambled over the edge as three men stepped onto the upper deck, waking several of the sleeping men near them. Ethan slipped and crashed to the river's surface. Nick swam to their craft where he hung onto the side with one hand, while trying to untie it from the sloop with the other. He loosened it enough to pull it free and launched himself into the boat onto his stomach. Ethan swam over and took Nick's outstretched hand to help him on board. They looked up to see Frank with one leg over the ship and the other on the rail. A pirate had a cutlass raised, ready to come down on him. He used his foot on the railing to kick his attacker. The pirate stumbled backward, but his blade slashed Frank's arm as he lost his balance and fell. Frank cried out in pain as his grip on the rail loosened. He plunged into the river, landing in a belly flop. Ethan flung himself in after Frank and reached him in two long strokes. He turned him over and grasped him under the neck, pulling him to the jolly boat. Nick dragged the men aboard and Ethan collapsed on top of Frank. He recovered quickly and grabbed a set of oars to help Nick row as more pirates crowded the deck, firing their flintlocks randomly, shots landing in the river all around. A shot hit the canoe and water seeped into the bottom.

"Double-time it guys, or we will sink right here," Frank shouted over the commotion.

He aimed the Glock toward the ship and fired off a few rounds. He couldn't see anything in the dark, the fog now almost completely concealing the ship, but he hoped it would be enough to frighten them into a cease fire. His adrenaline surged as musket fire continued to pepper the water surrounding them.

They had rowed farther away from the ship when a loud splash made Ethan turn to Nick.

"Sounds like they launched a boat to come after us, mate. Row as if your life depends on it, because it does."

The pirates continued firing at them as the boat took on more water, adding weight and slowing them down. Nick cried out and bent over to clutch his right thigh.

"I'm hit!" he shouted.

"Can you still row?" asked Ethan without stopping to turn to him.

"Yes," he said, grimacing in pain.

"We're almost there. We have horses, they don't. Once we get to shore, we can lose them," Ethan said.

Nick turned to see the outline of the beach two hundred feet away. They reached land within minutes, and Ethan scrambled out of the boat. He helped Frank up and supported Nick as they half-ran to where they left Samuel. He saw them approaching and ran forward to help the injured men.

"Wrap Frank's arm and Nick's leg and get them on the horses. I'm going back for Alvarez," Ethan said, breathing fast, trying to catch his breath.

"The gunfire. Are they coming after us?" Samuel said.

"Yes. Ready them to ride. I'll be right back."

Ethan raced back to the boat and leaned inside. He checked Tony's pulse. It was weak, but still there. He lifted him and heaved him over his shoulder, grunting with the strain. He heard the pirates—they were close. A shot hit the ground near his feet, causing him to jump. He adjusted the weight of the man he carried and jogged toward the others. Samuel met him as he came into view. He grabbed Tony's legs, and they settled him on Ethan's horse. The man who led them there stood frozen, watching the surrounding turmoil. Ethan threw several coins at him without a word. His hands swept through the dirt until he found them, then he disappeared into the night. Ethan mounted his horse and motioned to Samuel when he heard the pirates shout as they came ashore.

"I have no idea where we are, you lead."

Samuel kicked the animal, and it took off in a fast trot. Frank rode behind Nick, who winced in pain with every bounce of his horse. Ethan took up the rear, Alvarez strapped to his horse. After an hour, they stopped as the sun rose. Ethan re-dressed Frank's arm and tightened the tourniquet on Nick's leg.

"You all right?" he asked Frank.

"Fine, just grazed me, but it hurts like a son-of-a-bitch. I'm more worried about infection than anything else."

"That looks like more than a graze. We'll be home tomorrow and get you an antibiotic. We need to stop his bleeding," he said, eyeing Nick. "He's lost a fair amount of blood, and the shot is still in his thigh."

"What about that one," Frank said, lifting his chin to Alvarez on Ethan's horse.

"Alive, for now. He has severe bruising on his midriff. He may be bleeding internally. If he makes it back to the settlement, I'm not sure Adams can do anything for him."

"Well, there's nothing to do but hope for the best. But if he survives, I'm going to kick his ass for this," Frank said.

They had a quick meal and built a fire to dry as much of their clothing as possible. An hour later they mounted their horses to start for home again. They traveled in silence but for the sound of Nick's cries when his horse jostled his leg too much. He got paler by the hour, and perspiration ran down his face, despite the cold.

They encountered no one on the road until midday, when three riders blocked their path ahead. They stopped on the trail, and Frank and Ethan guided their horses beside Samuel. The other men rode slowly toward them. When they got nearer, Frank shook his head and muttered to himself under his breath.

"I've got this one, guys," he said, grabbing the gun from his waistband and pointing it straight at the middle rider.

Horatio Travis and his henchmen appeared unimpressed with the modern-day weapon. Frank released the safety and positioned his finger over the trigger.

TWENTY-THREE

Alexandria, Virginia 1791

The men were not home from tracking Alvarez yet. Linda didn't voice it, but I could tell it worried her. It did me too. They only expected to be gone for two days, but as we entered day four, there was no sign of them, and no word either. Prudence kept telling us the Lord would protect them, but I saw the worry in her eyes.

Jeremiah went to the marketplace and heard of recent Indian raids. One on a settlement just west of our land, and another on White's Fort, fifteen miles south. The brutal details of the attack shook us. Annabelle and me more than the others. We both realized what this meant. The assaults were getting closer, and with each attack, our risk increased. Witnesses said the natives killed twenty settlers, many scalped, and several more were missing. I relied on Prudence and her experience in this timeline to reassure me. But all she said was there are those who live in fear and those who die in fear. I wondered where I fell on the spectrum. Maybe I was both.

I was alone in my cabin, a rarity in those days. I lifted the edge of the mantel and slid my hand inside the cavity behind it, searching until I found my transponder. It felt heavy and unfamiliar in my palm, so I was uncertain why it made me feel better to hold it. I couldn't use it to go home—I *wouldn't*. Not unless everyone else agreed. And definitely not without Ethan, Michael, and Maddie. Perhaps my homesickness brought on my melancholy. Whatever the reason, it seeped into my very soul with a vengeance and refused to budge. I hid the device in its secret place again and peered out the window at Annabelle and Emory working in the garden. Pulling on my wrap, I strolled across the field to join them.

"Want some company?" I asked.

"Hey there, of course. You can help me pick green beans," Annabelle said.

"Hi, Emory," I said, smiling at her.

She glanced up and gave me a quick grin, then resumed her work. Annabelle and I chatted over the next twenty minutes, until I noticed Emory hunched over, hands on her knees.

I walked over to her and placed my hand on her back. "You okay? You look a little green."

"Yeah. I don't understand what's wrong with me. I'm kind of sick to my stomach and really exhausted lately," she said.

Annabelle took her basket from her and led her out of the garden to the grass. "Here, sit down and rest a minute, hon."

I plopped on the ground next to them. "Let's all take a break."

Emory sat down, then almost immediately bolted up and ran several yards away, where she got sick.

I exchanged a glance with Annabelle and we both jogged over to her. "You all right?" I said, pulling the hair off her face.

She nodded, inhaling a deep breath. We helped her back to the grass where she lay down, staring up at the gray sky.

"How long have you had these symptoms? Anything else abnormal?" Annabelle asked.

"I'm not sure. A few weeks, I guess. No other symptoms, I'm just tired, like I said."

"How's your appetite?" I asked.

"Surprisingly good. Even though I'm sick sometimes. Often, actually. I kinda get better after I eat. I hate most of the food here, but Linda makes some stuff that I really enjoy. But, jeez, the smell of that fish. I could spew just thinking about it," she said, screwing her face into a grimace.

I looked at Annabelle. My eyes darted to my stomach then back to her. Her eyes grew wide, and she mouthed *Oh My God* to me. I raised my eyebrows and gave her a slight shrug.

"Emory, when was your last cycle? Do you track it? I'm not trying to get too personal, but are you on contraceptives?" Annabelle said.

She sat up straight and glanced between us. "Well, yeah, I take the monthly pill, since Jeremiah and I got married," she said, blushing as she looked away. "But I forgot it last month, and it's not time for me to have it again."

"Did you have a cycle last month?" I asked.

"I can't remember. I used to keep track of it back home. Not that it mattered then, but I marked it on my tablet. I'm not even sure why."

"Were you regular when you tracked it at home?"

"Yeah. Oh my God. Do you think I could be pregnant?"

"I don't know, it's possible. The fatigue, the sickness, those are common symptoms," Annabelle said.

"How about we go see Adams before we jump to any conclusions? You could just have a stomach bug. There are lots of things here that can cause that. But he might have a pregnancy test. Do you want to get your mom?" I suggested.

"No! Not yet. Will you both come with me to see him? This is so embarrassing."

"Sure, let's sneak over and find him while everyone else is busy with chores," Annabelle said, standing up and offering Emory her hand.

We located Adams in the barn, grooming the horses.

"Hey. We need your help," I said.

"Yeah, what's up?" he asked, glancing between the three of us.

"Can you give Emory an exam? Discreetly?" Annabelle said, gesturing over her shoulder at the girl.

"Okay, a checkup for what? That's a very vague request."

Emory stepped forward. "I don't remember if I had a menstrual cycle last month. I'm tired and nauseated. I've thrown up a few times. It's been going on for a few weeks."

He stared at her a moment before he spoke. "Shouldn't your mother be here?"

"I'm eighteen now, Nathan. I want to be sure I'm pregnant and not just sick before I tell her. Please. I need to know."

"All right, I understand. Why don't you stay here while I grab a few things from the house? Have a seat on the bench, and I'll be back in a few minutes."

He headed out of the barn, leaving us alone again. "Do you think he is going to give me like a physical exam?" Emory said, biting a nail.

"No, not the kind you're thinking of. If you are only a month or two along, it's way too early for that. Besides, I'm not sure he knows anything about gynecology, other than the basics," Annabelle said.

"It's been so long for me, I can hardly remember pregnancy and childbirth," I said.

"Well, it's still fresh in *my* memory," Annabelle said.

Adams came back into the barn carrying a small bag. "Okay, let's take a look at you. I don't have a pregnancy test. I never thought to bring one."

He instructed her to lie on the bench where he took her temperature, listened to her heart, and clocked her pulse. He checked her throat, lymph nodes, and examined her stomach for any distention, asking her a battery of questions during the assessment.

"I can't find anything out of the ordinary. If this has persisted for three weeks, I have to conclude you are pregnant. You have no fever, no reflux, no signs of an ulcer, and intestinal worms would be evident in your waste. It's not gallstones, or you would have some level of pain. Consistent nausea with no obvious illness, my bet would be you're carrying. You aren't showing yet, but if you are expecting, you will notice a little baby bump in a month or two, assuming you are four to eight weeks into your pregnancy. Typically, sometime between twelve and sixteen weeks you will start to show."

Emory sat silently. I settled next to her and grabbed her hand. She turned to me and grinned widely. She giggled a little and stared off dreamily.

Then reality set in.

"Oh, my God. I'm gonna have a baby," she said, softly.

She was quiet after that, stunned into silence. Annabelle gave her a minute to let it sink in before she yanked her back to the present.

"How do you feel about that? Are you okay? I understand this can come as a shock. I've been there myself," Annabelle said.

She eyed Annabelle, tears threatening to fall. "I don't know. I think I'm good with it. I mean, I love Jeremiah, and we're married, so. . ."

"Why don't we sit here for a bit while you collect your thoughts and get used to the idea. Then you can find your parents and Jeremiah," Annabelle said, gesturing at Adams to leave.

She swiped at the corner of her eyes. "You two have to come with me to tell them. Who knows how my dad is going to take this news? You know how he is. No way can I do this alone."

I slumped against the wall of the barn. "Okay, give me ten minutes to gather my courage and we'll head out," I said, knowing I would need much longer before I was comfortable telling Gray his teenager was pregnant in a time without modern medical help. It was possible I was more anxious than she was to break the news to her parents.

It went about as well as expected. To Gray's credit, he tried to be understanding, but I could tell it worried him. I was certain Emory saw it too. Kira cried, but only out of fear for her daughter's health. Childbirth in this timeline was difficult and not without significant risk. We had no pain medication safe to take while pregnant or in labor, and no modern medical facilities in the event something went wrong. However, the news thrilled Jeremiah, and he doted over his new wife like she was fine china that might shatter at any moment.

Then Gray brought up vaccines. Without them, the baby was high risk. Over twelve percent of all infants born here died in their first year. Thirty-five percent of children passed before the age of six, and a whopping sixty percent did not live to see sixteen years old. I was only aware of those grim statistics because Annabelle told me later, when we were alone. Before she agreed to bring her toddlers here, she studied the mortality rate and the most common causes of death in children. She wanted to be sure she prepared for her girls' safety. Now, with an unplanned pregnancy among our group of travelers, those numbers were more frightening than ever.

I knew what Stephen and Kira were thinking. The same thought crossed my mind, and Annabelle's too. Someone must transport to 2072 and bring back vaccines for the baby. Without them, he or she could easily become another child who didn't make it past their first year. And we could not allow that to happen.

TWENTY-FOUR

Alexandria, Virginia 1791

"Horatio, 'tis naught betwixt us we cannot mend another time. Injured men ride with me, and we must not tarry. Their very lives depend on it," Samuel said.

"Yer fellow does not agree. He aims his weapon my way," he said, lifting his chin in the direction of Frank, who still held the pistol eye level with him.

"And make no mistake, l will not hesitate to use it either," Frank said.

"Ye stole land from me," he said, his eyes never leaving Frank's.

"Stand aside, Travis. We stole nothing from you. Mrs. Blanchard did not want to sell her property to you," Ethan said.

"Mister Ward speaks the truth. Now, stand yonder and let us pass. We wish no war with ye, Horatio," Samuel said.

"We settle this now," he said, drawing his flintlock from his saddlebag.

Frank did not hesitate, firing the gun at the ground in front of the man. Horatio's horse whinnied, and hooves clawed at the air as the animal reared back. The pop of the gun sounded unlike their muskets as the bullet fired into the dirt, causing a puff of dust to fly up from the road. The other men flinched, their eyes wide, but Travis maintained his composure.

"l don't miss, Travis. That was a warning shot. The next one is right between your eyes. And the bullet will go clean through you, tearing up anything it touches on the way out. You'll be dead before you even realize you were hit."

Travis pursed his lips, nostrils flared as he guided his horse around them. His glare bore into them as he passed.

"Ye have declared war with me. 'Tis not over yet," he hissed.

"Anytime, asshole. Take your best shot. You know where to find me. On the land we bought from Mrs. Blanchard. I'll look forward to putting that bullet between your eyes," Frank said, matching the man's glare.

Once they were out of earshot, Samuel turned to Frank. "If not save for yer unusual weapon, I fear Horatio Travis 'twas determined to put ye in yer grave."

"I am in no mood for the likes of him today," Frank said. "My arm hurts and I want to get home. And he looks worse by the hour," he said, motioning toward Nick.

Ethan twisted to see Goebel bent over on the horse, barely clinging to the animal.

"Samuel, can you lead him? I don't think he can ride unassisted any longer," Ethan said.

Samuel secured Nick to his mare and tied it to his own horse. Nick barely registered being manhandled into position. How he had stayed upright that long was a mystery. His eyes rolled into the back of his head and he was unconscious again.

They carried onward, only half a day's ride from home. Samuel glanced at the man they rescued, slung across Ethan's horse, at Frank's arm, which was bleeding anew, and finally to Goebel. Godspeed, or half of them would not live to see home again.

* * *

I was rinsing clothes in the barrel outside our cabin when I saw them on the trail, on the bluff above our land. I dropped the clothing, grabbed the hem of my skirts, and ran to the edge of the field. I picked Ethan out right away. Tall and blonde, he sat high in the saddle. There was something on his horse with him, but I didn't realize it was a body until they were closer. Samuel led a horse tied to his, with someone straddled across it. As they rode nearer, I noticed Frank's left arm dangling limp at his side, a bloody cloth wrapped around it.

"Adams!" I yelled.

By this time, others saw them coming and everyone spilled into the common area between the cabins. Adams came to the door of his house and peered out. He took one look at the approaching men and ducked back inside for his medical case. He jogged toward the group, with me right behind him.

Ethan dismounted and gave me a quick hug while Adams unloaded instruments from his bag.

"I am going to need to run this just like a field triage. Give me the worst patient first," he said, glancing up at Ethan.

Ethan lifted Alvarez down and laid him on the grass near Adams. "Round to the chest. Has not regained consciousness."

Adams leaned down to listen for breathing, then checked his pulse. He put the stethoscope on Tony's chest, glanced up, and shook his head. "He's gone. Let me see him next," he said, motioning to Goebel.

Ethan and Gray carried Nick, still unconscious, to the grass in front of Adams.

"Round to the thigh, unconscious since this morning."

Adams cut off Nick's pant leg as Suzanne ran toward us. "Oh my God, is he alive?" she cried.

"He just started the exam," I said, taking her arm and leading her a few feet away. "Let's give him some room."

She sobbed, watching Adams. Annabelle comforted Suzanne as Linda ran to Frank. Samuel and Prudence embraced and set about helping get things organized. It was a tense situation for the first several minutes.

"I need to pull the round out and get antibiotics in him," Adams said.

They moved Goebel to his cabin where he could perform the field surgery. I followed behind Frank and Linda while Michael and Gray moved Alvarez's body to an outbuilding until we could bury him.

Adams removed the lead from Nick's thigh and gave him a shot. He set the leg in a splint, wrapping it tightly to prevent him from moving it, the closest we could get to a cast.

"When he wakes up, he is going to need pain meds. And I should check his wound every few hours to make sure the infection is receding. It's best if he stays here in my cabin," he said to Suzanne.

She knelt beside the bed to take his hand and bowed her head. I couldn't tell if she was crying or praying. Both of which were completely understandable, considering the circumstances.

Next Adams tended to Frank's arm. It was not infected yet, but the cut was deep. He cleaned it and stitched it up. Once he rewrapped it, he gave Frank antibiotics and went back to Goebel to check his vitals again.

Adams stepped out to the living area where our group crowded the space, waiting for news, while Suzanne stayed in the room with her husband.

"It's going to take him a couple months before he'll be able to walk without a cane. The bullet hit his femur and broke it. He's lucky. It missed his femoral artery, but not by much. We'd be having an entirely different conversation if that weren't the case. What the hell happened?" he asked.

"What didn't happen," Frank deadpanned. "We found Alvarez on a pirate ship, had a run-in with them, then met Horatio Travis on the way home."

"You were in a fight with actual pirates?" asked Linda.

Frank responded with a shrug and glanced to Ethan.

"We lost Alvarez, as you all know, but we got the gun," Ethan said, running his hands through his hair. "I'm not sure if we should destroy it or keep it for emergency protection."

"Well, I guess we can speak freely since Prudence and Samuel went home and took Jeremiah and Emory with them," Gemma said.

Gray filled them in on the recent Indian raids, and his daughter's pregnancy.

"It feels less and less safe here," Maddie said.

We all agreed, but no one offered a solution.

"Listen, we have everything sunk into our settlement here. We have to make the best of it," Annabelle said.

"We've been okay so far. We'll just have to be ready for an attack, should they try to hit us," Michael said.

"How are we supposed to do that?" asked Joe.

"I know it's only one weapon, but we have the semiautomatic now too. That's a lot more fire power than our muskets," Frank said.

"If I may extrapolate for a moment, please," Ethan said. "Indian raids will not stop. They get closer to us every day. I think we must do the best we can to fortify our homes against an attack. What other choice do we have?"

He was so stoic and composed. As if we were discussing what to have for dinner and not a potential assault from natives who scalp their victims. That was the difference between us. My emotions drove me most of the time, while he relied on fact and *extrapolated* logic. Somehow, we balanced each other out, although I could not for the life of me figure out how at that moment.

"There's something else," Gray said. "I am going back to 2072 to get vaccines for my grandbaby."

I glanced over to Kira, but she refused to meet my gaze. They were united in their decision, it seemed.

"Maybe someone else should go. If natives attack, we need you here," Annabelle said.

"It's too dangerous. She's my daughter and it's my grandchild. I can't ask any of you to do that. I'll get in and out, a day or two, tops. I may even be able to secure more supplies while I am there. If the CCEA still has a skeleton crew, then the cafeteria might be stocked."

He had a valid point. We could always use more medicine and nonperishable foods. I couldn't be the only one who fantasized about a bag of chips or a piece of chocolate. I glanced around the room and read their faces clearly—they all agreed with him. Plus, we would have news from home. And good or bad, that was what we all craved more than anything. Even more than junk food.

TWENTY-FIVE

Alexandria, Virginia 1791-92

We buried Tony Alvarez in the woods the following day. Goebel was awake, but confined to bedrest, leaving Suzanne the only person there who had ever met him. It felt completely insincere. We bowed our heads over the grave of a man I not only didn't know, but who bore responsibility for injuring two of our own. I realized he did not wield the sword that cut Frank or fire the musket that shot Goebel, but he may as well have. If not for him, none of it would have happened. But he *was* a CCEA agent and a traveler from our own timeline. We owed him the respect he deserved for that. However, his death served as a stark reminder of the perils we faced here—dangers none of us wanted to think about just then—and our mood was somber.

As the days turned into weeks, and then months, with no sign of hostile Indians, we worried less about an attack. We focused on survival and improving our lifestyle. Gray set a date for his trip forward to 2072, about two months before Emory was due to give birth. Once Nick recovered enough to use a cane, he volunteered to go, but Gray flat out would not agree. It seemed so far off now that I measured my life in sunrises and sunsets, not by a calendar. The monotony also meant I was bereft of any anticipation for the future. I hated the person that made me, and I tried everything I could to overcome it. Instead, I became good at faking a brave exterior. But after the spring thaw finally came and summer was around the corner, it buoyed my attitude, and my pity party melted away along with the frost.

We continued to work hard. Hunting and planting more crops, we provided Linda a wide variety of foods to cook. Emory got bigger every day, and we assigned her to kitchen duty. That way she sat on a stool and it spared her any hard manual labor. She didn't complain, but I recognized the look in her eyes, the one only another woman who had been pregnant could appreciate. The universal expression we got about halfway through when all you wanted was to be normal again. The backache, the extra weight, the swollen ankles, it all took a toll. You allowed yourself to think of the birth as the end of the crisis. But we mothers understood it was only the beginning of a lifelong journey.

The men built a bateau boat we kept tied at a deserted cove on the river near the houses, where our stream emptied into the Potomac. I hiked down to where they worked most days, just for something different to do. I saw ships sail past, and I wondered if they were pirates. Could they be the marauders who took Alvarez? Or maybe that held me hostage when I was here rescuing Hannah? I really didn't want to find out—I was sure of that much. But it reminded me once again that the dangers of this era were many.

That day, I sat cross-legged on the grass, watching the men install the shade cover over the back of our completed vessel. Our boat was not much to look at, but large enough to hold all of us at sixteen feet long and six feet wide. It was flat-bottomed and double-ended, with oars on either side and one at the stern to act as a rudder. We planned to take it up and down the Potomac to trade with other settlers. Our vegetable enhancers were working well, and our crops were coming in faster than we used them. If we took the river to Alexandria, we could transport pumpkins, squash, and corn to the marketplace. Loading the cart with heavy goods and traversing over the hilly terrain into the city was difficult to do. The boat would save a lot of effort wasted on travel.

After a while of watching the men struggle to install the boat cover, I became bored and strolled back home. I took my time, following the creek along its windy path through the shaded forest. I found early-season berries and gathered them in my apron, humming a favorite song from before. I divided life into two categories—before we left and after we got here. The two times seem so far removed from one another it was impossible not to think in those terms.

We were now only a month away from Gray traveling back to Los Angeles. Or forward, I guess, was more accurate. We were all eager to find out what the world was like in 2072. I prayed we could go home, but I would not allow myself to dwell on it. I had already mentally prepared to stay as long as necessary.

I exited the woods next to Adams's cabin where Annabelle and Gemma mended clothes while their children played nearby. I emptied the berries into a basket and sat at the picnic table with them.

"Well, I must admit, this is not where I imagined I'd find you, Annabelle."

"Is that a dig on my domestic skills, Christine?"

"Never. You're my BFF. I just know how much you love to sew. Let me help. I'm bored to death," I said, grabbing one of Willow's torn dresses.

We talked and mended for the next hour until my eyes stung and my fingers cramped. I set the sewing tools down and glanced around our settlement. Smoke rose from Linda and Frank's cabin where she was cooking. I watched Goebel use his cane like a cricket bat to send Wyatt's pinecone ball sailing across the grass. Annabelle's girls giggled as they tried to get it from Wyatt, but he was too fast. Emory stood on Linda's porch, hands massaging her lower back, while her sister Rose carried a bucket between the cabins and the animal pens. Everyone was busy and going about their chores. A normal day in our settlement.

I moved to pick up the needle when motion caught my attention out of the corner of my eye. I scanned the edge of the field closest to us, where I spotted an almost imperceptible movement among the trees. My hand froze in midair. I squinted and focused on an area to my right. I was not imagining things. He was there. The Indian stood perfectly still, only his loincloth moved in the breeze. Wisps of hair danced across his face, the paint casting eerie shadows. The scene rooted me in place. I allowed only my eyes to roam from side to side as I scrutinized the surrounding forest.

And then I spotted the rest of them.

I blinked slowly to confirm what I saw. My heart slammed against my ribcage, trying to beat its way out of my chest. Indians posted at the edge of the tree line several yards apart stood ready to charge. I discovered six more of them as I studied the trees. There were probably others, but I didn't risk moving my head to search for them. I swallowed hard as my gaze wandered back to the first one. His eyes locked onto mine. Even from that distance, I could tell he fixed his gaze directly on me. His stare eviscerated me, and in that moment, I was never more certain of anything in my entire life.

They were there to kill us.

A shudder ran through me as I let the needle fall, not noticing it had dug into my palm. Tiny droplets of blood trickled down my arm and landed on the table.

"Get the kids and go in the house, right now," I whispered.

Gemma stopped her work and furrowed her brow. "What? Why?"

Annabelle raised her head, and her eyes met mine. She knew me well enough to recognize the terror in them, and she didn't hesitate.

"Gemma, on the count of three we are going to get up from this table and run as fast as we can to our kids. Grab them and drag Wyatt if you have to, to the nearest cabin. Once inside, we barricade the door," Annabelle said.

"I don't understand. What's happening?"

"Gemma, do what I say if you want to live. If you want Wyatt to live," I said. "There are Indians in the woods watching us. They are not here on a friendly visit. Trust me on this."

Annabelle took a deep breath. "One, two, three!"

I sprung up and grabbed the hem of my skirts as we scrambled from the table and I ran beside Annabelle for the girls. My lungs burned as I tore across the grass, getting to the children my only goal. Gemma was right behind us, shouting to Wyatt. Rose dropped the pail she carried on her way back to the cabins and stood fixed to the spot.

I screamed as loud as I could, "Indians!"

Emory ran for Rose as Jeremiah appeared on the porch. I was vaguely aware of others in my peripheral vision who stopped their work or came out of their cabins. Frank and Ethan were shouting, but I kept my focus on reaching the children. Someone might have yelled at me. I wasn't sure. I didn't stop. I felt like I was in a dream. I got to them at the same time

Annabelle did, scooping Heather into my arms as she snatched up Willow. Both girls screamed at the chaos, but there was no time to soothe them. Wyatt stood frozen in place. Gemma grabbed his hand and pulled him toward Adams's cabin. We followed her as Maddie intercepted our path.

"What's happening? Christine, what's happening?" she cried.

"To the cabin, now, Maddie!" I screamed at her without slowing down.

She ran beside us. Nathan met Gemma halfway, where he knelt and aimed his musket at the woods. I heard shots fire, not sure if they were ours or theirs, or if the natives even had guns. I didn't dare turn to check. I continued my crusade to the cabin. I reached the porch and pushed Heather into the cabin.

Maddie clamored up the steps. "Where is Michael?" I asked her between gasps for air.

"He's still at the cove working on the boat with Joe and Gray," she cried.

"Get inside," I said, pushing her through the door.

She stumbled over the threshold as I turned to watch Nathan fire on the approaching natives. I twisted to my left, and the dread somersaulted in my stomach. Emory ran to Rose, who was halfway to the house, having snapped out of her daze, an Indian not far behind her.

Other Indians broke into our houses. One entered my empty cabin next door and came out with an armful of supplies. He piled them on the grass and went in for more. I turned my attention back to Emory, who ran for her sister. Rose waved her arms wildly, screaming the entire time as she sprinted to Emory. But Emory was in her eighth month of pregnancy and moved slowly. I was ready to leap off the porch for Rose when Jeremiah rushed past Emory and reached her in seconds. He grabbed her hand and pushed her toward Emory and the house.

"Run! Go to Frank's!" he yelled.

I was still on the porch, unsure of how to help. Frank stood in front of his cabin, the semiautomatic aimed. He fired, and the Indian I didn't see making his way closer from my cabin collapsed within a few yards of me with a loud grunt. Emory and Rose were almost back to the cabin where Linda waited on the porch, her hands over her mouth in shock. An Indian on horse galloped toward Jeremiah, who pushed Rose farther ahead and continued to shout for her to run.

Time seemed to slow down then. Jeremiah turned to face the Indian, buying Emory and Rose the precious seconds they needed to reach the safety of the porch. The native was upon him quickly, and I knew what was going to happen even before he raised the tomahawk. My eyes darted back to Frank, who was still facing the other way, just in time to watch Adams shoot the Indian running for Frank's back. The native on horseback reached Jeremiah. I shouted to Frank, but he turned a moment too late. The Indian swung, and the tomahawk connected with Jeremiah's skull. I gasped, unable to fully process what I witnessed. The vicious blow spun him in a circle before he lurched forward to collapse on the ground, as his attacker raced onward after Rose. Frank aimed and shot, and the Indian fell from his horse.

Everything happened so fast. In a split second, it altered our lives forever.

Jeremiah lay still on the grass. A ring of deep crimson spread slowly in a circle around his head. Emory's screams were guttural, like nothing I had heard before. Her sorrow echoed across the settlement as Linda held her back. More Indians emerged from the woods, forcing Adams and Frank to retreat into their respective cabins. Shots rang out from the other side of the camp, and I realized it must be Ethan. He was near Gray's cabin. I didn't know where Kira was, I could only hope she was there too, safe in her house. The last time I saw her, she was headed there with Suzanne and Nick.

I rushed inside after Adams, helping him bring the heavy board down to secure the door. Annabelle pulled the shutters over the only window in the great room and put the board in that locked them in place. I turned to Gemma, Annabelle, and Maddie. Nathan reloaded his gun and went to the bedroom window to peer outside. The children were all crying hysterically. I took an inventory of our group. Ethan and Kira were in Gray's cabin, with Goebel and Suzanne. Frank, Linda, Emory, and Rose at

Frank's. Michael, Joe, and Gray with the boat. The rest with me in Adams's cabin. And Jeremiah laid dead in the field.

My son at the river.

Did the sound of the firefight reach them? Were they rushing back here only to have the Indians ambush them? My breath came in ragged gasps.

Annabelle was at my side in an instant, knowing why I was close to hyperventilating. "They're all right. They either heard the shooting or will realize something is wrong the minute they see the houses," she said.

I had been in perilous positions before and kept my cool. But the thought of my son in mortal danger pushed me to the edge, and the helplessness overwhelmed me.

TWENTY-SIX

Alexandria, Virginia 1792

"Christine, I wish we had time for you to calm down, but right now, we have to get a plan together. I need you here with me, okay?" Annabelle said, grasping my shoulders.

I dragged in a deep breath and nodded, forcing myself to breathe slowly.

Michael will be fine. He is with Gray. They won't do anything stupid.

I repeated this in my head over and over until I believed it.

The Indians pounded on the door, trying to break it down to get to us. It shuddered with each assault, causing the children to scream. Adams reached behind the mantel and slung his medical bag over his shoulder, knowing that was the most crucial thing to save above all else.

"What do we do?" cried Gemma.

Annabelle leaned against the front door, her hands flat on the surface, her face pressed up against the crack at the hinges.

"Smoke. I smell smoke. I think they are burning us down," she said, her voice cracking.

She twisted around to face us. "If we stay in here, we will burn to death or die from smoke inhalation first."

As she spoke, wisps of smoke curled their way inside through the seams of the logs.

"The bedroom window, it's our only chance," said Adams.

He pulled masks out of his bag and handed them to us. I helped Annabelle get them on her girls and adjust them tightly around the back of their heads. We crowded into the bedroom as he raised the window.

Smoke rushed into the room as the sound of timber crackling and burning fueled my rising dread. Adams climbed out first. I moved the chest under the window as a stool while he reached in for us one at a time. Once we were all out, he went to the corner of the cabin and snuck a glimpse. Indians on foot and horseback roamed freely through our settlement. They were looting everything they could from the unoccupied cabins. They tied our livestock to their horses. Adams snapped his head back and stood flush against the cabin. He signaled toward the house next door.

Fire raged through Michael and Maddie's cabin. We ran for cover behind it, trying to get to Frank and Linda's beyond that. I could not hear the children's cries over the roar of the blaze, the entire place now engulfed in the inferno. I glanced back to the window we just climbed out of and shivered, despite the heat from the fire. The first flames licked the edge of Adams's cabin, and within minutes the roof was fully ablaze.

Adams began the path to Frank's. As we ran across the expanse behind the houses, an Indian appeared out of nowhere, weapon raised. Adams stopped and struggled to pull the cock on his musket when the Indian lurched forward and collapsed face first in the dirt. Frank appeared, followed by Linda, Emory, and Rose, the semiautomatic in his hand. Sweat from the heat of the fire covered their faces, dirty streaks trailing down their cheeks. Frank joined Adams at the front of the procession. They led us on to Gray's cabin. Smoke poured from the cabin like a huge billowing cloud, swirling and circling its way toward the sky. I ripped my mask off and pulled it on over Emory's head, adjusting it on her. Annabelle did the same for Rose. The moment it was off, the acrid stench of smoke hit me full force and I choked on the thick air. Ash fell all around us as our homes burned to the ground. My head swiveled back and forth as we made our way closer to the last cabin, searching for any sign of Ethan, Kira, Nick, or Suzanne.

We finally reached the back of Gray's cabin. Frank peered through the window, then smashed it open. Blood ran from his hand as he scrambled over the ledge into the room. I must have been in shock, because even in our current state of danger, it pained me to watch him shatter the glass. That was the one thing we splurged on for the cabins. My mind didn't connect that our cabins were destroyed and the glass no longer mattered. I got past that quickly as Adams threw his backpack down and followed Frank through the window. I ran to peer in and saw Ethan carrying Kira to Frank. Suzanne was next through the opening. Goebel's leg was still not healed, so Ethan boosted him over the sill. He handed Kira to Adams, who hoisted her through as Maddie helped me lay her on the ground. Adams stumbled out and immediately began CPR on her. Ethan and Frank landed on the dirt beside him a moment later. Ethan had a nasty burn on his arm, so I took off my apron and wrapped it quickly, not knowing if that was the right thing to do or not. He winced as the cloth touched his skin. Tears fell down my cheeks. We didn't speak. There was nothing to say. We were glad to see each other, but Michael's fate weighed heavily on my mind, as I repeated the mantra in my head.

Michael will be fine. He is with Gray. They won't do anything stupid.

Frank assumed a defensive position to watch for Indians. Once Adams gave the signal, Ethan grabbed my hand and pulled me up as Kira choked and coughed her way back to consciousness. He helped Frank lift her and heave her onto his back, and we resumed our path to the woods. I took a last glance at our homes. The flames reached skyward like fingers trying to claw their way into the heavens. I studied Annabelle. Her tears came quickly. She carried Willow, who sobbed into her shoulder and grasped Heather by her hand beside her. The little girl was exhausted and frightened beyond belief. I bent down and picked her up, nestling her close to my chest to comfort her. She nuzzled into my neck and sobbed softly. Annabelle gave me a small smile as she wiped at her tears.

We followed the creek through the sun dappled woods. It was eerily quiet but for the sound of our footfalls. Not even a bird sang on this spring day. It was as if they respected our grief. No one spoke as we trudged down the familiar path. We all knew the boat was our only escape. I looked at Emory, who was in shock. She held her sister's hand and glanced at her mother every few minutes. Frank's face showed the strain of carrying Kira. So Adams took over that duty. Joe helped Goebel, his arm slung over Joe's shoulder as he limped along the trail using his cane.

When we were far enough away, we stopped to use the Lifestraws for a quick drink. Kira was fully conscious now, so Emory and Rose clung to her. We only planned to stop for a moment, but the stress and exhaustion of the ordeal overwhelmed us, and a delayed-reaction sense of shock overtook me.

I collapsed on the ground, my head cradled in the crook of my arm, where I watched a beetle crawl across a leaf. A few inches away, a colony of ants scurried about their routine, oblivious to the danger headed their way. Then the insect made his presence known, and the ants scattered in a panic. They ran in every direction in their futile dash to escape. We were the ants. We knew our enemy was out there, but blissfully ignored them, unaware of the impending danger until the last minute before they attacked. But just like the ants, by that time it was too late.

*** * *

Gray stopped hammering and stood up to stretch. He drew in a deep breath, the faint odor of smoke gone before he could be sure that's what it was.

Joe put his tool down and stepped back to admire the boat cover. "There, finally done. That was a sonofabitch to get on," he said, yawning. "Does anyone else smell something weird?"

Michael stood up and sniffed the air. "You think someone is burning leaves for bugs?"

"Nah, too early in the year for that," Gray said. "Probably making a campfire in the woods somewhere. Maybe they docked along the inlet near here."

Michael climbed onto the side of the boat, balancing on the narrow rail.

"Jeez, Michael. Don't fall. Your mom would have our heads on a platter," Joe said.

Michael scanned the horizon, his gaze stopping at a northeast direction. A thin plume of black vapor floated upward over the trees before vanishing with the breeze.

"Hey, guys. There's smoke coming from over there, toward home," he said, pointing.

"You sure?" asked Joe.

"Yeah, I'm sure."

Gray climbed up the side of the boat and stood next to Michael. Joe followed next. They shielded their eyes against the sun, staring into the distance.

"I don't see anything," Joe said.

Another puff of black smoke rose and vaporized quickly. "There, did you catch that? Smoke, right?" Michael said.

"I saw it. I don't like that. They wouldn't burn leaves today. There are no bugs out yet," Gray said, hopping onto the deck.

"Yeah, something isn't right," Michael said.

Joe's stomach turned at the thought. Michael's words were like lighter fluid on a flame. He only hoped that flame wasn't a bonfire by the time they reached home.

"Come on, let's get back there," Gray said, slipping into his backpack.

"What about the boat? Shouldn't we cover it to hide it or something, like we normally do?" asked Joe.

"No time. We need to get home and find out what's going on," Gray said, already headed down the trail away from the water.

Michael and Joe grabbed their packs and followed Gray. The men reached the woods and ran along the creek that led to their settlement. As they grew closer, the smell of soot was undeniable. Wisps of smoke drifted through the forest randomly. Gray carried his hammer in his hand, his musket tucked into his waistband. Michael's gun dug into his side with every step, so he held it instead, ready to fire. Joe saw him and did the same, as the dread rose in his throat like bile. They crashed through the woodland when Gray halted. The rest of their group lay scattered around the small clearing, looking as if they had just come through hell and survived.

* * *

I heard someone approaching but didn't have time to react swiftly enough. I was moving in slow motion, no matter how hard I tried to rise. I turned, expecting to find an Indian lunging for me. Instead, I saw my son. I sobbed out loud when I saw he was safe. The three men all talked at once, trying to get details from us. Maddie ran to Michael. They embraced, and I waited until they pulled apart before I went to him. I touched his face, so grateful he was all right. So thankful we all were. Injuries aside. All but Jeremiah.

"Indians," Ethan said, his voice hoarse from the smoke. "We need to get to the boat."

Frank filled them in while we made our way to the cove. We had no idea if the Indians would come after us, or if they only wanted to loot the farm. But we all agreed we needed to get to our boat and on the river quickly. I knew they were after the women and children. I was certain of that. I didn't share my opinion with anyone, but I knew I was right. They went straight for Rose and the babies first. I shuddered, thinking of what that would have meant for them. For any of us.

We reached the inlet in fifteen minutes and boarded in record time. The men each took an oar and steered us to deeper water, and we set our course for downriver, toward the Johnsons'.

We were all traumatized, and it showed. Soot covered our faces and clothes. Vacant eyes stared back at me from around the boat. This was nowhere close to how I imagined the maiden voyage on our boat would take place.

Emory wept for her murdered husband, with hands placed firmly on her growing abdomen. Adams cleaned and wrapped Frank's and Ethan's wounds and checked the children for injuries.

I lay down again. The stress and adrenaline crash sapped every ounce of strength left in me. My eyes fluttered shut where Emory's screams continued to haunt me, and the sight of Jeremiah falling to the ground was etched on my memory. The raid replayed in my mind on a continuous reel, each image another weight on my shoulders. Heavy. Remorseful.

I dozed off until voices woke me an hour later. I sat up as we rowed toward an inlet. Michael stood on the rail of the boat for a better view, but I didn't need anyone to tell me what I already guessed we would find. Tendrils of smoke crested above the treetops. I felt my stomach lurch and leaned over the side to be sick.

Ethan stood beside me, his hand on my back.

"Let's go ashore and check on them. We owe them that much," Frank said.

"I'm coming too," I said.

I followed Frank, Adams, and Joe. The others stayed behind to make sure our scant supplies and the rest of our group were safe. We walked in silence, dreading what we would find when we reached the Johnsons' farm. I braced myself because my instinct told me they were already gone.

TWENTY-SEVEN

Alexandria, Virginia 1792

The familiar stench of smoke permeated the woods the closer we got to the Johnsons'. We crouched behind the last trees before the clearing and watched. We wanted to make sure we were alone. The front of the house was still intact, the door wide open. Fire engulfed most of the rear of the house and barn. As we started across the field, I fixed my stare on boots, top side down, that were just visible from the yard. My heart sank. I knew it was Samuel. Frank handed Adams the semiautomatic, and he started for the interior with Joe. Frank and I continued on the path to the boots. We rounded the corner and saw Samuel face down, a gaping wound in his back. My gaze traveled to his head, where his hair once was. They had scalped him. This kind, gentle man died a horrible death. I dropped to my knees and sobbed, not caring if Indians were near enough to hear me. I leaned over to be sick again, but my stomach was empty, so all I managed was a cough and gag. Frank kicked the cabin and cursed. Only the flames snapped and flared in answer. He took my hand and pulled me into an embrace where I screamed into his shoulder. He let me stay this way until I composed myself. Then he led me to the porch, where I sat on the steps while he went in search of Adams and Joe.

The three of them joined me on the porch a moment later.

"They're gone. Prudence, their sons, and Jeremiah's sister," Adams said.

"We'll find them," I said, rising.

"No, Christine, we won't," Frank said. "They took them. There was a struggle in there. Jeremiah's mother is dead inside. They looted the house, like they did ours. They are hours ahead, and we don't track like Samuel could."

"They outnumber us by who knows how many," Joe said.

"We can't let them go without trying," I cried.

"It's too late, Christine. I'm sorry," Frank said, wiping a tear that rolled down his face.

I cried and cursed until Frank wrapped his arms around me again. "Shhh. There's nothing we can do. You know I'm right."

I realized he was right. It was just not in my nature to give up like that. They were good people who helped us when we needed it most. And now they were all gone. Samuel lay dead in the yard, and Prudence and the children suffered who knows what fate.

"What about Samuel and his mother? We should bury them," I said.

"There's no time," Frank said gently. "We've got to get back to the group to plan for our immediate future."

I allowed myself another moment before I straightened up and steeled myself for whatever we must do next.

We hiked through the woods to our boat in silence. The Johnsons' fate devastated me. And I was angry. My fists balled at my sides while I thought of all we'd lost in the last twenty-four hours. We arrived at the boat thirsty and beat. The others peered at us expectantly, and Frank shook his head, letting it drop to his chest. Emory stared at me, the tears flooding her eyes. Her mother sat beside her and stroked her hair while she sobbed.

To their credit, the men never mentioned my breakdown to anyone, and I didn't reveal what we saw at the farm. It would do no good to foist that vision on the rest of them. It was enough that Frank and I must live with the knowledge of what happened to Samuel and his family. The image of him in the grass would never leave me. Nor would the thought of what his family surely suffered.

I needed a few minutes by myself to gather my thoughts. I was alone on the beach, watching the waves lap at the shore. But somehow, it seemed crowded. I felt their presence with me. All of them. Samuel, Prudence, their children, Jeremiah, and his sister, Nellie. I understood the Indians outnumbered us, and we were way out of our league against them. But I believed we let the Johnsons down. We should have gone after them. Alone on that beach, I tried, but failed, to justify our decision. Then I prayed for their forgiveness.

Back at camp, we gathered on the boat, unsure of our next move.

"So what do we do from here?" Goebel said to no one in particular. "We've lost everything."

I hesitated, but only for a minute. What I was about to say scared me, but I said it anyway. My misgivings were minor enough that I pushed them aside for now to lay out my plan.

"I have an idea. You might think I'm crazy, but just hear me out," I said, glancing around the boat.

No one replied, they just stared back at me blankly. In all fairness, maybe it was because the last time I said something similar we ended up here. That irony was not lost on me, and I treaded carefully, choosing my words cautiously.

"We are going to need to transport."

I was certain I heard Joe groan.

"Transport? You heard what we told you about our timeline, right? There are food shortages, medical services are scarce. It's as bad as this hellhole. Drones are down, internet is spotty, cell service was out in many areas, everything was failing. Terrorists poisoned water and released biochemical toxins. We can't transport home. We're stuck here," Suzanne said.

"Not back to 2072. Forward, but not that far," I said.

Frank furrowed his brow. "Where the hell can we start over with nothing, Christine?"

"I can think of only one person who might help us. Jacob," I said, turning to Ethan to gauge his reaction.

He sat still for a minute before answering. "Blimey. It just may work."

"Who is Jacob?" Gemma said.

"And where and when is he?" asked Kira.

"He is Malcolm and Hannah's son. Gray, Adams, and I met him twice in 1868. If I know Malcolm and Hannah at all, and I think I do, they would have told him I might be in touch someday."

I forged a strong friendship with Malcolm and Hannah, and I knew they were both thankful for my bringing them back together when Gray,

Adams, and I rescued Hannah from 1790, Alexandria and took her back to 1868, Oklahoma. I was certain Jacob would recall that and help us.

"But you said transport forward, not back to 1868," Goebel said. "I don't understand."

"He was only a kid when I met him," I said. "But he became a doctor and practiced on the East Coast for years before returning to Oklahoma in 1908, after Malcolm's death. He didn't pass until 1938. If we go to 1908 New York, he can help us. It's a perfect place to blend in and be anonymous. He would be in his early fifties, well established, and if we time it correctly, we won't interfere with Malcolm and Hannah's history. Malcolm passes in April 1908. If we show up right after his death, before Jacob uproots his family to Piedmont, it will have the least impact. We would only need to survive here for a couple of weeks before we leave."

"But what about Hannah? She doesn't die until 1909," Ethan said.

"True. But I'm certain I can convince Jacob to keep our transport confidential and not reveal it to Hannah. If he knows telling her could disrupt her timeline, he'll do whatever is best for his mother. I'm sure of that."

"We would still be there with nothing. We have no money," Maddie said.

"Yes, we do," I said, glancing over at Gray.

He acknowledged with a quick nod. "When we were packing up in Los Angeles, there was too much silver to bring it all. It was too heavy. Christine and I hid a good amount of it in our lockers in the CCEA building. We figured if we needed it, we'd make a quick transport home for it. I planned on bringing it back when I went for vaccines."

"Then we can stay here. If we get money, we rebuild. Figure out where to go. Nothing in the past few days prepares us to move forward over one hundred years in time. We don't have the right clothes, and we would need to convert those coins," Adams said.

"It was just an idea," I said, trying not to sound bothered by their dismissal.

"I understand this place has lost its appeal at the moment, but what if we get the silver and vaccines as planned, then rebuild in the city? It would be safer there from Indian raids, at least," Annabelle said.

"That's true," Kira said.

"It's also very expensive," Frank said. "Exactly how much money did you stash?"

"I don't have an exact figure, but maybe a couple hundred coins, anyway. Probably not enough to build places in Alexandria. We would have to double or triple up families in each house," Gray said.

"Yeah, that went so well last time, I'm sure we all can't wait to live on top of each other again like we did at Mason's," Gemma said.

"Let's have a think about it today and we can discuss it tomorrow. We are all exhausted, and we need a day to recuperate," Ethan said.

"I say we take this boat farther downriver, dock there for the night and regroup," Goebel said.

We all murmured our agreement, and the men maneuvered us to deeper water.

An hour later, we secured our boat in a cove under the cover of low-hanging tree branches. We caught two ducks for dinner and roasted them over a fire we built on shore. The drumsticks went to the kids, and we made sure Emory got enough protein. We split the rest between us, each taking a small piece. Even with two birds, there was little meat to go around for fourteen adults. We barbequed some corn we had stashed on the boat to take to market, and that helped fill our stomachs.

The fire snapped as we gathered around it, each lost in our own thoughts. We were discouraged and unsure of our future at that moment.

"I think we should escalate the trip home," Gray said, breaking the silence. "I'd like to go tomorrow. Check out Los Angeles, grab the vaccines and silver, and we can vote on a plan after we confirm how much money we have. Maybe going home is an option now. We won't know until we get there."

"I don't see where we have any other choice. We need to find out what's happening back there and how we stand with money," Frank said.

There it was again. That no choice business. I was really nearing my limit with our lack of choices, but I was too drained to devote any energy to doing anything about it.

With our decision made, we curled up on deck for a fitful night's sleep.

Early the following morning Gray was up before anyone else. I motioned for him to follow me ashore, where we rekindled the campfire that went out last night. We warmed our hands as the fire flared.

"So I was thinking. I should come with you to LA. It's safer if two of us go. I'm the logical choice. Ethan and Frank both have injuries to their arms, and Goebel is still using a cane to help him get around. Annabelle should stay here with her babies, and Adams has to be here because he's our medic. If Emory goes into early labor, she needs him here. And before you even ask me about my son, don't. That's off the table. Worrying about him would only send me over the edge of the cliff I am currently teetering on," I said.

"All right," he said, rubbing his hands over the fire.

"All right? Just like that? I had an entire rebuttal prepared."

"Well, if it makes you feel better, I'll listen to it. But you may want to save it for Frank and Ethan."

"You make a good point. Will you back me up on this to them?"

"I will. I happen to agree with you. Who knows what waits for us in 2072? An extra pair of eyes and an experienced agent could only help."

Convincing the others not to give me a hard time would be more problematic, but I wanted to see Los Angeles for myself. I had already made up my mind. I was going. With or without their blessing.

Our group woke and joined us at the firepit, one by one. We ate the protein bars Adams had in his medical pack, and each took a meal replacement capsule.

By my own admission, I possessed a talent for being too blunt. It was often hard for me to control myself, a filter being a new concept to me. So I sprang my plan on them as nonchalantly as I knew how. Which meant I blurted it out and counted on Gray for support.

"I am going to go with Gray back to 2072. Backup for him is the safe way to do this, and, given the injuries in our group and the children who need their parents here, I'm the logical choice." I turned to Gray and waited for him to respond.

He caught my eye and didn't let me down. "Oh, yeah, I agree. It will be safer and faster with two of us there."

Ethan started to say something, but I stopped him. "It makes sense, and you know it."

He closed his mouth and stared at me for a long moment before dropping his eyes and bowing his head. I glanced over to Michael and gave him my sternest mom look. It worked, and he stayed silent. I heaved a sigh of relief when Frank didn't comment. For once, he conceded defeat without a fight.

Normally, we would bring a few essentials with us for a transport like this, but we literally had nothing left. Adams had the lone pack with the medical supplies and our one and only transponder. No one else, me included, had the opportunity to grab packs from their hiding places behind our mantels. We were too busy trying not to burn to death or allow someone to scalp us.

We said our goodbyes and took the transponder. I smiled at Michael and winked at Ethan, as Gray punched in our destination—CCEA headquarters in 2072, Los Angeles.

TWENTY-EIGHT

Los Angeles, California 2072

I had a vision in my mind about what we would find in Los Angeles. I was completely wrong. It was much worse than I imagined.

Looters had ransacked the offices, computers and equipment were broken and scattered everywhere. Overturned desks, their built-in computer screens cracked and missing parts, filled the space with smashed wall units. The only intact area was the jump room we landed in, only because it had a coded, solid steel security door, to which only top-level managers had the code. Thankfully, Frank was one such manager.

The elevators were not working, so we used the stairs to go down to the cafeteria. It looked as if there was nothing left, but we searched anyway. I was glad we did, because we found three cans of spaghetti sauce, a multi-pack of pasta and 3 boxes of instant cereal hidden behind a box of trash bags under the industrial sink. That wasn't much, but all we had was corn and squash on the boat, so anything edible was a welcome discovery. The ChefAid might contain food, but there were signs that someone before us has tried to access it unsuccessfully. The appliance was solid lightweight steel, and we decided not to waste time on what was probably a lost cause. We both wanted to get out of there as quickly as possible.

I moved to the ceiling to floor windows at the edge of the room and gazed out over Los Angeles. No drones crowded the sky as they normally did, and the interactive billboards were all black. The 101 freeway was empty but for a few military vehicles. The ChefAid factory was visible from my vantage point, and a queue of people a mile long waited to get inside the building. I watched them come out with boxes, which I assumed was food. If not for the line of people, the entire city would be deserted. Debris littered the sidewalks, but they were vacant of any life. It was clear trash service was no longer operating, and a pack of stray dogs who were once someone's pets appeared to scavenge through the garbage. After a minute of digging, the beagle, poodle, and chihuahua moved farther down the street in search of better prospects. Abandoned cars sat parked along the sidewalk, many with doors open, as if their owners had simply walked away, leaving them to rot in the southern California sun. Random patches of smoke rose from structures in the distance. It was impossible to tell if they were factories or the last traces of a fire.

This couldn't be Los Angeles. But I knew it was.

Gray walked to the window and stood beside me.

"Holy mother of. . ." he said as his voice trailed off to a whisper.

"I know. Shocking, isn't it?"

"It's surreal," he said, setting the box of food we found on the table behind him.

I held out little hope for cell service, but I tapped my ear chip, anyway. Nothing. He tried his too, with the same result. I glanced at him, then back to the landscape of what was once the most populated city on the West Coast. Where were the people? Were they hidden away in their homes? Or had they all left for parts unknown? I thought of my family in their cabin in the mountains. I could only hope things were safer there.

"Let's grab the vaccines and money and get out of here," I said.

"I'm all for that. 1792 is better than this, and given our recent experience there, that's not saying a whole lot," he said, grabbing the food.

Next, we found the medical supply unit. It had the same security door as the jump room. I held my breath when Gray punched in the code Adams gave him. The lock beeped and clicked open, and we stepped inside. We each took a side and dug through the cabinets for vaccines and medications we could use. On an impulse, I searched the drawers to the only desk in the office and was rewarded with individual packages of chips, crackers, and candy.

"Yes," I whispered as I piled them into the box with our kitchen finds.

When we had gathered all we needed, we left for the locker room to get the silver. As we stepped through the double doors, the sight stopped us both in our tracks. Someone pulled the lockers from the wall and pried them open, strewing their contents across the floor. My hopes sunk. I followed Gray around the corner to his compartment and shook my head. He stood where his unit once was. The pack he stored before we left was not there.

"Dammit!" he hissed, kicking the downed metal cabinet.

"Let's try mine. I didn't stash much, but it might be there."

We strode across the hall to the women's lockers and found the same mess there. Mine was at the far back of the room, and I started my way there. To our surprise, the last two rows were intact, which included my locker.

"Looks like they couldn't finish. Lucky for us," I said, punching in my combination.

I pulled out the pack and gave it a little shake and heard the coins jingle. I reached farther inside and grinned. My sugar stash was there. Candy bars, cookie packets, and bags of trail mix. Way in the back I found a still-sealed lip balm and hand lotion and practically cried with joy. I threw it all into a backpack from one of the looted lockers.

"Sugar much, Stewart?"

"Don't judge me. I have an illness. I'm an addict, really. Where's the support?"

"Well, lucky for us you do," he said.

"Do you think we can break into these last few units?"

"Let's try," he said, already searching for something to pry them open.

Gray pulled the metal sink stopper from under the cabinet, and we used it to access the lockers. We scored a few more snack items, although no one was as sugar addicted as me, apparently. We found an old swiss army knife and added all of it to our supplies.

We didn't bother with the armory. Without a code for that door, it was useless. There were a few offices untouched, but none had anything of use. We were in an office at the back of the building, and I peered down into the parking lot. Our vehicles were where we last parked them, but someone had broken into them, and anything once inside was on the ground, tossed aside as rubbish. I felt violated. It was only a car, with nothing important in it, but even so, it was an intrusion.

"Should we go to wardrobe?" Gray asked.

"That's a great idea, actually. Our clothes are so dirty and now these are all we have," I said, looking down at my soot-covered dress.

"They'll have carryalls we can put stuff in too. If we pack right, we'll fit it all in a couple of large bags. We'll put our backpacks on, hold the larger ones, and transport out without a problem."

"I like it. Lead the way," I said.

Once in wardrobe, we both changed clothes. That took care of one of our outfits. He gathered garments for the men, while I went after dresses for the women. Of course, there was nothing to fit the children, but we got the smallest sizes for Wyatt and Rose. The babies would have to make do with washing theirs. As I gathered clothing, I rolled it into the large bag. I only used about half the space, even after taking two changes of clothes for each person. I considered grabbing more, but then an idea popped into my head. I ransacked the wardrobes by their date tags, stopping at early twentieth century. I narrowed it down to the rack labeled 1900 through 1910. I piled dresses, petticoats, and shifts on the ground like a mad woman. I wasn't sure why. I suggested transporting to New York to search for Jacob yesterday, and that was still at the forefront of my mind. For reasons I could not explain, I felt strongly that was a workable option, and I was not willing to let the notion go yet. I had learned to rely on my gut instincts, so I didn't question myself. I just kept pulling items and packing. I moved to the men's section and did the same for them. Gray gave me a quizzical stare but didn't comment.

I cast him a warning look.

"Before you ask, I don't know why. Call it women's intuition. Or maybe I don't want to accept that everyone shot my idea down so quickly. Whatever. It will just make me feel better if we bring them, so humor me," I said, rolling the menswear into his bag.

"Wasn't going to say a word. I know better by now," he said, helping me pack.

We completed the raid of the wardrobe department and sat at a table to take a break.

"Can you think of anything else we might cram into our backpacks?" he asked.

"Well, we can't get into the armory, but what if there are knives or something we can use for weapons in the kitchen?"

"It's worth a try. I was so focused on food I didn't even think about it before," he said.

"Me either. We should look though, before we leave."

We stashed our supplies in the jump room, taking two more small bags from wardrobe. We found a few good knives in the kitchen and tools left by a worker in the walk-in freezer. One last search yielded a single can of peaches and a few salt and pepper containers. I stuffed them in my pack and started for the door. Gray noticed a cart pushed in front of a cabinet and moved it aside just to be sure we had missed nothing we could use. The drawer was full of one-cup instant coffee packets and powdered creamer. I thought he might pass out, he was so elated. We filled our packs and made our way upstairs.

"Definitely the find of the day," I said, giving him a high five.

It winded us, hauling the heavy loads up seven flights of stairs to the jump room. Transferring everything to our backpacks, we realized we had a ton of stuff, but we determined it must all go with us to 1792. We repacked them a couple times before we loaded them to the brim, barely able to close the tops.

We had no experience in programming the pods, Frank always did that for us, so we used Adams's transponder. We secured our backpacks, grabbed our larger packs, and left for the outskirts of Alexandria.

TWENTY-NINE

Alexandria, Virginia 1792

Annabelle watched her girls play while she sat cross-legged on the grass, eager for Gray and Christine to get back from 2072. She glanced over at Emory. Her pain had increased over the last twelve hours. Adams wasn't sure if she was having Braxton-Hicks false labor pains, or if this was the real deal. Annabelle was sure. She was in labor. It was too far along for false contractions. And it worried her. Giving birth now, she was a little over a month early, and without proper medical services that could be dangerous. If the baby's lungs were not fully developed, or Emory experienced hemorrhaging, there would be no way to help either mother or child. She kept her concerns to herself, knowing it would do no good to voice them out loud.

By midday, everyone realized Emory was in full labor. Her contractions came at random intervals and didn't stop. Without medication to regulate them, they could do nothing but let it play out. Maddie, Michael, Suzanne, and Joe watched the children, while Annabelle, Adams, Linda, and Gemma kept vigil with Emory and her mom. Frank, Goebel, and Ethan stayed away, but glanced at them often as Emory's moans turned into screams. Adams monitored her blood pressure and heart rate but could do little else. His medical training did not include gynecology, so a physical exam to figure out how dilated she was would be useless.

As day gave way to evening, the contractions came regularly, about every ninety seconds. The labor exhausted Emory, and she continually asked her mother when it would be over. Annabelle and Gemma knew from experience that a first child could take days to be born with no medication to hasten the process. So did Kira, but she told Emory it should be any time now. She counted back to how long she had been in labor, and it was nearing twenty-four hours. Maybe Kira was right, and it could be any time. They propped her in a sitting position to ease the pressure on her back, where she dozed between contractions.

"I'm worried because she is so early," whispered Kira.

"It was probably the stress with the raid and losing Jeremiah," Annabelle said.

Kira nodded and wiped her daughter's forehead. "She's so young to go through all this."

"She will be all right. She's strong. I think she's getting close," Gemma said.

"We are all here for her. We will all help with the baby. I have no grandchildren, so this is such a treat for me," Linda said.

"I don't know how we would get through this without all of you. Thank you," Kira said, tears rolling down her cheeks.

Emory startled them when she woke suddenly and bent forward in pain. She grunted and bore down to push.

"Do you have to push?" cried Kira.

"Yes!" Emory yelled.

Adams and Gemma positioned her for birth. "The baby is crowning," Gemma said. "I see the tip of the head!"

Annabelle moved closer to her. "Emory, I want you to give it everything you are made of on the count of three. We are going to hold that push for several seconds and then take a break before we start again. Do you understand?"

"Yes. Oh, God!" she said through clenched teeth.

"One, two," Annabelle didn't get to the last number before the girl wailed and bore down, her face twisting with the effort.

"Keep pushing!" shouted Kira.

Gemma helped Adams slide their only sterile drape under Emory to give the child a sanitary area to be born.

Sweat mixed with tears as it poured down Emory's face.

"I can't do this," she cried.

"Yes, you can. You're almost to the end, Em. Try, for your baby," Kira said, grasping her daughter's hand.

"Mom, I want Jeremiah," she sobbed.

Kira stifled a sob and kissed her hand. "I know, baby. He's here with you. I can feel him."

"Do you really think so?" she whispered, her eyes pleading for reassurance.

Her mother brushed the hair from her face and kissed her forehead, as Annabelle counted down to the next push. She pushed and panted with exertion as the baby's head emerged farther.

They repeated the push and rest process for the next thirty minutes until the baby was born.

"It's a boy," Adams said, smiling.

He gave the infant a quick once over as he kicked his tiny arms and legs and cried.

"Everything looks good," he said.

They cleaned him with sterile wipes and wrapped him in the cleanest apron they had. Emory slept, but not before she told them the baby's name—Jeremiah Stephen Stanton.

Kira cradled her newborn grandson, cooing and singing to him while Emory rested. It was dark now and the other women collapsed against the boat walls, completely worn. Adams continued to check Emory's vitals, and suggested she take an antibiotic because of the less than sanitary conditions of the birth, just to be safe. Her mother woke her for a minute to give her the capsule and snuggled next to her with the baby. All three of them closed their eyes, the gentle rock of the waves lulling them to sleep. They settled in for the night, too tired to even eat.

Linda prepared clam soup with corn and squash for the children. It went over like a lead balloon. But they chowed it down, anyway. There was nothing else to fill their bellies.

Early the next morning, the baby made it known he was hungry. His screams pierced the silence, and everyone was wide awake within seconds of the protest. Kira helped Emory breastfeed him and the day kicked into full swing. They were determined to find food today and planned to hunt. As they readied the gear, which consisted of the Glock, four muskets, and a couple of knives, the women made plans to search for edible fruits and more fresh water. They had one pot used to carry nails to the boat during the building stage, which Linda cooked the soup in last night. If the men brought back meat, they would roast that on a spit and barbeque it, along with the corn and squash, allowing them to boil water in the pot. The meal replacement capsules kept everyone nourished, but they were almost gone, and did nothing to fill the gnawing emptiness in their stomachs.

The group split off in search of food, while Kira and Maddie stayed with Emory and the kids on the boat. Both newborn and mom dozed on and off all morning, while Maddie and Kira entertained the children. They made a game out of digging for clams on the beach. If the men had no luck today, at least they had them for protein. Rose and Wyatt found duck eggs while exploring the brush near the river and added those to the bounty.

The other women foraged for berries but found none this early in the year. They gathered wild morels, arugula, beets, and spinach and took as much as their aprons would carry. They were back at camp to clean the vegetables before the men arrived. Linda was confident she could make a filling soup with the clams, using the produce to flavor it, and hard boil the eggs for a side dish.

Shortly after, the men strode into view, all smiles, with two huge turkeys. The others cheered their success. The poultry would feed them for a few days if they rationed it well. Linda set right to work, preparing the fowl, as they would take the longest to cook. Because her sous chef, Emory, could not help her, Gemma stepped in. An hour later, the turkeys were on spits roasting over a large firepit.

The mood in camp was the best it had been since leaving the settlement. They didn't talk about Gray and Christine going to Los Angeles. They should be back tomorrow, and no one wanted to jinx the trip. But below the surface, they all worried, eager to hear news from home.

Dinner was the feast they imagined. The turkey skin was crisp and flavorful, and Linda stuffed the birds with vegetables. She fried the clams in the pot with turkey fat and the gizzards, wasting nothing. She mixed them with arugula, and it made an excellent side dish.

"Linda, you've done it again. A bloody fine meal," Ethan said.

Everyone murmured their agreement while Linda smiled. "I love to cook, and it makes me happy you all enjoy the food."

Frank grabbed her hand and held it up high. "Kudos to my wife and her outstanding cuisine."

"Here, here," Adams said, holding up a turkey wing.

After dinner Emory joined them with the help of her mother, and they passed the baby around the group. The baby's tiny fingers and toes enthralled Rose, and she beamed from ear to ear when Emory asked if she would hold him while she ate.

Young Jeremiah was an excellent distraction as they waited for the two agents to return from two hundred eighty years in the future.

THIRTY

Alexandria, Virginia 1792

Edward Blake stood at the gun port near the mainmast of his ship, gazing out over the Potomac. He hated being stuck on this river. He longed to be in open sea. But that was not to be—yet. Until recently, he had possession of a most remarkable weapon. One the likes of which he had never seen before. But alas, his drunken crew allowed thieves to steal his new gun right from under their noses. Now he sailed this murky river in search of his property.

Unforgivable.

Several men paid for that mistake with their lives. His second in charge, Cyrus Coates, should have been one of them. But he relied on the old seadog too much. He had every intention of getting the gun back, no matter the cost. Coates learned the man's associates had clubbed and robbed him as he slept, while his inept crew lay passed out all around him.

Now he only needed to locate them. He went ashore thinking they had found them, only to find their houses burned in a clear Indian raid. The local savages may have stolen his only chance to get the gun back. But there was nothing to show they perished there. On the contrary. Only one body left behind. A young man. And he wasn't scalped. Which told him the settlers had escaped and the Indians either went after them or already had them captive. No dead women abandoned because they were of no use to them. Nothing. He believed they fled during the attack, and if they escaped, they wouldn't be far. With no horses for travel, they either fled to the wilderness or the river. From the look of the remains of their settlement, they would have had a boat. He was certain they took to the river for escape. Which was their mistake. The water was where Edward Blake ruled. And if they were on this godforsaken river, he would scour every cove, every inlet, every inch, until he found them.

Cyrus pulled him from his reverie with a shout.

"Edward, 'tis a boat in the cove," he said, handing him the spyglass.

He peered through the collapsible monocular at the small inlet. Hidden under tree branches and brush was a bateau boat. People moved about on deck, oblivious to the men observing them.

"Take us about and farther out. I do not wish them to see us," he said to Coates.

"Aye, sir."

He scrambled to carry out the pirate's orders, instructing the crew to sail the ship out of view.

"Wait until nightfall, then bring us closer, Mr. Coates."

* * *

We arrived slightly off course to our camp and hiked about a mile, dragging the heavy bags, before we saw our boat.

"Christine!" Annabelle shouted when she saw me.

Several others turned our way and ran to help with the packs.

They peppered us with questions, everyone talking at the same time. I glanced at Gray, who appeared as weary as I had ever seen him.

"Let's get these stowed on the boat and then we'll talk," he said.

We emptied the supplies on deck, rummaging through the food. The candy thrilled the children, and that occupied them while we talked. We counted the coins, and while we had enough to buy food and lodging for several weeks, we did not have enough to start over like we did when we arrived here.

We told them about what we saw in Los Angeles and watched their smiles fade with each word.

"It's bad. There is no way we can go back yet," I said.

"Believe it or not, we are better off here for the time being," Gray said.

"Yeah, but here where?" Suzanne asked.

"We have no homes, not nearly enough money to rebuild, and no crops to sell," Kira said.

"We need to talk about that, for sure. Figure out our next move," Adams said.

"We brought new clothes, two changes each." I paused for a beat before continuing. "We took period appropriate clothing for the early twentieth century too."

"Why?" Frank asked. "I thought we decided that wasn't going to happen."

"I know. I just thought it would be a good idea to grab them. If nothing pans out here, at least that's an option. We had room in the packs, there weren't any other useful supplies to take, so it couldn't hurt. We are running out of options here."

"I must admit, I am warming to the concept of New York," Annabelle said. "Between the Indians, disease, and nowhere to live, a big city away from here is sounding better all the time."

"We'll still have no money, or very little anyway. What's the point?" Goebel said.

"The point is, there is someone in 1908 who can help us. And we would be safer in the city," I said.

"You know, they introduce the model T in 1908. We might actually be able to buy a car and not ride horses. My old ass would appreciate that," Frank said.

"It bears a discussion anyway. It's almost dark, so let's eat and we can talk more tomorrow. If we decide to go to 1908, we shouldn't waste any money on lodgings here in Alexandria," Ethan said.

"Besides, the boat deck is such luxurious accommodations. Why would we ever give up all this?" Joe said, sweeping his arms out in front of him.

That made us laugh and broke up the serious mood. We sorted through the food and rationed a treat for each person. The kids were on a sugar high and only calmed down at dinnertime for more turkey. We added the spaghetti and sauce we got in Los Angeles to the menu, much to their delight. As we sat around the fire to eat, we theorized about Los Angeles and when it might be normal again. After what we saw today, I harbored serious doubts that would ever happen. But I bit my tongue and pretended that everything would return to the way it was someday. There was no sense in spreading my pessimism through camp.

Halfway through the meal, Goebel stood, gazing out to the river.

"There's a ship. With a British flag," he said, pointing.

A sloop, about a mile out, slowly passed out of view around a bend in the river.

"That flag means nothing. That could be anyone, including pirates," Frank said.

"Doesn't matter, they're leaving," Michael said.

"I still don't like it. They might have seen us. These branches can only disguise the boat so much," Gray said.

"It looks like they left, but let's keep eyes and ears open, just to be cautious," Ethan said.

With the ship out of view, we forgot about it and handed out fresh clothing.

Later that night, as we prepared to sleep, the men kept the muskets out, just in case. Adams took back our lone transponder and wrapped it in an extra piece of cloth used for the boat cover. He pushed it into a notch in the deck's corner and covered it with scrap wood. We did not want anyone to find that, ever. Without it we had no way home, or anywhere else.

* * *

Edward Blake watched the dying campfire on shore twinkle like a candlelight in a window, beckoning him home. He felt it in his bones. Those were the thieves who took his gun. It mattered not that he stole it from another. Once it was in his possession, that was the end of the matter as far as he was concerned. Luckily for him, when spirits flowed, tongues wagged freely, and he found his way to their settlement. It was only a question of *when* he would find them after that. And he would never allow a deed such as the theft of his property to go unanswered. His reputation for brutal retribution was not unearned.

His faithful first mate stood beside him, ever ready to carry out his commands. But his crew was restless after being at sea for months before the journey inland to find those scurvy dogs. They needed drink and women, and he would abide by their desires once he had his weapon back.

"Mr. Coates, bring all hands hoy. Heave to before shallow water and send the jolly boats to shore. When we reach them, run a shot across the bow to announce our arrival. Any man who resists, cleave him to the brisket. Give no quarter to any who fight, man or woman. And find my gun, Mr. Coates."

"Aye, Cap'n."

The crew set about readying the jolly boats. Several men climbed into each one, muskets and cutlasses in hand.

* * *

I lay on my back on the deck, gazing at the stars. The night was quiet, with only the croak of bullfrogs and the occasional howl from a coyote. My fellow travelers snored softly all around me. I was the only one awake. I shouldn't have drunk two cups of coffee after dinner. I tried to resist the temptation, but real coffee from our time was too hard to refuse. I was paying for it with the lack of sleep.

I closed my eyes, trying desperately to relax enough to doze off, when a splash brought me instantly alert. Another quickly followed. I strained to hear anything more, but the frogs resumed their nightly song. Maybe it was a beaver or a duck taking a midnight swim. My eyes fluttered shut again as I convinced myself I was being paranoid. Then a suppressed cough echoed across the deck. I definitely did not imagine that. I sat up and twisted my head from left to right. It could have been one of our group on the boat, but it sounded as if it came from farther out on the water.

"Hello, anyone awake?" I whispered.

I got no response. Ethan stirred next to me, but all else was quiet. I lay back down, chiding myself for allowing my paranoia to take control. I turned on my side, determined to fall asleep.

Ten minutes later, I dozed in that suspended place between sleep and consciousness when I felt something sharp poke me. I gasped and angled my face skyward. The outline of a large man loomed over me, the tip of his cutlass pressed into my hip. Several others appeared only as shadows as they boarded our boat and stood guard over the others. Before I could scream, a loud *boom* shook the boat, the water near us splashing with the weight of a cannonball.

THIRTY-ONE

Alexandria, Virginia 1792

All hell broke loose in a matter of seconds. The men outnumbered us and overtook the boat quickly with the surprise attack. They seized our weapons and tied our hands behind our backs. Baby Jeremiah's screams pierced the night, while the other children cried, huddled next to their parents. Michael sat directly across from me. I couldn't make out his face clearly in the dark, but I knew he was there. Tears rolled down my cheeks, yet I was helpless to wipe them away with my wrists bound. I glanced discretely in Ethan's direction to see him trying to release his bindings. He scraped the cloth against a piece of metal protruding from the rope clamp. It wasn't working, but he kept at it diligently.

None of the men spoke other than to bark orders while they tied us up and took our weapons. They got the muskets we saved during the raid and our bag of kitchen knives from the cafeteria at the CCEA. I didn't see the Glock anywhere. I was sure Frank had hidden it, but I knew they would find it. Now they stood aside, waiting. One of them readjusted the end of a gangplank on the boat rail where a short, beaded man climbed his way up to the deck. He peered around, taking in the scene.

"Silence that mite before I toss it into the briny deep!" he shouted.

A man stepped forward and reached for Jeremiah. Emory lunged backward, the baby on her lap.

"No! Please! Let me hold him, I can quiet him. Please," she sobbed.

Gray struggled to free himself to get to her, but another man planted a boot on his chest, pushing him flat on his back, and pinning him there with the tip of a cutlass jabbed into his sternum.

"Allow her to calm the babe afore Edward boards. I fear he shan't be as patient as I," the short man said.

"Aye, Mister Coates, betwixt my foul mood and the babe, I fear my patience is waning. Let the lass hold the mite."

The voice came from a tall, dark-haired man with a long beard and mustache, who walked up the gangplank. When he reached the top, all heads swiveled to him. He held a cutlass in his right hand, a musket tucked into his waistband. His knee-high black boots resounded on the deck as he jumped down.

Ethan and Frank exchanged a look between them I couldn't read. Ethan sat up straight and glared at the pirate.

"What the hell do you want, Blake?"

"Ah, a kinsman. And ye recognize me. The thieves I seek, I presume. From where do ye hail?" he said, sauntering toward me and Ethan.

"Dorset," Ethan hissed at him.

"Aye, Dorset. I have fond memories of my country. I am but a pirate. Ye may think of me as naught more than a swarthy gypsy. However, my fine English breeding 'twould never permit such a rude breech of manners. I should like to introduce myself," he said, turning in a circle to the others.

"My name is Edward Blake. 'Tis my ship that weighs anchor yonder. A few of yer gentlemen came aboard that ship and stole something from me. I am here to put all to rights and retrieve my property."

"We took back *our* gun, not yours," Frank said.

"Don't play the fool with me, sir. Careful or ye shall find yerself in the briny deep with the babe," he said, sneering at Emory.

She pulled Jeremiah closer, rocking him.

"Mister Coates, have ye relieved the gentlemen of their weapons and searched the boat for my gun?"

"Aye, sir. We still search for the musket ye seek."

He motioned to the crew, who rifled through our packs. They found the snack food, and muttered among themselves, the packaging completely foreign to them. They found the Glock under Frank's pack and confiscated it quickly.

Edward smiled as he turned it over in his hand. "Lead them to the ship, please."

"Wait, you have what you came for. You don't need to take us anywhere," Gray said.

"On the contrary, sir. Ye shall instruct my trusted gunsmith on the makings of this weapon. I shan't want my crew to be without their own."

"We don't know how to manufacture a gun any more than you do," Frank said.

"Nay, 'twould not fare well for ye, I fear. Ye shall be given but one chance. Mayhap yer memory will improve with the death of yer women?"

He yanked Linda up, the muzzle of his musket pushed against her temple.

"No! Stop! I'll tell your gunsmith everything!" Frank shouted, struggling to rise.

"Aye, ye shall," he said, lowering the weapon. "To the ship!"

They herded us over the gangplank and onto the jolly boats. It took three boats to transport our group and the pirates. The sun rose as they rowed us farther away from shore, toward their sloop. I was next to Adams, with Maddie on my other side. She whimpered softly, and her entire body trembled. Adams leaned closer to me and whispered.

"I hid the transponder on our boat."

My heart sank as I glanced back to shore. Each minute took us further from any hope of getting out of this.

My mind spun. I knew we must get back to our boat and transport out of there. Even if we escaped Edward Blake, if we stayed here, he would never stop coming after us. The only place to go was forward—to 1908, New York. There was nowhere else. Once again, we were out of options.

I stared straight ahead but whispered to Adams. "When we get on the ship, follow my lead. We need to convince them to take us back to the boat. We have to transport to New York. It's our only chance."

He gave me a brief nod but didn't respond as a pirate turned toward us. I didn't make eye contact, leaning closer to Maddie to comfort her.

"We're gonna be okay, trust me," I whispered to her.

She didn't even acknowledge she had heard me. I think she was in shock. Anger boiled inside me as the pirate ogled Maddie.

Now all I had to do was figure out how to convince them to take us back to our boat.

They untied us to climb onto the ship. Annabelle and Joe carried Willow and Heather, and Gray carried baby Jeremiah up the rope ladder. I wondered why they had not scoffed about us bringing the babies, and then it hit me all at once. The children were going to be their bargaining chips if we refused to cooperate. I felt sick to my stomach. I could not allow myself to complete the train of thought. It was just too horrible.

Once on board, they bound us and ordered us to sit on deck.

"Take us to Alexandria, Mister Coates," Blake said.

They went about their task silently as they readied us to sail.

I stared at the ship's deck as if the answer to my problem might appear there. I realized I must act quickly, before our last hope of surviving this unraveled. And I knew I would only get one chance.

The crew was drinking, getting louder and rowdier by the minute. It made me uneasy. I saw how they eyed our women, and I had to do something before it escalated. As if reading my thoughts, Blake had a brief conversation with his men I couldn't hear, then motioned to us. Three of them started toward us.

One grabbed Rose, pulling her up to him. "Up with ye, lassie," he said, leering at her.

Rose screamed, and Kira and Gray both lurched to reach for her.

"No! She's just a child! Take me!" screamed Kira.

My heart jumped in my chest as I realized what was happening. The other two grabbed Gemma and Maddie, pulling them to their feet. Michael shouted and one backhanded him. Everything was spinning out of control.

"Wait! Captain Blake! Please, I need to confess something before you allow this!" I screamed out so loudly the pirates stopped to face me.

Blake turned toward me slowly, and for a moment I thought I had made a grave mistake. He said nothing, so I continued.

"Please, I have something to say you'll want to hear."

He glared at me, then calmly made his way across the deck to stand in front of me. It took everything I had to say my next sentence in a way that would convince those savages not to kill me on the spot before they dragged Rose, Maddie, and Gemma away.

I took a steadying breath and looked him squarely in the eye.

"We have more guns. Just like the one you took from our boat. But if you allow your men to touch any of us, you will lose your only chance of ever getting them. We hid them, but if we are going to die on your ship anyway, we will never tell you where they are. Right now, you have a choice. Release our women. I'll not offer this again. I give you my word, we will give the weapons to you. But if any harm comes to them, you will not find the guns, ever. You will lose them forever."

He gazed out over the water as he considered my words.

"Dare I say, I do not trust ye," he said.

His eyes roamed past me in search of confirmation from the men.

"The woman speaks for ye?" he asked, scanning the men's faces.

"She's right," Adams said. "There are more guns. Just don't hurt them."

Blakes eyes widened, and I knew we had him.

Gotcha, you pirate asshole, is what I thought.

"I give you my vow. You will only kill me if I am lying to you. Why would I do that?" is what I said.

He leaned down to eye level with me. "Ye speak the truth. I shall kill ye myself, cleaved to the brisket, if ye lie to me."

I was really going to enjoy the look on his face when we transported away in front of him. I fantasized about flipping him the bird as we faded from sight, but I was sure he wouldn't know what it meant.

"Release the lassies," he said, waving his hand in a dismissive motion on his way back to the group of men.

The pirates pushed them down and stomped off, grumbling to themselves, clearly not happy I interrupted their plans. They readied the jolly boats, and Blake pointed to a few of our men.

"They accompany us, the rest stay here," he said.

I panicked, and my eyes darted around our group. We all had to be together for a group transport.

"No. We all go," Frank said. "That way we know they are safe, and the crew won't manhandle them."

"No man here 'twould dare to disobey my orders," Blake said.

"We won't reveal where the guns are unless they go with us," Frank said.

Blake glared at Frank. I could not let this escalate into a chest-pounding testosterone match.

"We are only women and children. Your men outnumber ours by twenty. What harm could we possibly do?" I said as calmly as I could.

"Aye, 'tis the truth. Ye shall be the first to die should any of yer men resist. As they wish," he said, motioning to Coates.

I tried to reassure myself the plan would work as they led us down the rope ladder and onto the jolly boats. I pushed my way into the same boat with the men, where I took a seat next to Frank. As they rowed toward shore, I leaned over to whisper to him.

"Adams hid the transponder on the boat. We have to go to New York, Frank. It's our best chance. When he transports us, be sure we get the twentieth century clothing bags, and any other packs we can grab. Pass the plan along, so everyone knows."

He leaned over and whispered to Ethan sitting next to him. Whispers traveled from person to person until I glanced around and got acknowledgments from everyone. I had a moment of concern regarding the travelers in the other boats, but there was nothing I could do about it. They would find out about the plan soon enough.

"Where in New York is Adams going to send us?" Frank said under his breath.

"No clue. We didn't have time to talk about that. Hopefully just outside the city," I said.

I leaned back against the side of the boat and breathed in the morning air. I said a silent prayer this went the way we needed it to. Because if it didn't work, Edward Blake was going to kill us all. Starting with me first.

THIRTY-TWO

Alexandria, Virginia 1792

We climbed the gangplank from the small boats to our bateau. I exchanged glances with Frank and Adams. My heart was beating in my chest like a bass drum.

"Where are my guns?" Blake asked once we were all onboard.

I glanced at Adams. "He can get them for you. He hid them."

Blake turned to Coates and gestured toward Adams. Coates untied Adams's wrists and followed him, cutlass drawn and ready to use.

Adams went to the loose board in the boat's corner. He bent down and lifted it, hooking his arm through his medical pack at the same time. Coates smiled, thinking the guns were stashed in the medical pack. Adams picked up the transponder and stood. All at once he punched information into the device. His eyes never left the screen as he barked out orders, speaking quickly.

"Annabelle and Joe, get your kids in your laps. Emory, hold on tight to Jeremiah. Everyone else, get whatever pack you can, even if you have to just lay on it to grasp it."

I moved for the clothing bag and threw myself across it, landing on my back and grabbing it firmly with both bound hands. Those who were on the same boat with me reacted quickly, securing packs any way they could. The others saw the transponder and worked out what was happening and followed our lead.

The pirates were at a loss. They couldn't figure out why we were flinging ourselves over bags of seemingly useless clothing. It surprised and confused them, allowing us the few seconds we needed. Coates waved his cutlass at an unseen enemy as he twisted from side to side, not sure who to attack or what to do.

"What is that instrument? Where are my guns?" shouted Blake, drawing the semiautomatic from his waistband.

Gray ran at him from behind while we distracted the pirates with our dash to the bags, knocking the gun out of his hand. It sailed through the air. We watched in slow motion as it spun and tumbled end over end before finally flying over the side of the boat and into the river with a splash. Blake rushed to the edge and leaned over, searching frantically for the weapon.

"I'll kill ye!" he screamed as he started for Gray.

Two pirates grabbed Gray as he tried to twist loose.

"Get ready!" yelled Adams, completing the transport instructions.

Gray stopped struggling and went slack as the pirates held him up. Blake stopped short as Gray vanished, little by little, before his eyes.

Dizziness overtook me, but I was still conscious enough to twist to Blake and fix my stare on him. We faded from sight as the band of pirates stood gawking at us in disbelief. I raised my chin and smiled at them as our transponder hurled me into the future.

* * *

New York City, New York 1908

We awoke on a hill overlooking the city. I could hardly believe we pulled off our escape and made it here safely. We grabbed the clothing, the medical bag, and a couple packs of snacks while on the boat. We had hidden the silver in the pockets of the new clothes, so the pirates never found it. They were so focused on the gun they missed everything else. Frank had disabled the Glock before he went to sleep that night, but didn't tell anyone yet, so it was never a threat to us while Blake had it. And if they ever recovered it from the river, it would be useless to them. Frank figured the gun was fired too many times in that timeline already, and he didn't want to take any more chances.

Everyone was glad to be out of 1792, and especially away from Edward Blake and his band of marauders. I felt like I'd run a marathon in concrete shoes. I was utterly exhausted. We all were. So we decided to camp out for the night and venture into the city tomorrow. We had earned a break.

We used the Lifestraws to drink from a nearby creek, took the last of the meal replacement capsules, and filled up on junk food. Even though we had little to start over with, we were safe for the first time in days. The mood around the fire that night was exhilarating, and I would remember it for many years to come. It would creep into my memory now and then and stand out as a pivotal point in my life.

The next day we changed into our new clothing. The dresses were not much more comfortable, but they were sure more attractive than our eighteenth-century undress wear. I brought dress clothes this time, knowing we would be in the city.

Our plan was to go to hospitals to search for Jacob. Since we knew he was a doctor, it made sense someone there would lead us to him. But first we needed to get settled in a hotel. It would do no good to drag the children and all fourteen adults from hospital to hospital.

Walking into New York City was mesmerizing. We had not seen a structure over two stories tall in over two years, besides our quick venture to Los Angeles, and the architecture was stunning. Packed cable cars wound through the streets, mixing with pedestrians, automobiles, and horse-drawn carriages. Shopkeepers swept sidewalks or cleaned glass store windows. Carts and stands held their goods, advertising for them.

We sold our coins to a dealer downtown, and settled in at the Knickerbocker Hotel on West 42nd Street and Broadway, in Manhattan. The French-Renaissance-style building was a sight to behold. The rooms were luxurious, and I was in heaven after sleeping on a hay filled mattress for so long.

On day two, Adams, Gray, and I left our temporary home to search for Jacob. Because we were the only agents who had met him, we didn't want to alarm him any more than we already would, by bringing more people. We had only aged a few years since we last saw him, so we hoped he might recognize us, even though he had not seen us since he was a young boy.

Automobiles and buggies paraded by us on the street in a steady stream of traffic. Women shaded themselves with parasols and elaborate hats, toting shopping baskets. Their skirts brushed the ground, stirring up dust from the street. Most men wore suits, and all of them had hats, even the young boys, who sported caps.

I stood in front of the hotel, rooted in place as my gaze swept over the scene. It was so overwhelming after being away from a real city for the past two years, and I found myself unable to move. The scene had the same effect on Gray and Adams.

"Wow," Adams said. "I still can't believe we're here."

"Isn't it amazing?" I said, smiling.

"It's better than I imagined," Gray said as another Model T drove by a few feet from us.

I inhaled a deep breath and stepped out onto the street after them. Our first stop was Bellevue Hospital in Manhattan. The nurses were busy and hardly acknowledged our presence when we asked about a Doctor Aldred. No one seemed to know him, but it was a large facility, so we kept trying.

After three hours, we gave up and moved on to the next hospital. After visiting two smaller clinics, I was getting discouraged. A nurse suggested we try Fordham Hospital in the Bronx. It was at least five miles from there, so we hired a buggy for the trip.

I was the quintessential tourist for the ride there, swiveling my head from side to side, pointing at sights and acting like an excited kid. I just couldn't help it. New York was fabulous, and I felt at home there immediately.

Our driver dropped us at the corner of Aqueduct and St. James Place at the Fordham Hospital. The neighborhood was not nearly as glamorous as Manhattan, but it fascinated me all the same.

We entered the lobby to people moving in every direction. Nurses pushed patients in wheelchairs, while others carried trays of medicine. We approached a nurse behind a desk in the middle of the room. She peered up at us with tired eyes. I smiled, but she didn't return the gesture.

"Good day. Are you familiar with Doctor Jacob Aldred? We wish to make an appointment with him."

"Yes, of course. Doctor Aldred volunteers here twice a week. Do you not choose to see him at his private practice?" she asked.

"Oh, yes, that may be best. What days does he volunteer here at Fordham?"

"He is with patients today," she said.

I exchanged a glance with the guys. "Might we be able to take a moment of his time now?"

"He is quite busy. There has been an outbreak of tuberculosis," she told us firmly before resuming her paperwork.

"I understand," I said, smiling.

It was clear she would not be coerced. I turned to leave, thinking maybe we could catch him later when he was off duty, although I did not know what he looked like at this age. I had an image of stalking doctors as they exited the hospital, and I couldn't see that working.

"Nope. We haven't come this far to have Nurse Ratched bully us," Gray said.

He spun around and motioned for us to follow as we approached her again.

"It is really of the utmost importance that we see him today. We can wait here until he is available. It's a most personal matter, one I'm certain he would be interested in speaking to us about," he said.

Her lips pursed for a moment, but she stood and disappeared through the door behind her. A few minutes later, a tall man with black hair in his fifties followed her into the lobby. He dried his hands on a towel, setting it on the edge of the desk. The nurse sat and pointed toward us. As he headed our way, I pictured the young boy I met all those years ago. I saw the resemblance and knew immediately it was Jacob.

"I'm Doctor Aldred. I understand you are most eager to see me. What can I help you with today?"

His accent had the faintest suggestion of British persuasion. His years growing up with Malcolm clearly influenced him.

"May we speak to you in private? Just for a moment?" I asked, gesturing to the room's corner.

He frowned and motioned us to the far end of the room, away from the crowd.

"I am most curious how I can help you, Miss. . ."

"Stewart. Christine Stewart. This is Stephen Gray, and Nathaniel Adams," I said.

I thought I saw the slightest hint of recognition pass over his expression, but couldn't be sure I hadn't imagined it.

"We were, are, friends of your parents. I don't know if they ever told you about us. We met you twice in Piedmont when you were a young boy, right after they adopted you."

A smile slowly spread across his face. "Christine. Yes. You're from the future time."

He didn't pose it as a question, more of a statement of fact. They *had* told him someone might contact him. I knew they would. They would have prepared him and told him the truth about their past. Too much happened they needed to explain to him. Even as a young boy, he would have known his parents were different somehow.

"Yes, we are," I said.

"You're aware of who we are then?" Gray asked.

"Of course. What took you so long?" he asked, grinning.

The remark threw me off balance. I was unsure what he meant. It must have showed on my expression because he was quick to rephrase.

"Forgive me, I could not help myself. That was a silly joke. Although, I *have* been expecting someone to show up one day. However, I always assumed it would be after my parents passed. They will be truly chuffed, as my father likes to say, to learn you are here."

"I'm sorry, Jacob, but you cannot tell them we're here. If you do, it could change their history. That's why we came to you, and not them. We do not want to disrupt their timeline together. If we show up in Piedmont, or they know we're here, it could alter the course they are on. We don't want to risk doing that. You cannot tell anyone about us. Not even your wife or children."

"I see. Well, this is a turn of events I did not expect. But I made my mother a promise many years ago that I would be receptive to a visit from you. And I am a man of my word. I understand what you did for them, for all three of us. If you had not saved them, my life would have turned out very differently. So it is without hesitation that I welcome you and offer my assistance in any way I can."

"Thank you, Jacob. That is wonderful news. Because we desperately need your help," I said.

THIRTY-THREE

New York City, New York 1910

The house was a flurry of activity, as it was every morning. Michael and Maddie clamored down the stairs, Maddie holding their ten-month-old, Christopher. She handed me the baby and they gave him a quick kiss on each cheek.

"Mama loves you," Maddie said. "Thank you for babysitting, Christine. We should be back by early afternoon. Frank is going to drop us off downtown this morning and then pick us up later."

"It's no problem. You two take your time," I said as my grandson blew raspberries at me and tried to grab my earrings.

"Love you, little man," Michael said to his son. "Yeah, thanks, Mom. Love you too."

I followed them to the entry of the Victorian brownstone we shared until renovations on their new home were complete. Shortly after arriving in New York, we bought a row of crumbling brownstones and renovated them, where we all lived now, next door to one another. Ethan and Gray were partners in a construction renovation business that did very well. They turned our extra downstairs parlor into a master suite, allowing the two bedrooms upstairs to go to the young couple.

Jacob loaned us the money, which we pooled with our profits from the silver we brought here, to purchase the brownstones. It took months to renovate them. Without Jacob's help, financial and otherwise, getting settled here would have been a daunting task. We insisted on paying him back with interest, and I was happy to have that done.

Later that year, from the same hotel we stayed at when we arrived, I would celebrate New Year's Eve after my wedding to Ethan and watch the first-ever ball-drop at midnight from the top of the New York Times Building.

Michael and Maddie married shortly after we got here, and Christopher was born not long after that. Now they really needed their own space with a second child on the way. They were both journalists for the *New York Times*. Michael covered politics and business, while Maddie wrote about 'women's issues' and covered the social page. Today they were both covering Joe Harris' political race for a seat in the New York State Assembly.

They jogged down the steps as Frank tooted the horn on his Model T automobile. I waved to him, and he grinned from ear to ear as he pulled out to the street. He had a fishing boat and three employees that he took out a few times a week to fish, then sold the catch to local markets and restaurants. He said he was living his best retirement. Ocean fishing and a classic car. It was classic Frank.

Linda was everyone's grandmother. She used any occasion as an excuse to bake over-the-top cakes. She owned a small bakery downtown, and while she sometimes complained about the early hours, we all knew she loved every minute and wouldn't give it up for anything.

Ethan came out of the kitchen, coffee mug in hand, running late as usual.

"Hey little guy. What are you and grandma up to today?" he said, tickling the baby's tummy. Christopher cooed and blew another raspberry Ethan's way.

"Well, we are going to Annabelle's to start a big order of duvet covers for the Knickerbocker Hotel. But first, a stroll around the park in his new pram," I said, bouncing the baby on my hip.

"Brilliant. Gray and I have a bid downtown and then back to work on the kid's place. We have a crew starting on the Livingstons' renovation, so I need to swing by there to make sure I line them out properly. Busy day. But I'll be home for tea," he said, giving me a kiss.

Now that Linda had taught me to cook, Ethan no longer avoided meals at home. Though I still couldn't break him of the habit of referring to supper as tea. Brits. What could you do? I must admit, dinner around here wasn't half-bad anymore.

"Don't let Gray give Daniel a hard time today. He's a nice young man, and Emory really likes him. Plus, he is great with baby Jeremiah. She deserves a second chance at love."

"You know Stephen—no one is good enough for his daughter. But I will try to keep him off Daniel's back. I think he does it just to test him."

I shook my head and laughed. I waved to him as he started down the street to Gray's house, Christopher's chubby little hand waving too. I grabbed the pram and settled him in, then picked up my parasol and started toward the park.

Annabelle and I started making quilts and duvets to make extra money when we arrived here. We had no idea that venture would grow so large. We landed a contract with the Knickerbocker and were in negotiations with a factory to move production there.

Any extra time Annabelle had was spent helping run Joe's political campaign for State Assembly. Women couldn't vote here yet, but in ten years, when that came to fruition, watch out New York. Because my best friend, Annabelle Harris, was a force to reckon with in any timeline.

As I approached Jacob's old medical office, I popped inside to say hello. Gemma smiled and stepped out from behind the counter to see the baby. Adams partnered with Jacob before he moved his family to Oklahoma, knowing he and Gemma would one day operate the practice himself. Gemma went to nursing school, although her husband gave her updated medical training, and she and Nathan ran the neighborhood clinic together.

Kira watched all the children when needed and kept the books for the construction business. She also led our twice weekly yoga class at her house. Edwardian society wasn't ready for me to resume my normal jogging routine, and I had to do something to stay in shape. I didn't understand how Kira managed it all, to be honest.

Nick Goebel and his wife ran an almshouse in the Bronx. The modern-day equivalent of a nonprofit shelter for the homeless. It was something they had always wanted to do, and it was a tremendous success. New York's public assistance was insufficient to the city's enormous need, and their shelters made a huge difference in many people's lives. Suzanne was expecting their first child this winter. Linda took her under her wing, fussing over her like a mother bear. She and Frank never had children of their own, and Suzanne and Nick became family to them.

After two years, we had adjusted to Edwardian-era life, although the first six months were challenging. We realized early on that to guarantee financial security, we needed to think like entrepreneurs. Working for others would be risky, and one more way we might accidentally reveal ourselves as time-travelers. It was a lot of stress piled on top of everything else we had to consider.

Our only transponder completely shut down after we were there for two months. We had to assume the CCEA was offline, and the program no longer in operation. We knew this was possible, but to be honest, I never expected it would really happen. After a year, we stopped checking it regularly, although Adams continued to inspect it randomly. But I was uncertain he even did that much after that first year. We stopped asking him about it. A testament to how happy we were there.

It was a magnificent time to live in New York. So much happened in the early 1900s. Railroads and automobiles, telephones, electricity, and natural gas were available. The subway cost a nickel to ride from lower Manhattan to Grand Central, in midtown. Vacuum cleaners and Victrola's were in many homes. And bathrooms. We had real bathrooms with running water and flushing toilets.

Even the Vitagraph, which was the closest to a movie we were going to get, made us feel more like we were home. A dark theater with its flickering images became date night.

The Wright Brothers took their first public flight. Multi-storied buildings graced the New York skyline, stretching upward in an unforgettable image. Cable cars ferried people across the Brooklyn Bridge for the view of a lifetime.

Vaudeville was popular in the theater district, and stores lined the streets, selling anything you could imagine. People from all over the world came here to chase their dreams. New York was a melting pot of expatriates all living in the largest city in the United States.

America was going to explode, technologically. Our country would advance more in the next decade than we had over the past one hundred years, and the United States was well on its way to becoming a world super-power.

I marched arm in arm with Maddie and Annabelle in the New York Suffrage Parade of 1908, and Maddie wrote about it later. We were there at the start of the New York to Paris Automobile Race.

We wanted to be in as many public pictures as possible. We theorized that maybe one or two would end up in a newspaper or history book online, and maybe, just maybe, one of our family members would see them one day and know we had been safe and happy. I held onto that hope firmly.

We were in the midst of it all. Ordinary people in extraordinary circumstances. And I couldn't have been any happier.

The downside to being here was the need to remain silent while aware of what fate had in store for the world.

The Titanic would sail in two years. I realized even if I voiced concerns about it, people would call me a crazy tea-leaf-reader, or worse. My objections would never be enough to halt the era's most famous or anticipated ship's maiden voyage. I dreaded seeing the tragic details play out in the newspapers. But we had to allow events to unfold as history meant them to. No matter how heartbreaking it was for those of us aware of the outcome.

Our time here was not without challenges or sorrow. When I received the telegram from Jacob about Malcolm's death in 1908, and then Hannah's in 1909, that hit me full force, even though I had beforehand knowledge of when they would pass. Jacob took his mother's passing especially hard. Left without Malcolm, her health declined quickly, and the doctor in him blamed himself for not being able to save her. After spending forty years married to the man she loved, I was sure she died of a broken heart after losing him.

And we all left people we loved behind. We missed our families. Michael left his father. My parents and sister remained in California. Ethan's daughter stayed with her mother in England when we left, and that was especially difficult for him to deal with. We knew we would probably never see any of them again, and it was tragic to live with that knowledge. Personally, I didn't allow myself to think about it much. It was the only way to get through it. I told myself they were safe. And I had to hold onto that belief, or I would crumble under the weight of the pain. Every one of us had our bad days, when our family's well-being was heavy on our minds. We had no way of knowing for certain our trip would be permanent when we left Los Angeles. We knew it was possible, but I don't think any of us really believed it would come to that. I imagined our goodbyes would have almost certainly been different, had we known.

But despite the hardships, I no longer considered going to 2072 to be the right choice. We embraced our lives here, and I wasn't certain any of us would choose to go back, given the chance.

Of course, I could only speak for myself. I was here with my husband, my son and his family, and my best friend. I had a gorgeous home and wonderful friends. 2072 couldn't possibly offer me any more than that.

THIRTY-FOUR

Los Angeles, California 2074

Jonathan Hoyt studied the hologram in front of him for ten solid minutes. He tried to make sense of it all. Running the plausible scenarios over in his mind one last time, he finally admitted he just didn't know what it all meant. He sent another message, one of many he'd sent over the last year.

Safe to come home. Is your device functional? Do you need a retrieval? Please respond.

-Hoyt

He waved the image off and settled back into his chair as he gazed out over the Los Angeles skyline. Drones of all sizes whizzed past his high-rise window, a few coming dangerously close to hitting it.

Los Angeles was on the way to becoming its former self. But it would be years before the American people would feel truly safe again, himself included. He tried to imagine what his friends were facing. Wherever they were, it must be worse.

He sent them to Colonial America at their request. And now only one of their transponders appeared operational. He had tried for the last year to reach them with no luck. Why were the other transponders not registering? Was their lone device malfunctioning too? Had they received his messages and could not respond? He had so many questions, and not one answer.

He had to decide what to do about this. They left him no alternative, so without prolonging it any further he tapped his cell chip.

"Call James."

He waited for the call to connect to his head of security.

"Hey, boss. What's up?"

"James, hello. I'm afraid I need to pull you off whatever you're working on and put you on an extremely sensitive project."

"No problem. You want to shoot it over to me?"

"No, I don't want a trail. Can you come up to my office, please?"

"On my way."

James arrived five minutes later, ready to receive his new assignment.

"I have a group of friends who are traveling. And by that, I mean they transported elsewhere when the war started. I've attempted to reach them over the past year but received no response. That worries me. It's very unlike them."

"Sure. How can I help?"

"I need you to find them for me. I sent them to 1790, Virginia. Three of them were stranded four years ago, and I can't have a repeat of that happening again. The last activity shows they programmed a single transponder from 1792, going to 1908, New York. That was two years ago. I'm uncertain if just one agent survived and moved forward, or if they did a group transport. I don't know why the system doesn't show the other devices as active. Maybe they only have one operational device and it is malfunctioning? I just don't know. But I owe it to them to search. You can trace them to the remaining live transponder when you get there. Let's have you plan to leave in a week. That should give you time to wrap up whatever you need to and make sure Simmons is up to speed to take over while you're gone."

"I'll start preparing tomorrow, Mr. Hoyt."

"Thank you, James. Let's see if these agents are ready to come home."

* * *

New York City, New York 1910

Seconds after Hoyt transmitted his message, text flashed on a screen one hundred sixty years in the past. The transponder sputtered to life for the first time in two years, where it lay forgotten, tucked away at the bottom of a chest under layers of blankets and quilts.

Life moved on in the house with the device, its occupants oblivious to the message it waited to deliver. With no one to see it, the red light continued to blink unanswered. Until five days later, when Adams discovered it.

"Gemma, where's the blue quilt Christine and Annabelle made for us? It's frigging freezing in this house," he shouted.

"In the trunk at the end of the bed. Where all the quilts are, Nathan," she called out from their son's room.

He dug through the chest until he saw the corner of bright blue fabric. He grabbed the blanket and pulled it out. His transponder came out with the quilt and skidded across the floor and under the bed.

"Dammit," he hissed.

Resting on his knees, he placed one hand on the mattress for balance, and slid his other hand back and forth underneath the bed. He felt nothing. Next, he lay on his stomach and lifted the duvet cover to peer under.

He froze at the sight.

The light on the transponder flashed like a neon sign on a dark desert highway. His heartbeat escalated and pulsed with each strobe.

He reached for the device and flipped it over to read the message. He sat on the floor at the side of the bed, leaning against it for support. He didn't call for his wife. He knew he should. But doing so would make it real.

If he didn't tell anyone, maybe it wasn't true?

He wasn't sure how long he sat there, unmoving and thinking. Gemma snapped him out of his reverie when she entered the room. Her gaze wandered to the pile of quilts on the floor near the chest and her husband sitting on the floor, staring into space.

"What are you doing, babe?"

His eyes met hers and he held out the transponder. She studied it with furrowed brows for a long moment, finally taking it in her hand. She glanced at the screen, then slid down and sat next to her husband.

"We need to show the others," she said.

"I know. I don't want to. But I realize we have to. Let's get this over with," he said.

She followed him to the candlestick telephone on the side table in the parlor. He called them all, asking for an immediate, urgent meeting.

By dinnertime, all twelve adults arrived at their home, children in tow. Some of them sat, others stood, all assembled in the parlor.

"What's so important, Adams, that you drag us out on a Sunday? I was just about to have dinner," Frank said.

"Yeah, I was catching up on some last-minute work at Michael and Maddie's new place. What's the emergency?" Gray asked, adjusting the tool belt strapped on his hip.

"Wyatt, why don't you take the younger kids upstairs to your room?" Gemma said.

Heather and Willow scrambled to follow him, while Rose took Christopher in one arm and Jeremiah by the hand.

"Well, what's wrong? You're scaring me," I said to Adams. He didn't answer right away, which made my stomach twist.

"I found this today. Or rather, the message. Apparently, the CCEA is online again. The transponder is working."

He handed the device to Gray, who looked at the screen, and passed it to Kira. It traveled around the room like that until everyone had seen it.

I glanced over at Ethan, and then Michael and Maddie. They appeared as stunned as I felt. I think we all were, as we realized what this meant.

I knew this day might come, but I was still completely unprepared for the wave of melancholy that washed over me at the thought of leaving. I loved my life here. It was uncomplicated. It was unhurried. It was everything I always wanted. I just didn't realize that until I got here. And we were thriving. Being a part of this community when America was advancing faster than any other time in history was inspiring.

I didn't trust my voice not to crack if I spoke, so I stayed silent and kept my emotions hidden. Frank was the first to react.

"You understand they can trace us now that it's working again," he said.

When no one responded, he stood and walked to Gray. He lifted the hammer from his friend's toolbelt and quietly placed the transponder on the table. We could have heard a pin drop at that moment. I held my breath, waiting for someone to object. But no one did. We all stood watching Frank, the hammer in his hand at his side.

"If anyone wants to stop me from smashing this thing to bits, now is your chance. If you want to go back, just say the word, and the transponder is yours," he said.

His eyes stopped on each of us as he spoke. Still, we remained mute. He raised the hammer.

"Last call," he warned.

"Wait!" I shouted.

All eyes were on me instantly. I turned to Ethan, who looked crestfallen.

"We need to tell him we don't need a retrieval. He's obviously concerned about us. I know Hoyt. He won't let it go unless he finds us, or we tell him to stop," I said.

I was sure I saw the relief surge through Ethan's body like an electric current. They all thought I wanted to go back to our timeline. Nothing was further from the truth.

Frank handed me the transponder and stood before me, waiting. I punched in a response.

All is well. No retrieval needed. Safe and happy. We are home where we are. Thank you, and be well, my friend.

-Christine

I glanced at Ethan as he reached for my hand. Couples around the room did the same, holding hands with the person next to them. You know what they say. If you are unhappy with the story, turn the page. On that Sunday evening, in 1910, New York, we turned the page. We began an entire new chapter of our story.

Frank didn't hesitate as he brought the hammer down on the device. Bits of plastic and metal splintered and skittered across the table before landing on the carpet. I stared at the shattered pieces of the transponder as tears of joy filled my eyes. We were completely on our own now, with no way back to the future. But instead of feeling trapped, I was truly free for the first time in my life.

I said a silent prayer no one came after us and the CCEA never discovered what we had done. Or where we were. I chided myself and tried to push the negative thoughts out of my mind and just enjoy my newfound liberation. But instead, an unrelenting worry clawed at the back of my brain. I shook my head and forced my attention back to the present, trying to convince myself I was being irrational. I wasn't sure how our future would play out, but I let the uncertainty go for the time being, allowing myself to live in the moment.

I inhaled a deep breath as I squeezed Ethan's hand. A smile slowly spread across my face before I joined my family and friends in a roaring cheer so loud it drifted out of the brownstone and all the way to the street below.

THE END

ABOUT THE AUTHOR

Christy Cooper-Burnett is an award-winning author based in California with a degree in Administration of Justice. After retiring early from the new home construction industry, she now divides her time between northern and southern California.

She has a grown son who inspired her to write her award-winning debut novel, *No Way Home*. Although she began her writing career later in life, once she started, she couldn't stop!

Her work focuses on creating relatable stories and characters that transcend genres and encourage her readers to imagine what they would do if thrown into the unique, imaginative situations her protagonists end up in.

NOTE FROM THE AUTHOR

Word-of-mouth is crucial for any author to succeed. If you enjoyed *Escaping Home*, please leave a review online—anywhere you are able. Even if it's just a sentence or two. It would make all the difference and would be very much appreciated.

Thanks!
Christy Cooper-Burnett

Thank you so much for reading one of
Christy Cooper-Burnett's novels.
If you enjoyed the experience, please check out our recommended
title for your next great read!

No Way Home by Christy Cooper-Burnett

"Immersive science-fiction and a moving character drama."
–Brian Carmody, author of *Hellish Beasts*

View other Black Rose Writing titles at
www.blackrosewriting.com/books and use promo code
PRINT to receive a **20% discount** when purchasing.